Prince With Benefits

A Billionaire Royal Romance

Nicole Snow

Cover Design – Kevin McGrath – Kevin Does Art.
Photo by Allan Spiers Photography.
Formatting –Polgarus Studio

Description

HE BOUGHT A WIFE. I BOUGHT INTO MAKE BELIEVE...

ERIN

Cinderella had it easy. I'm lying to millions of people, and it's all Silas' fault.

Yes, *that* Silas. Billionaire. Prince. Scandals galore. Downright royal bastard.

Everything that screams run. If only it weren't for his rock hard edges and wild tattoos, tempting anything female on all seven continents.

But I don't care about his looks. *Really.*

Our deal is simple. He needs a pretty little lie, a wife to cover up his dirty deeds. I need a fortune to buy the treatment that just might save my father's life.

Match made in hell? Totally, and I'm going to make it work.

No, I'm not stupid. I'm not getting played by this billionaire prince. Forget his banter, his charms, the rumors I've heard about his ridiculously over-sized...ego.

What's that phrase he teases me with - Prince with benefits? Not in a billion years.

Yes, I'll lie for him. But I swear, my panties are absolutely, positively *not* melting every time I imagine his kiss...

SILAS

It's almost perfect. An engagement with an American girl, desperate as she is beautiful. Anything goes with Erin, except one rule.

Her body's off limits. She's joking, right?

Charming any girl I want into my bed doesn't mean a thing when there's only one on my mind.

I want Miss Make Believe. My fake, sassy, sexy fiancee. She, who says 'no,' and makes me so obsessed I'm about to trade in my designer suit for a straitjacket.

I convinced her to wear my ring, easy. I'll get her clothes off next. Show her what the world's most infamous player does when he's on fire. Then I'll move on.

No more playing castle. I'll have my Princess with benefits on her knees, treating me like royalty...

I: Tripped Up (Erin)

"Look, I know American reporters, and their little interns. I've worked with plenty. You think you can get away with anything as soon as the cameras roll, but let me remind you again. We have rules. No flash, no interruptions, and absolutely *no* unauthorized social media. His Highness keeps a very strict media presence, and it's my privilege to enforce it."

How I stopped myself from rolling my eyes at this pompous, self-absorbed bitch, I'll never know.

Serena Hastings flips her long blonde hair back, giving me the stink eye one last time, before she moves through the gaggle of media and finally takes her seat.

Eyeballing the stage, I'm wondering if I made a huge mistake taking my summer off campus to come to Saint Moore.

It's my father's crowning career achievement, though. An interview with Prince Silas Erik Bearington the Third.

It isn't hard to understand dad's excitement. It's taken his whole life to get here, and I'm just along for the ride. A very hellish, testing-my-patience-every-damned-day kind of ride.

From the brutal jet lag flying from LA across the Atlantic, to the correspondence dinners where I have to be on my best behavior to avoid embarrassing him, to the constant entourage around the palace who think they're sent by God...sweet Jesus.

Now, I'm sitting here in these stupid heels that are *way* too tight, wishing for a miracle. What comes next dwarfs *everything*.

Don't worry, dad said. He told me he'd show me how it's done. I wanted to follow in his footsteps, didn't I?

When the lighting adjusts and a hot, narrow beam shines on my face, pulling sweat from my pores, I really have to wonder what the hell I've gotten myself into.

Of course, dad isn't even sweating before his interview with Prince Playboy himself begins. Yes, *that* Prince.

The twenty-something, six foot and then some giant who's scandalized several continents. The Prince who's brought the tabloids and dirty blogs more gossip than a hundred celebrity wardrobe malfunctions.

He, who my friends used to swoon over during late night truth-or-dare sessions in our freshmen year dorm, putting him at the top of most eligible celeb bachelors they'd love to have between the sheets. A man I've never been able to stand, much less crush on. A living argument against any country having kings and Queens in modern times, when all they're likely to get out of it are media scoundrels.

Prince Charming, Prince Skirt Chaser, Prince Hung, and a thousand other names.

The Prince, the bastard, the legend.

Silas.

"One minute, Mister Warwick!" the camera man shouts to my father as he climbs up onto the stage, taking one of the two empty chairs beneath the halo.

The other, with the gold and burgundy back, is reserved for the devil himself. I wonder if he's going to walk into this interview late, and throw my dad one more complication.

That would be just like him, wouldn't it? It's not like he takes this Prince thing seriously. It's just the world's biggest license to be a dick, to drink and fuck himself stupid every chance he gets. That's what the blogs have told me, anyway.

None of it fazes dad, ever the professional. He sits up there in his finest suit, his silver hair slicked back, the same prim smile on his lips that I've seen him use in a hundred interviews growing up.

Game time. It's the look that makes me wonder if I'm really cut out to follow in his footsteps. He's wearing the calm, measured, controlled mask I've tried to don before, and failed every time.

I don't have to wonder long because there's new commotion surging through the room. The door off to the side opens, and in walks four strong men in designer suits, the Bearington family crest pinned to their lapels in royal purple and gold. It's a double-headed eagle holding a crown.

A taller, younger, stronger man steps out between them. They part like water, making way for His Highness.

My heart skips a beat. It's him. For real.

3

Prince Silas, arriving in all his smug, unwavering, damnably sexy glory.

Okay, so maybe the SOB really is what they say in the looks department. If I had any doubt, it's blown to pieces, now that he's quickly stepping toward the stage, taking the five stairs up in two big strides.

My father stands respectfully, extending a hand. The Prince takes it, towering over him by nearly a whole foot, and dad isn't a short guy.

"Charmed, Mister Warwick." The Prince has that foreign, not-quite-English accent everybody in the kingdom does, except his is somehow thicker, more refined.

"It's my honor, Your Highness. I've been looking forward to this for a long time," dad says, nodding.

"Twenty seconds!" Another cameraman roars out, flinching for a second in the hopes that his interruption hasn't upset the Prince.

Based on what I've read, I don't think that's even possible. Nothing upsets him. He basks in every scandal and fresh jab the media takes at him like they're triumphs.

They both take their seats across from each other. I can't believe they look so casual, like it's the most natural thing in the world, when there's so much on the line.

If dad pulls this off, he's going to be seen by billions over the next week. Serena, bitch that she is, has reminded us since day one that the Royal Press Corps is looking for a new American correspondent. And with rumors swirling about how much longer Queen Marina will continue to rule before passing the crown to her grandson, my father could be front and center at the Bearington's wild court for a very long time to come.

As for the Prince, it's his time to shine with something besides his dick. It's no secret the world's been holding its breath, waiting for him to shape up, and act like a statesman for one of the wealthiest countries in the world. A future King.

Saint Moore is virtually the last monarchy in Europe where the ruler is more than just a figurehead. For fifty years, Queen Marina has rallied her country to good causes and swayed more than a few votes in their parliament, even if she's been very respectful of democracy.

As for Prince Hung – who knows? He's taken his pleasure demonstrating all the things he'll do with modern day concubines throwing themselves at him. Not politics.

"Five…four…three…two…one…"

Cameras roll. Dad looks into the closest one confidently, and begins to speak.

"Welcome to this special edition of the Warwick Report, ladies and gentleman. Today, I'm coming to you from the Kingdom of Saint Moore, where I'm sitting down with a man who needs no introduction." He pauses, three seconds, just long enough to let everybody tuning in remember the insanity that surrounds everything Silas. "Prince Silas Erik Bearington, heir to the island's throne, one of the most powerful, scandalized, and adventurous men in the world."

"Tom, you flatter me too much," Silas says, that wicked smirk above his chiseled jaw pointing up like pitchfork ends. "Let's get it on, shall we?"

"Absolutely, Your Highness," dad says. If he's rattled at all by the Prince's need to control the conversation, he doesn't show it. "You're recently back in the kingdom after completing your duty in the Royal Marines, serving in Afghanistan. Tell me, sir, how has that experience changed you? I think everyone was surprised to hear about a Bearington Prince flying into an active combat zone. Thankfully, on our side, this time."

The Prince smiles. Smug as ever, but a little darkly.

"Yes, we always did like to play both sides, up until the Second World War. It's been good for me, Tom. Reminds me why I'm really here, next in line to the crown, how fortunate I am to be born into this royal lineage. There's pride in serving a man's kingdom, and beyond. I'd never imagined Afghanistan until I stepped foot there. Some truly awful circumstances, just beyond our borders. Life and death. War. Poverty. Terrorism. A lot more exciting than who's wearing last year's style at the next big charity ball, I'm sure you can imagine. Also, a much bigger challenge for me, and I *love* those."

"Oh, yes," dad says, returning the Prince's smile. "They called you a hero in the press after Kandahar. Said you single-handedly thwarted a terrorist attack on an allied base, saving your own troops and dozens more from several different countries, including the United States. What really happened?"

"Please. The media embellishes everything." Silas shakes his head, waving it all away, pushing his stern hand through the air. The perfectly tailored gray suit he's wearing fits him like a glove, exposing more of that powerful body each time he moves, even subtly. "I gave the orders, sure, as soon as I saw them creeping up on our base. Still took everyone in uniform that day to stop the attack, to swarm out and hit them at the right moment, before the suicide bomber could plow through the main gate and do God knows what."

Dad straightens in his seat. I can tell by the look on his face that things are about to get serious. The tension in the palace room thickens, and even the ornate ceilings soaring into the air can't hold it.

God, I wish I'd picked different shoes. These heels are totally *strangling* me now.

"That's a very modest account for those who know you, Your Highness," dad says. "Some might say unnaturally modest. More like the kind of attitude a future King should have, rather than the playboy Prince."

"Look, Tom, we all know what's bound to happen one day. Truth is, any talk about it now is shoveling Her Majesty in her grave while she's still very much alive and kicking ass." Prince Silas pauses, the dimples in his cheeks deepening. He knows he's about to blow his carefully crafted tact.

Several people behind me suppress snickers. A woman coughs. I'm trying to pay attention to the interview, read dad's body language, to see how he's going to handle things if they take a nasty turn.

But damn, I can't take my eyes off Silas' face. Those deep blue eyes of his betray nothing, perfect royal compliments to his dark black hair, and a day's worth of shadowy stubble on his chin that probably makes every woman in the room wonder what it feels like against their skin.

Myself included. *Shamefully.*

"Certainly, Your Highness. We all hope Queen Marina will be around for another hundred years, but you and I both know what's realistic." Dad pauses, the confident smile on his face disappearing.

He swallows something hard in his throat. "Frankly, you have people in your own kingdom saying you may be the last Prince, and your grandmother could well be its final Queen. They want a referendum once she's gone. That could mean trouble in a time when royals are an endangered species all over Europe, and indeed, the world. Let me just come out and ask – are you trying to *save* the monarchy?"

"Really, Tom? You think my bloodline needs saving from a joke protest movement like Republic First?" Silas' dark blue eyes storm angry, full of disbelief. "The Bearingtons have ruled this island for over a thousand years. We'll do it again for a thousand more, when we can all drive across bridges to Scotland and Iceland. We've kept our people safe in war and guided them into the modern age with wealth, class, and good sense. I know that might be difficult for someone like you to understand, when your own government has barely been around for three hundred years."

Dad's chest swells as he quietly inhales a big breath. He sinks back in his chair, his hands tightly folded in his lap, staring at the Prince.

Oh, God. What's going on? He isn't…offended? No, too unprofessional.

But I've never seen him shaken in an interview like this. I can't believe it's happening because he's face-to-face with this Royal Prick.

Prince Silas senses it, too. The tension in his face softens, and he looks at my father, cocking his head ever-so-slightly. "Tom, you're just asking the tough questions, and I appreciate it. That's why I agreed to this interview personally. Let's move on, shall we? You've got plenty of ammo left, I'm sure. Ask me about the latest supermodel I'm bedding, or the hot new custom sports car I've added to my stable. I just broke in one of those things yesterday. We both know how history and politics gets damned boring."

Silas has a huge grin on his face. I can't tell if he's joking, trying to ease the tension, or if he's just in a mad rush to deflect more questions about the kingdom's future.

Dad doesn't give up that easily, even when his subject is getting pissed. I wonder if he'll press on with the same questions, or circle back to them later, after he's probed the bastard Prince a little more.

For the first time in my life, I'm not sure who'll crack first.

He doesn't do either. Instead, he grabs the sides of his chair, his hands visibly shaking.

Jesus. Something's wrong.

Stiffening in my seat, I watch him lean forward, reaching for something that isn't there. The shadows shift around him, changing the bright light.

For the first time, I notice he's completely drenched in sweat, the collar around his jacket stained wet.

Time to panic. Several murmurs run through the crowd.

The Prince stands up at the same time I do, and he sees me, several rows behind the other journalists. Our eyes lock for one intense second. We share our confusion, dismay, and utter shock before dad rolls out of his chair and goes crashing down on the podium.

Everybody jumps out of their seat, searching for a better view, chattering away. Cameras snap, hyenas feasting on daddy's suffering. Several swarms of guards flood the stage, surrounding my father and the Prince, one carrying a small white box with a red cross on its side.

I can't see what's happening. My heart races, and I try to push forward, shuffling through the purple rope separating the media from the interview stage.

The kingdom's official cameras have got to be off by now. Even if they aren't, it's too late to worry about embarrassing myself or my dad any further, when he's up there seizing up, sick or dying or maybe both.

I don't bother with the tiny staircase. I move right past it before anybody can notice and haul me away. My hands clench the edge of the podium, and I pull myself up, cursing the skirt I'm wearing for tangling up when my leg finally gets enough leverage.

Somehow, I manage it, without getting yanked away by the guard. My eyes turn to dad and the little crowd hunched around him, barking orders back and forth in that rich, regal accent that's becoming chalkboard on my ears.

"Hurry, boys, hoist him up! Get this man the hell out of here. I want an ambulance out front in the next sixty seconds."

No, I can't just stare. I have to move.

One step forward, and my fucking heel catches on the stage's edge, throwing me backward. It's a long enough fall to do some damage if I slip, so I throw my weight forward.

I don't know what's worse. The fact that my dad is having a stroke or a heart attack right in front of me, or that these stupid, *stupid* shoes are twisting my ankle, sending me crashing to the floor next to him.

There's no time to brace for impact. Next thing I know, I'm falling, face first into the podium's hard black surface. I wonder if I'll get to share a room at the hospital with dad when I break something.

But I don't hit the surface. Something catches me, yanks me back, saving me from hitting the floor.

Make that two big somethings.

Hands. Thick, strong, determined, and locked around me.

Blinking back the dizzying confusion, I open my eyes. Prince Silas' dark blue irises widen when they see my face.

Like my heart wasn't already beating a hundred miles an hour. I'm lost for words.

Any words.

He's holding me in his arms like we've just done the last move in a fiery dance. His fingers press into my skin, tense and surprised, but completely unshaken. In control.

What the hell does a woman say when she's literally been swept off her feet by one of the most powerful, handsome, and arrogant men in the world? A man I'd scoffed at every time he showed up in the tabloids or in clickbait on the web?

The Prince, the heir to the throne, who's probably laid the female population of a small country. The Prince, with those ridiculously deep, beautiful blue eyes that are always saying *fuck me.*

And right now, they're trained on me.

Me, Erin Warwick. Intern. Nobody. Damsel in distress.

She, with the worst heels in the world. Him, with the icy, dominating eyes a woman could lose herself in forever.

"That's my father!" I stammer, trying to explain, hoping I'm not about to get tasered and thrown to the floor when the royal guards catch up to me.

"Don't move, love," he says, never breaking eye contact. "Everything's going to be fine."

Easy for you to say, I want to tell him. But I can't find the words.

Everything starts spinning again. This time, it's got nothing to do with the crappy shoes. I'm on the verge of blacking out.

"Stay with me," Prince Silas growls, his fingers pressing harder in my skin.

Dad groans, several feet away, reminding me why I'm up here, mysteriously thrown into a Prince's arms by my own clumsiness in these God forsaken heels. They're starting to move him.

Wait, damn it – dad! I have to follow him. I have to –

I never get a chance to do anything. The guards I've been expecting surround us, but the Prince holds one hand up, telling them to stand down. His hands tighten on me one last time.

One on my shoulder. One against my lower back, holding me up, helping me back on my feet.

"See that she has a ride to the Royal hospital, and wherever she'd like to go after that," Silas snaps, looking away from me at last.

I'm barely able to stand on my own without collapsing again. Thankfully, I don't have to support my own weight for long.

"Right this way, madame."

Several guards tug sternly, but gently on my arms, leading me down the stairs, right behind the entourage that's ferrying dad away.

Just a few minutes later, I'm outside the palace, led down the hundred marble steps, and into one of the sleek black sedans below. A man sits next to me in the back. The driver stomps the gas as soon as my seatbelt is on, without saying a word.

I'm grateful for the silence. I hate it, too, because it lets me think. Exactly what I can't afford to do just yet.

I won't let myself comprehend what a complete disaster this is until I know dad's going to be okay.

* * * *

A couple hours go by just waiting. Then, I'm in his room, staring at my father laying feebly in bed. It's a tiny, clean, white chamber. Sterile looking. Maybe just a little more stylish than the bland, depressing places I'd find back home in LA.

Nobody ever said the kingdom didn't have a great medical system. Its reforms and upgrades were personally encouraged by Her Majesty, whose reign has always turned a lot of attention to her subjects' health and wellness.

That's what the Wikipedia article says, anyway, something I lazily gloss over while I wait for dad to wake up.

His hand feels so cold in mine. Whatever they've given him, he's out like a light.

It's early morning the next day, and I haven't slept a wink. We're both waiting for the initial test results to come in.

They've checked his heart, done several x-rays, and determined there's no need for immediate surgery. I'm not sure if that's good news, or a sign there's something worse lurking in his system. Something much harder to fix.

Morning light drifts over us, somber as it is bright. I'm starting to drift off myself, when dad finally groans. He sits up while my grip tightens on his hand, easing him awake.

"Christ. Feels like I got hit by a damned freight train. How long was I out, Erin?"

I shrug. "All night. It's early morning now."

Dad reaches up, running a shaky hand across his face. About a second later, his eyes stretch huge, and suddenly his fingers tangle around mine.

"The interview – shit!" He pauses, like it takes the full

horror several seconds to set in. "I blew it, didn't I? Jesus Christ."

"Don't think about that now, daddy!" I lean in, stroking his fingers, kissing him softly on the forehead. "You need to get some more rest. There'll be plenty of time to sort out what happened later with the palace, I'm sure."

I hate having to lie to him.

He knows damn well nobody gets second chances in this business after a meltdown like that.

Maybe the Warwick name will salvage his career, carrying him to new prospects. But as far as I'm concerned, we probably won't hear a word from the royals, except when they're going to send us on our merry way with impersonal wishes for good health.

"Fuck." Dad slumps back in his bed, pulling his hand from mine. The IV in his arm stretches as he rubs his eyes.

My heart sinks like a stone. He isn't really...crying...is he?

Oh, God.

"Dad, no," I say gently, wondering if there's any combination of words to ease the dagger cutting through him. "Work doesn't matter. You have to get well. That's the only thing worth worrying about right now. Whatever else is on your mind, forget it. Don't let it take over. Turn it off. You're a smart man. You'll bounce back from this...all of it. You've got more experience and connections than anybody else in this business. The world won't end just because you need a little time off, I promise. Dad, I –"

"Erin..." he cuts in, a defeated expression turning his face gray. "Shut up."

I do.

Hell, I don't know what else to do. I've never seen him like this.

His rudeness hurts, but I try not to let it get to me. Standing up, I walk toward the window, staring out into the early sunrise.

The hospital overlooks a ragged shore, where the wind sends foamy waves crashing against the rocks. My hands become fists at my sides, and the only thing that keeps running through my mind is that I have to forgive him.

He isn't in his right mind.

He's hurting.

We don't even know what's wrong.

I won't let myself cry – not even when I hear him gently snoring again after a couple minutes pass.

Holding in tears is worse than anger. They sting my eyes, my soul, make me question everything about why I'm standing in this foreign hospital after watching my father's career self-destruct, waiting to find out how much longer we need to stay here before we jet back to the States, completely humiliated.

There's a TV in the corner. It's been muted since the moment I stepped in, and now the early morning programs are starting. I see two prim reporters at their desks, smiling, going through the latest news on the continent.

Another bailout coming in the Eurozone. Something about nuclear security in Belgium, and then a thirty second segment on military drills near the Russian border.

Then another headline. The one that twists the knot in

my belly and the rock in my throat at once without mercy.

BOMBSHELL INTERVIEW! PRINCE GOES FROM HOT WATER TO HERO!

Turning nervously to make sure dad's still asleep, I look up at the screen, that anger in my eyes beginning to pour out in hot, salty streams down my cheeks.

I see it all again.

The painful look on dad's face before he rolled out of his chair, collapsing in front of the Prince.

The swarm of security and paramedics. Panic. Commotion.

A flash of myself jumping onto the stage, my hair a mess, lunging to save myself from toppling off the ledge. I'm less than a foot from planting the ground face first when Prince Silas grabs me, jerks me up, straight into his arms.

Jesus, it looks even more picture perfect seeing it in the third person, like something from a movie. They didn't bother capturing anything after that, the long, awkward stare between us, how I gazed into his deep blue eyes.

The footage cuts off. I storm over to the TV, lean up on my tippy toes, careful not to let these overly tight heels screw me over again. I punch the off button, without bothering to give the other dramas and kids shows from Saint Moore and Europe a chance to take the edge off.

I'm pissed. Hurt. Worried.

Scared.

There's another chair in the corner, and that's where I park my unsettled ass for what seems like the next hour. I wish to God I hadn't flipped on that stupid program.

I should be thinking about dad, brushing off his outburst.

Instead, I'm thinking about the Prince. The first and last time I'll ever be close to him. The way he held me – firm, but gentle. Almost like a decent man should.

Sure, the media was eating up the drama, recasting it as a heroic spectacle.

I wasn't fooled. Even utter bastards can be gentleman in the right time, right place.

Hell, I wouldn't be surprised if Silas drove off the second we were gone, straight to his little mistresses. Maybe that flashy club for royalty and multimillionaires he owns, the one I've read about on the trashy blogs, hosting parties for the most eligible supermodels in Europe.

His own private hunting grounds for sex.

My hand reaches for my phone. I'm about to pull it up, and read more gossip about Prince Not-So-Charming for reasons I don't even understand, when the door pops open. The noise wakes dad, and he groans, sitting up in bed while the visitor enters.

A tall man in a white coat with salt and pepper hair steps in. "Ah, you must be Miss Warwick, I presume. So glad you're here so I can update you both on the news. I'm Doctor Jameson."

The physician rounds the bed, standing next to dad, and begins pulling something from a manila folder. I'm studying his face. It isn't hard to notice the complete lack of any pleasantries or warmth.

He's serious business. And serious is never good when it comes to medicine.

"Mister Warwick, there's no easy way to say this, so I'm just going to come out with it. We've found a shadow near your pancreas in scans."

My ears start ringing, and his voice fades out. *A shadow? A shadow?! What the hell does that mean?*

"Shadow?" My dad repeats, just as confused as me.

The doctor holds up three x-rays on a sheet, and begins going through them, pointing at the areas in question.

"Yes, an unusual growth, of sorts. Not benign. We'll know for certain once your labs come back. Regardless, it's something we'll need to deal with shortly." The doctor pauses, straightens his spectacles, before he goes on. "Regrettably, it's near a nerve cluster that's likely to cause intense nausea and a shock to the system that stresses the heart. That's why you had the attack yesterday. The good news is, it's fully operable. I'm recommending surgery soon, once you decide whether you'd like to have it done here in Saint Moore, or back home."

"Home," dad says, without a second's hesitation. "Don't want to spend a second longer on this damned island than I really need to."

Doctor Jameson's face tightens. Dad gives him a sour look and mutters an apology.

"It's okay. He's been under a lot of stress," I say weakly, looking at the physician.

"Yes, yes, I understand. Well, the two of you ought to talk things over and try your very best to remain calm. We'll have more news for you this evening. Assuming this isn't anything to *really* be concerned about beyond the surgery, we can have it done in under a week, wherever you choose. The Warwick Report can be back on the air in no time at all."

"No, I'm taking time off," dad snaps, his eyes going dark. "Whatever the outlook here."

I want to reach out, squeeze his shoulder, but I know him too well. He's always been so high strung, the sort of man who has zero tolerance for failure.

"And if there's more to worry about?" I ask, fighting to ignore the sickly feeling building deep in my stomach.

"We'll deal with that scenario when it's on the table." He collects the x-rays and shoves them back in his folder. "I have some other business to attend to. Rest assured, Miss Warwick, your father is getting the very best care here. Not just because it's our duty, but because His Highness himself has requested extra attention to detail."

"The Prince?" I squeak, doing a double take. "Why?"

"I don't know. He didn't divulge any further details, madame. He's requested nothing but the best to handle your father's case by name. Since I'm at the top of this field available at the royal medical center, well, here I am. Suffice it to say, His Highness cares very greatly about all his guests, and he's deeply sorry for the trouble your father ran into the other day."

"Trouble my ass." Dad snorts, tips his nose up, and rolls over, facing away from both of us. "He can't possibly be more sorry than I am. Believe me."

"If you'll excuse me…" Doctor Jameson looks at the door awkwardly.

I nod, and he's gone without another word.

As soon as he's out, I take the chair next to the bed. Dad never turns around to face me, drifting off yet again after a few minutes.

I don't know if I should be grateful he's getting his rest, or worried about his dark attitude.

Just now, my own exhaustion catches up to me. Turning in the chair, I tuck my head against the back, and close my eyes.

Prince Silas Bearington, and fact that he might know me by name, is the last thing on my mind.

* * * *

I don't have a clue how long I'm asleep. It seems like evening by the time I'm awakened by a light tap on the shoulder.

Looking up, I see Doctor Jameson standing over me, his face more grim than before. "Miss Warwick, could I speak to you outside for a moment, please?"

"Of course," I say, looking down at dad, still fast asleep in his nest of tubes and bedding.

I follow him out and watch as he closes the door gently behind us. We're alone in the long corridor, where it's eerily quiet. I take one look at his face and know I'm about to get bombed.

"What is it? What's wrong?" My heart moves ten times faster than my lips, pure adrenaline in every pulse.

"Your father's growth is cancerous, Miss Warwick. A rare, aggressive cancer. Very difficult to eradicate in this area. Something I've never seen." He pauses, as if he needs to stoke his bedside manner, to prevent cold scientific fascination from taking over. "I'm very sorry."

That's it then. Cancer.

What was that word he used again? *Aggressive?*

I'm devastated.

Or else, I should be. The weird thing is, I just feel numb, standing there underneath the bright white lights overhead while the doctor waits for some kind of reaction.

"How does this change things?" I ask softly.

"He'll need additional treatment, of course. If it were up to me, I'd recommend a full round of chemotherapy immediately after surgery, a regimen we call..."

I'm listening, but all the terminology washes over me. So does the pain, the disappointment, the sad realization our nightmare isn't over. I thought the worst was behind us when dad collapsed during his interview, and I fell into the royal bad boy's arms.

No, it's only beginning. I couldn't be more wrong.

"Let me assure you once again, Miss Warwick, your father is more than welcome to make full use of our facilities and expertise. We have plenty of experience working with American insurance. But just between you and me..." He pauses, looking around, and leans in when he's sure nobody else is around. "I told you this is rare. We have our own research wing, yes, and we're doing well, all things considered. However...we can't make miracles happen. If it were me, I'd go abroad. Opt for something more experimental. Only the best of the best."

Experimental? Abroad? Obviously, he's used to dealing

with billionaire royals who never think twice about their finances. Even more obvious he doesn't have as much experience working with insurance as he let on.

Despite his success, daddy isn't a rich man.

He's done well as a journalist, sure. He's comfortable. But his last divorce took him to the cleaners not so long ago.

He barely has the money for globe trekking and time off if he wants to keep his condo. Let alone for things like experimental treatments abroad.

"I don't know if we can afford it," I say, trying to stop the anger from creeping into my voice.

Doctor Jameson cocks his head, quickly scratching his nose. He looks at me like I've lost my mind.

I still can't believe it. How a perfectly normal trip, the highlight of dad's career, has turned into *this*.

"Well, you certainly don't have to decide now, Miss Warwick," the doctor says reassuringly. "You have time – a little time – before any difficult decisions need to be made. Know that they *do* need to be decided in a timely manner, though. As soon as you're able, if I'm frank. The quicker you move against this sort of the thing, the better his chances."

God. The people on this island all seem to have a way with being 'frank.' They're too honest, everybody from Prince Playboy to his subjects, and always in that haughty not-quite-English accent that makes me want to slap them across the face.

You can't get angry, I tell myself. *For dad's sake.*

"I understand," I lie, right before a new worry takes over.

"Should I tell him the news?"

"No, no, that's my responsibility," he says, surprise flashing in his eyes. "We'll let him rest awhile longer. I'll make the rounds later today, and inform him when he's awake. Better to get the shock out of the way so both of you can begin running through your options in earnest. I'll bring you more details about the experimental option, if you'd like. Now, if you'll excuse me…"

You have no idea. I'd love to excuse you, Doctor Dick, and this whole stupid, pompous island.

I'd love to excuse my father's cancer, his heartbreak, and these brutal heels still attached to my feet.

Raw emotion paralyzes me while he disappears down the hallway, leaving me alone.

Slumping against the wall, I try to hang onto the anger, the frustration. It's the only thing that's stopping me from breaking down into an ugly crying fit right here.

That's twice as hard to hold back when I realize just how achingly alone I'm about to be. More lonely than I've ever been in my entire life once dad starts to go through treatment.

Not to mention if it doesn't work. If, God forbid…

No, I won't let myself think the rest.

I won't let myself cry.

I definitely won't let the scream I'm holding in out, even though it's tearing me to pieces.

Several people walk past, nurses holding charts, slinging medical jargon back and forth. It's just another day for them, and why shouldn't it be?

They belong in this twisted fairytale kingdom where even the Prince is bad when he isn't playing hero for the cameras.

I want to go home. I want to help dad get well. And then, I never want to hear about Saint Moore or any of the royal assholes running this place ever again.

They've brought nothing but terrible luck into our lives.

When I finally force myself to move, retreating to his room, my right foot is so numb it almost drags across the floor. My heel catches, and I barely stop myself from tripping yet again.

I have to be more careful. I definitely need to pick some better shoes.

There's no Prince waiting for me if I stumble again. And there damned sure isn't a glass slipper at the end of all this suffering. There's no reward, no magic, except my father's survival.

I'll do anything to make sure he's got a fighting chance.

II: Grown Up (Silas)

The women in this club don't fuck around.

When they know I'm watching, they go all in, shaking their tits and asses off. Too bad for them, I'm barely paying attention tonight.

I can't stop thinking about the American girl with the chestnut hair, the mahogany eyes, the hips so round I wanted to smack them when they caught my hand, just to see how they'd bounce.

Of course, even I'm not a big enough bastard to give a girl a spanking after her father's having a fit in front of her.

My eyes scan the drunken sluts on the dance floor beneath my private balcony. At least half the two dozen or so girls out there know this place is crawling with cameras I can access anytime. Whenever I'm not looking down on them behind the tinted window like a god.

I'd be lying if I said I didn't feel like one. Comes with the territory when you're born a Prince, heir to a fifteen hundred year old throne, entitled to virtually any prime pussy in the realm, plus a hundred countries over.

They're desperate to please. Delusional. So fucking fake

I can practically taste silicon every time I glance at their basketball sized tits.

Their dreams aren't a mystery to me. They think they're next in line to audition for Princess and future Queen. Every one of them out there, from the redhead with the double D's, to the blonde with the perfect ivory skin, thinks she's Cinderella. Think I'm going to drop to my royal knees and propose the morning after my cock fits their magic pussy like a glove.

Doesn't work out that way. Never has, and never will.

Sure, I'm a bastard and a heartbreaker. Took me my first few flings to make peace with that, and most nights I don't give it a second thought. I let my dick lead me on like a magnet to whatever I'm in the mood for, then have my personal valet escort them out of my chamber the next morning, with a free ride home and a bouquet of roses.

The girls who try to show their faces around this club again wind up banned. The ones who try to get close to me in public get a stern talk with my bodyguards.

Most of them listen. Every so often, they go out ugly. Crying, screaming, wailing my name and threatening to sue me penniless from the rooftops.

Every so often, when I see those scenes, I question if it's really worth it. Mostly, I laugh, because I've got ten more girls ready to polish my royal scepter for every one who has a conniption fit.

For all my power, wealth, and women, I'm not free. I play by rules most people will never understand.

I've been bound to God, Queen, and country since the

day I drew my first breath. If I had to add one more principal, it'd be *one and done.*

Tonight, for some fucking reason, I'm not feeling it. I can't even settle on a girl who looks enough like Little Miss Warwick.

Why the hell am I fantasizing about an American girl who probably doesn't have a million to her name? Especially after her father went for the throat, before he just went down cold?

I'm still wondering when there's a knock on my door. I turn around, cup my hand across my mouth, and yell like always.

"You already know it's open."

Victor steps in. My personal valet is about ten years older than me, pushing forty, a transplant to Saint Moore from a distinguished Russian family. He steps up to me, that prim and proper smile on his face, the same one I've seen a thousand times before he's about to drop a load of horseshit in my lap.

"Pardon the interruption, Your Highness. I'm here to tell you that Her Majesty has requested an audience." He steps aside, making way for me to pass, wanting me to walk with him this instant.

I take my damned time. Sip my thousand Euro glass of scotch slowly, letting the liquid fire bathe my stomach and plate my veins in gold.

"Yeah? What's grandmom doing up at this hour? She's usually turned in before nine."

Victor clears his throat. "It seems she's heard about what

happened during the interview yesterday. It's been all over the press, sire. She's very eagerly awaiting your company so she can discuss –"

"My fucking image, right?" I smile and wink at him, draining the last of my scotch. "Come on, Vic. I already know."

Pausing, I sigh. Victor shifts uncomfortably. I've busted his balls a million times by now, and he always takes it like a champ, even if he's never sure exactly what to say.

"I hope she realizes I'm trying, Vic. It's not like I gave the guy a stroke when he was lobbing his questions. Didn't have anything to do with the hero shot either. That was all the daughter, racing up there and falling straight into my arms. Don't tell me what the blogs say – I didn't engineer a damned thing."

Yeah, the jackal's daughter, I think to myself. His very sweet, very pure, very fuckable daughter.

"You know you have my trust, Your Highness," Vic says, respectful as ever. But his eyes don't agree with his voice.

"Stop looking at me like that. Look, if it wasn't for that fairy tale embrace when I caught her, they'd be throwing a lot more shit in our faces right about now. Grandmom has to understand that, doesn't she?"

Victor straightens, folding his hands across his lap. "It's certainly not my place to say, sire. I have a car waiting to take you to the palace. At your convenience, of course."

Convenience my ass. I let my glass drop loudly on the wooden stand in the corner. Then I grab my gray jacket, the one with the purple and gold lapel. It's shaped like our national symbol, the double-headed eagle holding the crown jewels in his talons.

I'm wishing I could summon that mythical SOB to swoop down for a day or two, and give the chattering class something else to fixate on instead of Prince Playboy's latest antics.

Victor moves behind me, a subtle offer to help me slip my jacket on, as if I'm too damned drunk to do it myself.

I step forward angrily, out of his reach. I'm sober, and I'm damned sure old enough to dress myself. I haven't let the attendants anywhere near my body since I was eight years old. Mom was still around then, able to order her servants to have me up and dressed by nine o'clock sharp every day.

"I'm ready. Let's get this over with."

"Right behind you, Your Highness." He really is. Vic trails me like a loyal, if annoying dog the whole way out, radioing to my entourage for the usual security checks before we reach our ride.

This isn't the way I wanted my night off to go. I wanted to forget today's circus.

The pussy and scotch will have to wait. Duty calls, as long as my veins are soaked in royal blood.

A jet black luxury SUV waits on the curb. There's one brief glimpse at the subjects lined up near the entrance, waiting to get in. The bouncers have orders to pat them down thoroughly, making sure the girls who pass my looks test also aren't packing anything nasty like drugs or weapons.

The palace was scandalized enough when Victor found a joint in my room after my twentieth birthday party. He told me he'd keep it to himself, but I knew who had his true loyalty: the unbearably perfect, larger-than-life woman I'm on my way to see right now.

Hell, I stopped smoking completely after that. Nothing's worth risking another week at rehab in the lowlands. Sure, the scenery is gorgeous, but it doesn't make up for the distinct shortage of women, booze, and bright, shiny lights.

All the things engraved on my heart and soul.

It's a short hop to through the capital to our royal palace. The light nighttime traffic clears the streets when they see my motorcade coming. Outside, I watch the people sitting off to the side in their cars, a few stragglers waiting on the streets.

They wave. They put their hands over their hearts. Every so often, they shoot me the middle finger.

This division in the kingdom is what it's all about, what's gotten Her Majesty so nervous.

Grandmom wants me to shape up before she croaks, and the people are looking at King Silas. We both know Prince Hung will be done for then, but his memory will live on.

They'll be forced to decide whether they want me wearing the crown, or if they're going to use their votes to abolish centuries of wealth, guts, and glory.

"Right this way, Your Highness." A man opens the door for me.

I step out, moving quickly through the line of guards to

the back entrance. The lights in the palace are always so subdued; soft, gold, and otherworldly. It smells like a damned museum, and the décor matches one, too.

Whether I'm a lock for the throne one day or not, I can't imagine living here again. I'm walking swiftly down the long hallway, portraits of our ancestors towering down at me, glaring.

I can recognize my face in some of theirs. We all share the same vibrant blue eyes. I won't be caught dead in their furry robes and heavy gold jewelry, outside formal ceremonies, but it never fails to creep me out how easily I'd look exactly like my ancestors with just a change in wardrobe.

Victor leads me to the big three hundred year old door with palace scenery hand carved into it, stopping in front of it. *Great.*

It's the royal reception hall, a place she must've chosen to really make her damned point. It takes two men just to open the heavy door, revealing the chandelier, the amber and gold walls, and the huge fireplace inside.

The whole atmosphere takes on a different quality. Like it's somehow absorbed a piece of the royalty, billionaires, and Presidents who have stepped inside it across the centuries. Creaking, yawning, and ominous, the big doors smack the walls when they finally come to rest.

There, on her burgundy chair in the center, sits Her Majesty. Grandmom looks like a living ornament, holding up her monocle with one white gloved hand, her evening crown perched in her thick white wig.

"Come in," she says simply, the only person left alive who can take that commanding tone with me.

I step inside and wait for the doors to close, taking the leather chair she motions to, perfectly positioned several feet away from her.

"How are you this evening, Your Majesty?" I ask, pretending I give a shit.

"Unwell. Have you seen what's been going through the news today?" She knows I have, but it's not really a question.

It's an early warning before her claws really come out and she tears into me for fucking up the throne's reputation yet again.

Her valet, Patricia, walks up like it's all been rehearsed, and gently pushes a tabloid into the Queen's hand. "Special issue, Your Majesty."

"Swept off her feet! Shocking new conquest for Prince Silas after American girl falls into his arms?" Hearing her reading the headline sounds...ridiculous.

Christ. I want to bust out laughing, but thinking about the Warwick girl helps me hold it in. The tabloid shows my hand on her ass – that perfect ass – the girl's chocolate eyes beaming into mine like she can't wait to taste my lips.

"Come on, we both know what happened," I say, straightening up in my seat, hoping like hell I can stop thinking about that precious ass so I won't have to hide an erection from my royal grandmother. "It'll burn itself out like it always does. You know how these things work, Your Majesty. They'll be onto something else next week."

"I only know one thing," she says sternly, giving me that sour look I know so well, lowering her monocle. "This – *this*, Silas – has got to stop."

Her white gloved hand crumples the tabloid in half and slaps it against her knee. It barely makes a sound against the thick, flowing fabric she wears.

"I'm all over it. Victor told me this morning that they're being treated at the royal hospital. I ordered the very best for them. Way more than that jackass really deserves after his line of questioning."

Jackass? *Shit.*

I know I've slipped up in her presence – again – but I act like it doesn't faze me. Honestly, why the hell should it?

A little course language is the least of grandmom's worries, judging by the anger tugging at the lines on her face, a look that could give the Medusa a run for her snakes.

"You, Prince, are not on top of anything. Nothing that truly matters, anyway," she says, glaring. "Perhaps you're on top of your drinks, your parties, your greedy little tarts who don't have a drop of royal blood in their veins. Let me be perfectly clear, grandson – I've had it with the drama."

Her Majesty stands up, folds her arms, and twists that invisible dagger she just put through my guts deep. I'm taken aback. She's been cold and pissed off before, but never like this.

This isn't grandmom talking to me. This is Queen Marina Bearington the Fifth, preserver of the kingdom, holder of billions in wealth and millions of hearts.

"What are you saying? You don't think I'm sick to death

of this shit myself?" I'm shaking my head. "I don't understand, Your Majesty. We've seen these storms a hundred times, and this is just one more. We'll wait for it to blow over."

"Look at you, Silas. You're all grown up. Some days, I tell myself, I should've seen this coming." She pauses, narrowing her eyes. "Your father would've been just as big a disgrace, if I may be frank. He was off with his mistress on that yacht when it sank in the Mediterranean, taking him to his grave. You, I'm afraid, are heading down the same ugly path."

The whole damned floor drops out beneath me. She's *never* mentioned the accident since the funeral. Never breathed a word about the wicked rumors everybody in the kingdom knows are probably true.

My old man was a player, too. Like father, like son.

He would've been next in line to inherit the crown, saving me from all this, if only he hadn't sailed into a once in a hundred year storm off the Greek islands.

"Your Majesty…grandmother…" I'm trying like hell to find my words. "I haven't disgraced anything. I haven't even had a chance to fill your huge crown. Why do you think I sat there like a good little boy through the interview, while Warwick took his shots? I'm trying to shape up, embrace all the pomp and duty you've groomed me for. Really."

"Really?" she repeats, questioning me, slowly descending the three steps leading up to her secondary throne. "Silas, I'm entering my ninth decade in this world. You ought to know by now I'm not a fool."

Goddamn. When we're on the same level, she's a lot shorter, barely coming up to my chest. But those deep blue Bearington eyes rip through me, one with her aura, making me feel like I'm only half her size.

"You'll do better," she says, ordering me with a tone she never uses, not even with the servants. "You must. I don't have much time for your embarrassments anymore. I ran out of patience ages ago."

Patience? She really wants to talk about shit?

Mine is shot to hell.

I cock my head, trying my damnedest to return the death stare, without letting the warm buzz from the scotch muddle my words.

"What do you think I'm doing, Your fucking Majesty? I mean, really? *Really?* You think I'm some overgrown kid who's acting out? I must be enjoying this, yes, ruining our dynasty? You want me to admit it – is that it?"

Maybe a small part of me loves self-destruction. Subconsciously. If the crown goes to hell, all these ugly worries go too.

But I won't let that happen. I'm pulling out every stop to reshape myself in the eyes of the people, and she thinks I'm jerking everyone off.

"Fuck," I growl, running a hand across my face.

She doesn't even flinch. Over in the corner, Patricia stirs, one hand on the phone in her pocket, ready to summon the guards if she needs to.

It's the first time in months I've dropped F-bombs in the Queen's presence. It's the first time I can remember being this pissed, because I've actually tried. I'm standing there, wishing I could rip that stupid silver tiara off her head and throw it into the fire crackling behind her.

Everybody in Saint Moore worships the ground this woman walks on.

I don't.

I can't.

I've been her round peg since the day my father died, and she's been jamming me into a square hole I'll never fit through. I don't understand why she won't stop trying.

It isn't good enough that I become King. No, I have to carry on her water-to-wine routine, acting like a saint sent to Earth, adored by millions I'll never truly relate to.

I have to pretend it's vital to preserve this crown, when we could just as easily step down, ride off into the sunset with all our wealth, and let go of this medieval bullshit for the sake of prestige.

"Don't you dare take that tone with me again, Silas," she snaps, stopping when we're less than a foot apart. "I want you to listen, grandson, and listen good. You don't get to destroy fifteen centuries of tradition, wisdom, and grace. God knows this family has had its share of scoundrels and rakes going backward through the ages. We've survived them all. We'll survive you, too, because you're bigger than your antics."

Oh, fuck. Here comes the pep talk, where she tries to remind me I'm born for this, bound to a destiny I never chose.

"Let me guess, you want me to straighten up, fly right,

and start acting more like you? Everything I've promised for the last four years, yeah?"

"Act, yes. *Act.* I want more than talk, Silas. I'd like you to honor your family and your kingdom," she says, one more remark that puts me on guard. "Your mother was a wonderful woman. Out of her element with royal life, certainly, but she had a graceful heart. Look to her example."

I can't believe what I'm hearing. She's laid the guilt trip on thick before, but she's never stooped to using my dead mother.

I want to pivot and walk the fuck out. Too bad that's a breach of protocol even I can't bring myself to do, not when I've been raised to believe it's like slapping my own grandmother across the face.

"What's mom got to do with any of this, Your Majesty?" I say quietly, letting the last of my buzz wash over me.

"If you won't act for me, for this bloodline, or for this country, then please do it for her. I'm asking you to consider it seriously, Silas. I know full well by now I can't *make* you do anything. All the titles and power in the world can't do much for a man with your stubbornness."

"How about specifics? How the hell can I prove to you I'm already serious? Every time I try, the bastards in the press turn it into the butt of another joke. I can't control that, and you know it, Your Majesty."

She pauses. Thinking.

Damn. Have I stumped the Queen?

"You need a calming influence, something to prove that

you're mature," she says slowly, turning her head, studying my reaction for what comes next. "A woman, Silas. Not another whore you'll have for one night and never look at again. Find yourself a wife."

I think I blink before my eyes pop out, but I can't say for sure. I can't even feel my face when her words sink in, anchor, and drag me down with them.

"Jesus. You're asking me to get married? Just like that?" I snort, turning around. "Surviving bombings in Kandahar was easier than that."

"I never said it would be easy. I'm giving you a difficult, but effective alternative, son. The people never loved your father, Silas. They loved your mother...loved her almost as much as they adore me. If they can't learn to respect you, then maybe they'll respect your family, your children. I can't save you anymore. I've already accepted that." She pauses, a sad glaze coming over those eyes I know so well. "I can only save the family, the office, and the crown. Everything I'm bound by God, oath, and blood to salvage."

I want to ask why the fuck she's talking from both sides of her mouth. Telling me I need to shape up, but acting like I'm beyond redemption.

And marriage? She's talking crazy. I wonder if she's going senile.

One thing's for sure – I've had my royal limit tonight.

"Are we done here?" I growl, the only words I can get past my numb lips.

"You're dismissed. Think about everything I've said. Please."

I can't. Not now. Maybe not ever.

My head dips in the shortest, angriest bow I've ever thrown her way. Then I spin so hard my designer shoes squeak loudly on the delicate tile, probably leaving a streak.

I don't care. I have to get the hell away from this place, this asylum I've always hated, the world's most opulent freakshow.

It takes half my body strength to shove the heavy doors open. I'm not waiting for the guards. Victor doesn't say a word to me on the way back to my car.

He knows when to keep his damn mouth shut, and this is definitely one of those times.

I want to get back to the palace with a few new bottles at my side. I want tits in my face and tight, hot pussy sliding up and down my cock, draining this venom from my system.

Mostly, I just want to get out the latest orders to my entourage. Tell them I'm tired, pissed, and not to be disturbed with any business, official or petty, until past noon tomorrow.

* * * *

Sleep won't come, no matter how many times I flop down on my Egyptian cotton sheets and shut my eyes.

Only thing worse than the anger throbbing in my temples is that ache in my balls. The one that's been there since I grabbed Little Miss Warwick's ass, looked into her dark brown eyes, and wondered how they'd roll with her riding my cock.

I need to shake this. I'm going for a walk.

I'm drunk, staggering downstairs from my VIP room, sometime around two A.M. Half the girls have left, disappointed I haven't made my appearance, several of them taking off with the bodyguards changing over their shifts.

All I need is one.

One pussy to take the edge off.

One pussy to remind me I can make a woman sing like nobody else.

One hot, sweet pussy to claim for the night, have my way with, and never see again.

"Silas!" A voice rings out behind me. The only one that's ever gotten away with calling me that name, without putting Prince or Your Highness in front.

The last fucking voice I want to hear tonight.

I stop dead in my tracks, halfway to the bar. That's all the time she needs to jump me, throw her arms around me, and spin herself around until we're face-to-face.

"Get out of here, Serena. I'm not in the mood," I growl. Inwardly, I cringe.

I don't have to wonder what this woman's eyes look like when they're rolling back in her head. There's no mystery here. Last winter, I fucked my press secretary, a two week tryst in the mountains north of Bearington City. I was home for a couple weeks on leave from the Marines, and I was desperate for the only pussy still in season.

I remember exactly how she screams. How she twitches and calls out my name, over and over when I'm between her legs, bringing her off for the fifth time in one night.

I remember that I'm *one and done*, and the fact that I fucked this girl more than once, violating my own cardinal rule, is the reason I'm standing here looking into her desperate, hurt face.

"Jesus. You're drunk again, aren't you?" she says with a sigh, slowly taking her hands off me.

I start walking again, without saying anything. Already know it isn't going to stop her from trotting after me. Her heels scrape the floor, catching up after about ten seconds.

"Silas, you don't have to do this to yourself. You can drop the lonely, broody act when I'm around. Talk to me!"

I don't slow down or say anything until I'm at the bar. At least out here, she'll have to talk business, keeping up the pretense that she's never been anything more than my damned press secretary.

"You've got business for me that can't wait until morning, or what? I don't recall scheduling an appointment at this ungodly hour." I reach out for the fresh glass of scotch the bartender has laid out for me without asking. We have a special understanding between us, one that lets him read my mind when it comes to spirits.

"Actually, yes," she says, flipping her light blonde hair back.

I turn and stare at her. If she's trying to be flirty, she's out of her fucking mind.

And business? She can't be serious. That's the last thing I want in the middle of the night, when I can't decide if my cock is throbbing worse than my head.

I was simmering before, but now I'm pissed.

She's staring at me like a puppy waiting to throw her a bone.

"I wasn't serious. You think I'm really going to sit here and talk about my goddamned image at two o'clock in the morning, half blasted out of my mind?" I snap, draining my shot in one pull, and then putting down my glass for a new one.

"I think you will, yes, because I want you to consider something new. New idea, all mine. Strictly off the record, Your Highness." She adds my title almost as an afterthought, purely because the bartender is eyeballing her. "I haven't vetted it yet with any of my staff."

"You've got less than a minute," I tell her, picking up my glass, focusing on how the light hits the scotch on the rocks. Everything glows like gold and crystal coming together.

"You have an image problem. You've been defined, sire, boxed in by the press. There's a dozen playboy jabs every time they say hero. Doesn't matter. Whether you're doing something wonderful, like you did today for that girl and her father, or something…a bit less noble, everybody sees a playboy."

Yeah, they do. I barely stop myself from snorting and rolling my eyes.

They see the truth, I want to tell her, taking another long drink instead.

The player behind the medals and money is the whole reason I've got at least a dozen girls lined up here every night, offering themselves to me like I'm able to give them the universe.

In the bedroom, I do. I give them a few glorious hours they'll remember until the day they die, pounding them halfway to heaven with the biggest cock they're ever going to take.

And then I move onto the next. *One and done.*

"What's your point?" I say, my eyes running up and down her trim, skinny body. She's not a bad looking girl, but damn, she's nothing like the models I've had night after night.

Nothing like the curves I felt on that American broad today.

"It's not too late to break the mold. *We* can force the media to redefine you. It's worked for other royals and men in your class for ages. You've heard about Prince Lukov on the Baltic, right? A year ago he was just a womanizer, a drunk, a man they said had ties to the Russian mob…"

"Please." I quietly balk at the comparison, sipping my scotch. "I don't have skeletons like Lukov in my closet."

"Of course not, Your Highness. All I'm saying is, look what at the reports about him now. Loving husband. Family man. He's only a year into his marriage, and with the royal baby, nobody remembers the old Prince Lukov." She pauses, seeing the skepticism in my eyes. "Or that Sterner kid, the billionaire in the States. He married his stepsister, for God's sake, but nobody cares about that scandal. They just see charity, family, the handsome married man."

"And? I'm not shoving a ring on anybody's finger, or adopting a kid tomorrow, Serena."

She smiles nervously, and leans in, just far enough so her leg touches mine. "Even a public courtship could go a long way, sire. A kiss for the cameras with a steady lady, stepping out of your cars with her at the next palace functions, having her come to dinner with you and the Queen. I think –"

"No."

I only say it once. But I'm thinking *no, no, fuck no* to all that crazy.

No, no, no, goddammit, because I've heard the same thing tonight. It can't be coincidence.

I don't know what kind of game her and grandmom are playing, but they're hitting me from every side. Trying to push this marriage scheme.

It doesn't take much to see right through her. She clams up when I give her the heavy look, knocking back the last of my scotch.

"Silas, look, I'm not saying you need to get engaged to the love your life. It doesn't even have to be real. You can use me."

Don't have a clue how I stop myself from choking on the booze. *Shit.*

I'm staring to see what's going on here. Grandmom's using the stick, and Serena, she must be the carrot.

And does she seem…warmer? I'm used to the stone cold bitch barking orders at the press corps and corralling reporters. Not this soft, smiling stranger I've only met a few times when she shared my bed.

I wonder how many she had down here before me to put her up to this. And she's still talking, trying to convince me with words she can't be crazy enough to believe.

"Use me," she says again, words that would be sexy if they were coming from anybody else. "I'll do anything you want. We'll be perfect when in front of the cameras, and what a story it'll make! The Prince and his secretary. Can you see the headlines now? If they think you've found love, that you're starting to settle down, all those playboy stories vanish. Poof."

She snaps her fingers. Smiling like mad. There's crazy eyes, and then there's hers.

I realize I'm sitting in front of a lunatic, drunker than a highland beach skunk.

I'm already feeling my hangover. The buzz burns through me, hotter than hell, completely overwhelming the desire to fuck that drove me down here.

Or is it all this asinine conversation?

"I knew you were desperate, Serena. I understood, and I cut you a break after everything that happened because it was my own damned fault. Still, this has got to be your stupidest idea yet." I lean in, ignoring the twitch in her green pupils, so different from the way I made them shake six months ago. "Next time you decide to bother me this time of night, it better be good. Not because you want to talk about a fucking fantasy."

I stand up, anxious to get upstairs to my suite. She reaches out, catches my wrist with both her hands, clutching at me like a mouse in a storm.

"Silas, we *can't* be through."

"Babe, we never started. If you want to keep the position

you've got without stirring up any crazy questions, you'll forget last winter. Everything. You'll remind yourself you're nothing but the royal press secretary, assigned to the Prince, and nothing more. Even if I entertained your fucked up suggestion for more than two seconds, there's no way I'd ever make you my...what? My pretend girlfriend? My fiance? My wife?"

Raw anger is the only thing that suppresses the savage laugh in my throat. Her eyes are soft, sad, maybe a little scared. Time to go, before I pull the trigger that sends fire straight through her heart.

I turn around and walk, praying she isn't stupid enough to follow. This time, she stays put. I can hear one of the bodyguards shuffle over just before I get into the elevator, and see him whisper something into her ear.

They hand out warnings like candy whenever I need to be alone. And the bitch has gotten to me, yeah, just enough for the guards to sense it, step in, warn her not to follow me. She'll listen, if she wants to keep doing anything in a royal capacity.

The elevator door closes, taking me back to my private level.

I've forgotten about the pussy I came down for. I'm finally ready to crash, and forget this brutal day.

Nobody ever said being Prince was easy.

* * * *

I'm eating a late brunch the next day, wondering why I can't stop thinking about Selena's idiotic suggestion.

Maybe it's because the damned thing is…well, not so stupid after all.

Anything involving her would be a disaster, of course. But stepping out, finding a girl I can use to play pretend, just to get the media jackals and grandmom off my ass…no, that's not insane.

I've always been a fan of making my problems disappear overnight. When I see an opportunity, I don't let go.

Right now, a big, fat one is staring me right in the face. I can practically see it now.

Just a few minutes of playing pretty with my fake love a week. Maybe a dinner or two, just to keep up appearances, and keep her on good terms.

That's all I want. All I need to pull this off before I go back to drinking, whoring, doing whatever I damned well please.

My hero shine didn't last long when I left the service and Afghanistan, no matter what the nicer boys in the press try to say. Not like it suited me anyway.

I'd rather do scandal than play hero a thousand times over. Hero is a role I don't understand, and never will. It's dangerously detached from reality.

No, fuck hero. Afghanistan taught me life is short, more than anything else, and I'd better make the most of every day in case there's not another.

Hero's something I'll never understand. A suit that won't ever fit.

That's for grandmom, with her pomp, her tradition, her endless charity balls. Me, I know exactly what I am.

I just need to dial it back enough to prevent the Bearington crown from falling into the streets instead of my hands once grandmom's done.

I need a girl to play the part, to give me a new image. An actress, that's what I'm after.

Preferably, a girl who doesn't know a thing about who I really am, and who won't think twice about upsetting the whole arrangement because she starts to get attached.

Smiling, I sip my coffee, tasting all the sweet notes of the Hawaiian plantation it's imported from, just for me. Truthfully, everything seems bright and decadent and beautiful today.

It's glorious, because I woke up with my head straight, instead of a hangover. And it's only going to get better, damn it, because I have a plan.

I'm finishing up my goose eggs and coffee when Victor knocks. "You know it's open!"

He comes in, a somber look on his face, very much back to being my personal servant instead of my chaperon for Her Majesty.

"Your Highness, I heard about Miss Hastings and her chat last night with you in the club. I'm deeply sorry, particularly because I'm the one who's warned her about inappropriate discussions before. If you'd like me to discharge her from her position immediately, I certainly would have no qualms."

"No. It's my fault for bringing her to bed. She's crushing like a stupid schoolgirl," I tell him, owning up to it, as much as the bitch annoys me. "She's doing her job, giving me ideas to iron out my image. As long as she's doing that, she ought to keep what she's earned. She'll get over the rest of it, I'm sure, she's a professional at heart. Don't let her go, Vic. Just...keep her the hell away from me for awhile. Please."

"Understood, sire," he says, the look on his face telling me that's going to be easier said than done. "Is there a reason you've called me up here?"

"Yeah. I've been thinking about the Warwicks, wondering how they're doing."

Victor narrows his eyes. Probably wondering what I'm really up to.

Screw him. He doesn't need to know. Not until it becomes absolutely necessary to spell everything out. Not a day sooner, because I know he'll try to talk me out of it, if he even gets a hint of what I'm after.

"If you're certain, Your Highness, it would be my pleasure to find out and relay the message for you."

"I'd like that. I'd also like to know exactly what's wrong with her father, and what their finances look like."

Victor blinks. "Prince, I can find out the details of his condition without issue. The financial arrangements might be another matter. As you know, they're both foreign nationals, and the kingdom has no agreement in place with the United States to look so closely at their private details."

"Give me a damned break." Shaking my head, I fold my arms and glare at him. "No more games, Vic. You know as well as anybody that they've had special agents checking over the island's bank accounts forever. Trying to catch the rich assholes who tried to use our banks as a conduit to Switzerland to avoid their taxes. It was all over the news, just a year or two ago."

"That's true, Your Highness, but I don't see how American nosiness has anything to do with –"

"No buts. I'm not asking you to comb through the personal accounts of anybody at the US embassy. I'm just asking for the financials on the Warwicks. Two journalists nobody's going to start an international incident over. Can we do that?"

I wait tensely for the answer, and it better be *yes*. Vic hesitates.

Finally, he bows his head slightly. "Of course, sire. Anything you wish. I'll have to file a request with the intelligence office. You know how these things go. Hopefully, they'll process it promptly, and pass along something I can give to you by late tonight."

"Make it happen. Mark it high priority, or whatever. I want that file." Dismissing him with a wave of the hand, I stand up and head to the shower.

This bathroom is bigger than most people's homes. I've taken a couple dozen girls underneath the mock waterfall and the marble benches. Just last week, I fucked a brunette with fake tits here, pressing her against the wall, stretching her hair so tight in my hand the water sprayed her in the face when my cock took her over the edge. She took it without complaining, all for me.

Fuck. My dick wakes at the memory, pulses next to my belly button when I lather fine soap and water across every rock hard inch of me.

They all love it, this body.

The eagle tattoo crisscrossing my chest, wings spread wide, eyes set like a bird about to tear any lesser man's eyeballs out. The mad, dark stripes going up my arms, tapered like the royal flourish.

I'm a living tapestry. Something the press has always screamed about when they've caught little flashes of my tattoos sticking out my collar, or coming out the cufflinks near my wrists.

A million men would laugh all over the continent if I came out on the front pages shirtless.

Their wives would get wet, guaranteed, imagining what this wild, royal, unforgiving body could do to them.

And their nasty little fantasies about me – every last one of them – would be right.

I've got nasty on the brain, too. I grab my cock, all ten inches, and start stroking it like a demon.

It isn't that nameless brunette I fucked last week in this shower I'm thinking about. Isn't even the supermodel from Poland I sent home with a sore pussy several weeks further back, the one who's shared beds with half the billionaires and royals left in Europe.

I'm thinking about the girl I'm going to pretend to love.

Erin, Little Miss Warwick, with her soft American accent and hips begging to be wrapped around a good man's waist. Too bad for her there's nothing good about me.

I'll fill her anyway, fuck her, take her in ways she's never seen with those sweet, innocent eyes.

I want to corrupt her. Bad.

Even more than I want to use her to get my personal bullshit off my back, once and for all.

Christ, I'm a bastard.

Doesn't stop me from leaning into the wall, grunting like a bull, when I finally bring myself off, thinking about how she'd convulse on every inch of me.

I'm straining for precious breath by the end of it. Then I finish washing up, a sour frown pulling at my lips.

"Fuck you for thinking this'll be easy," I tell myself, staring into my own ripped reflection while I towel off.

I'm sure she'll take the offer, when I find her weakness, and throw it in her face. They always say yes to me, every woman who isn't related by blood, or wearing a thousand year old crown on her head.

No? That's a word I can't imagine.

Erin's going to be the perfect cure for all my woes. If only I can go several months without sinking my dick into her, making things complicated.

She'll either save me from the vultures who won't stop picking at me and the entire royal line, or else.

Yeah...or else she'll ignite the biggest scandal the monarchy has ever seen.

By the time I've got the towel wrapped around my waist and I step up to the huge mirrors to comb my hair, I'm smiling.

Whatever else I am, I love a challenge. I love a high. I'm the richest, most famous adrenaline junkie in the world.

Prince Hung is officially on the prowl, and he never comes home empty handed.

This whole wicked situation promises excitement. Sexual, emotional, scandalous, glorious excitement.

And that irresistible risk is the reason she's in my sights. I'm making Erin Warwick the hottest fake Princess the world's ever seen.

III: Make Believe (Erin)

I'm downstairs in the lobby, waiting in line to check out.
Dad's finally well enough to travel, and we're about to get
the red eye flight home.

It's going on midnight. Honestly, I can't wait to get the
hell out of here, to leave behind this miserable, evil island
that's shattered both our dreams and given us nothing but
tragedy.

"Checking out," I say, stepping up to the counter.

The man behind the computer nods politely, takes my
card and info, and begins typing away. Just before I think
he's about to print out a receipt, he frowns, deep lines
crossing his forehead.

"Miss Erin Warwick, right? Hmm. I'm terribly sorry, I
can't process this request."

I blink in surprise, wondering what kind of new
complication is about to bite us in the ass. "Huh? What're
you talking about?"

"There's a hold on your account, madame. VIP request,
you understand, from someone in the government. I need
you to step outside near the front, Miss Warwick."

The government? I resist the urge to turn around, wondering if I'm about to be arrested and detained.

Anger takes over. My fist comes down, banging loudly on the wood. "I don't have time for this crap. My father's upstairs, very sick, and we can't be late for our flight. I have to get home. If there's some kind of hangup processing his credit card, just bill us later."

"No, no, nothing like that," he says, slowly looking through me like I'm a ghost. "I need you to step outside and meet with the party waiting for you. Please."

He talks like a mouse. Practically begging me to do what he says. A chill runs up my back, and I slowly turn, sensing the five big men in their perfect suits before I even see them, standing next to the door.

"Are you done yet? You've scared the poor man enough," a voice that shouldn't be here says.

It's a voice I recognize. Regal, cocky, and completely in love with his own power.

No way. It can't be him...can it?

Oh, but it is. Prince Silas steps out from behind the guards like he's here for a stay, and annoyed with me for holding him up.

"There's the lady I'm looking for. Hello again, Erin," he says, that trademark smile forming dimples on his handsome face.

"Prince Silas?" Total shock rips through my core as he closes the distance between us, grabs my hand, and pulls me forward.

"My driver's waiting for us. If you'll come along kindly,

there's something I need to talk to you about."

He's pulled me through the door, and I'm halfway down the stairs when I start to completely lose it.

"No, no! I can't go now. I have a flight to catch soon. I need to get my father to the airport..."

"Nonsense. I'll make sure he's personally helped to the gate by my aides."

"I *need* to be on that plane, Your Highness." I bite my tongue when I use his title. I say it the same way I want to call him a *jackass* to his stupid, smug, mysterious face. "What's this all about? Have I done something wrong?"

He doesn't tell me until I'm in the car, plopped back in the wide leather seat with him. It's a big SUV, and the back feels a lot like a limo, with a cool black interior and more leg room than any vehicle should have.

"You'll be fine. My promise, love."

Love? Is he fucking kidding me?

"I really don't think so. It's going to take at least an hour to get through security. I ought to be bringing dad down right now, heading for the gate."

He laughs. Chuckles in a rich, deep tone like I've just told him a dirty joke. He's shaking his head when my heart beats mad, and my fingers twitch, ready to slap that wicked smile off his face.

I don't care if it'll get me detained and cause an international incident. If he doesn't stop, it'll be worth it, I swear.

"What's so damned funny?" I say, glaring at him.

"You're so procedural, aren't you? It's like you don't

realize you're riding with the second most powerful person in the whole kingdom. Do you really think I can't bypass the usual red tape, love? Get you and dear old dad a private jet back to the States the instant I snap my fingers?"

He holds his hand out and the cabin echoes with a loud *snap*.

I can't take this anymore. I grab him with both hands, shoving his arm as hard as I can. I keep going, reaching forward, falling into his chest while I try to slap him with both my palms. The momentum from the SUV lurching around a tight turn only helps me topple into him.

I grit my teeth. Prince or not, he's being a royal asshole, and I'm nobody's doormat. Nobody's – not even to the man who has everything.

"Hey, hey! Easy, now," he says, dangerously cool, getting a hold on me. Calmer than he should be, considering I've just assaulted his majestic, princely ass. "Don't hurt yourself, love."

I look up, the deep blue gems in his face swallowing me up. That's when I realize he's gotten me under control with no more effort than if he'd picked up a kitten. He's overwhelmed me. Holding both my hands behind my head, sternly but gently, a skill he probably learned overseas in uniform.

"This can't be easy for you," he whispers. "You've every right to be pissed, to lash out. I get that. I've practically kidnapped you."

"Yeah, you have," I say, feeling my muscles go slack. There's something vaguely gratifying about hearing him admit it. "You'd better start talking to me, Your Highness. Told you, I have a plane to catch, and I'm going to scream bloody murder if it leaves without me."

Folding my arms, I look away from him, settling back in my seat. Everything outside is whipping by us. The SUV is flying through the capital, with men on motorcycles all around us. The royals must have a special pass to drive through the city like a bat out of hell, faster than any emergency vehicle I've ever seen.

"It won't. I'll see that it's personally grounded by my orders. I'll have the fucking captain hold the door open for you, with a pillow, a blanket, and a martini in hand. Or are you more of a wine girl?"

Slowly, I turn to him, disgust twisting my face. He's wearing that smirk again – the one that would almost be sexy if it wasn't for smugness. We must be staring at each other for about three brutal seconds before he winks.

"Hold tight, Erin. We're almost to the castle. Then I'll be more than happy to fill you in on why I'm so eager to sit down with you."

No. I want to know now. I really do, and that's what I want to tell him, but the huge, imposing vista appearing through the window behind him puts me at a loss for words.

He wasn't joking around when he said *castle.* It's got to be Lucius, a medieval fort with huge gold capped spires I've only seen in the distance on the edge of the capital when the sun hits it just right.

Suddenly, they're a lot closer. And we're rolling across the literal drawbridge going over the moat, right into something from a fairy tale.

Except I'm not feeling charmed.

More like someone who's been taken captive, against her will, completely at the mercy of this strange, arrogant man for reasons I'm nearly afraid to find out.

The SUV jerks up a winding road past the castle's walls, and then we're next to a huge red door. It's smooth and modern, a more recent addition to the historic structure.

A man comes to Prince Asshole's side, pops the door, and he jumps out. Much to my shock, he rounds his way to my side himself, opening the door for me, reaching out with a hand.

"Come with me, love. You're the one in a hurry, aren't you?"

I jump out and brush past him, refusing his hand. He's right about the rush, but I'll be damned if I'm going to admit it.

I still can't wrap my head around this situation. And that goes double when he leads me into the castle, walking inside it like he owns the place.

Ugh. Technically, he does, and this could be his main home for all I know.

The place looks like a lodge, a luxury hotel, and a museum smashed together in one grand jumble.

Gold chandeliers, masterful paintings of the wilderness, handcrafted furniture in every corner. Classical music pipes through the hallways he leads me down, slowing when I start to lag, waiting for me with just a hint of impatience on his princely face.

We stop and wait for an elevator leading God knows where. My eyes finally aren't on him, but rather, on the huge ram's head protruding from the wall overhead, a long horned animal that's preposterously big, strong, and possibly extinct.

"My great grandfather bagged that one," he says, catching me looking. "One of the last ones, back when the crown owned every square inch of the mountains for hunting. You know what they say about the horns on those bastards, right?"

I shake my head. The way the smirk on his face tightens up just a little more tells me I probably won't like the answer, but he's going to throw it in my face anyway.

"Ground them up into dust, and they'll make a man crazy. He'll go all night. His dick will grow another inch or two – no bullshit. He'll become the beast, focused on nothing but fighting and fucking." He pauses, his nostrils flare, and he cocks his head. "Probably all rumors. Probably. It's hard to believe these creatures went extinct a hundred years ago if they were so good at fucking, isn't it?"

Jesus. For the first time since I've gotten here, I feel like I'm about to pass out.

I can't handle this. I wonder what I've done to deserve it, standing here in a castle with this Prince, this infamous playboy. Yes, the man saves my life and possibly dad's one day, and then talks to me about rams *fucking* the next.

The elevator door opens, and I step inside another hallway with Prince Playboy. He taps his perfectly polished toe the whole way up. I'm too busy grabbing the golden banister around the edges so I don't pass out, feeling the blood drop to my stomach as the elevator carries us up what feels like more than a dozen stories.

I look at him, my eyes burning in disbelief. He looks so good, so ordinary here, in his lair.

He's all suit and tie again. Everything clinging to his strong, thick, angular body so custom and expensive I wouldn't be surprised if his shoelaces cost a thousand dollars.

He stops in front of a door with gold trim, pulls a key from his pocket, and unlocks it. Then we're in a round room flanked with circular windows, a fireplace, and a view that would make heaven itself jealous.

"Take a seat," he says, moving to a small cabinet in the corner. "Before I offer you a drink, I'd like to come clean. I lied about the flight, love. Don't worry about dear old dad. My men are making sure he's on a jet to Mexico as we speak."

"Mexico?!" I choke on the word, feeling my chest tightening. "You're kidding me. Please tell me that's what's going on here. This is all some strange, elaborate joke...right?"

He turns around with that hateful fucking smirk on his face again, carrying a bottle that looks like crystal wrapped around some amber liquid, plus two glasses.

"I did what I needed to get you here. You can forgive me later, babe," he says, so fucking sure that I will. Then he sets everything on the little black walnut coffee table between us, popping the cap.

Slowly, he fills our glasses. "The finest bourbon in Europe. Something like fifteen thousand euros a bottle. It's a very special day, and the drinks should match the mood."

It rolls like gold over the perfectly round scoop of ice in each glass. He slides mine over to me, and I grip it tight, letting the cold numb my hands. I can't promise I won't hurl the heavy glass at his face, first chance I get.

If I'm going to hurt this royal asshole for what he's done to me, I'd might as well do it in style. Picturing him with a knot rising on his damnably handsome head almost makes me smile.

"What's wrong with you?" I say through clenched teeth. "Really. I want you to explain what's going on here, and I mean *now*. I'm going to call the embassy if you don't. I'll tell them you've taken me hostage."

"Hey, no need to get ugly." He frowns, pulling away the glass he's just taken a long sip from. "Yes, I suppose you need answers, don't you? It's only fair. How do I say this delicately?"

He turns his head. Both of us know full well that *delicate* isn't in this man's makeup.

"Fuck," he says, making me blink. I still haven't gotten used to hearing a Prince drop the F-bomb like he's one of the frat boys on campus. "How do I put this?"

"What?" I ask quietly, feeling my heart slow to a patter, bringing my drink to my lips with the hope it'll steel my nerves. "What is it?"

"I need you to marry me, Erin Warwick."

Oh.

Oh, Jesus!

Just like that, it's out. An answer that only invites a thousand more questions, if only it didn't completely stop my heart.

I shouldn't be sipping this whiskey, or bourbon, or whatever the hell it is. The sting in my throat causes me to cough, and turns the world upside down.

I can't see straight. Can't stand up. Can't even breathe.

Prince Silas' strong arms wrapping around me is the last thing I sense before I completely black out.

* * * *

It hits me in the face. Just a cold, crisp bite to the nose, bringing me back to life.

Gasping for air, I jerk up in his arms, and feel the water dripping off me. No, it's more than that. He has an ice cube on my head, gently positioned in his lap, of all places.

We're on the couch. It takes him a minute to see me blink before he moves, realizing I'm awake.

"Perhaps I ought to work on softening my delivery after all," he says. I'm too weak and confused to be bothered by the smirk on his face.

This can't be real life, can it?

"You were out for five minutes. I was going to call a medic. These blackouts must run in the blood, though I know your poor father has more reason than you do to lose it."

I sit up, hearing the heavy ice slip off my head and hit the floor like a baseball. "Fuck you. You said you'd give me an answer, asshole. You've only left me wondering. I need to go. My flight..."

"Whoa!" Prince Silas gets up and stands in front of me. He's too big, too fast, and too damned imposing to maneuver around. "Let's talk this out. I'm only asking for three years, love. Not a whole bloody lifetime."

"Three years *of what?!*"

"Marriage, of course." He narrows his eyes. "Maybe I should get that medic after all, so we're sure you didn't bang your head..."

Marriage. That word again. As ludicrous as it is heavy.

"Why – for the love of God – *why* would you want to marry me? This is insane," I tell him, trying to push past him again.

It's hopeless, I know. But I'm going to faint a second time if I don't keep moving, trying to make myself believe this isn't just a twisted nightmare.

"Because I know everything about you, Erin, and I've got all the leverage in the world," he says softly, grabbing my wrists and pulling me against his chest. "That's the funny thing about being a Prince – I have an obscene degree of control over everyone's life except my own. And let me tell you, I have my issues. You're the answer to about ninety-nine of them."

"You're insane," I tell him, finding my new favorite word. My eyes scan the table for that glass.

Just my luck that I spilled what was left of my drink when I blacked out. Otherwise, I'd have thrown it in his face and followed it up with a resounding slap, right across that five o'clock shadow he wears, dangerously close to my skin.

I'm sweating, flushed with heat. It's not just the alcohol or the fainting spell.

Wait. *No.*

This is already fucked up enough. You can't be turned on right now, I tell myself, shaking my head.

"Yes, yes, I know what it sounds like," Prince Asshole says, thankfully mistaking my gesture. "Believe me, Miss Warwick, it's nothing but business. I'm making you an offer. Proposal, I should say, but getting down on one knee and shoving a million dollar ring on your finger is only going to send mixed messages."

"Let. Go." He releases me, and I stumble back, throwing one hand out when he approaches, thinking I'm going to fall over again. "I need some fresh air."

He gently leads me over to a huge private balcony door. A soft ocean breeze caresses my face the instant the door opens. We step outside, and I've never been so grateful for sweet oxygen.

"I know your father's very sick," he say softly, helping me over to a big lounging chair. "I also happen to know your family doesn't have the resources to give him the chance he deserves. I can do that. As a show of good faith, that's the reason he's off to Mexico on one of my planes – they can do marvelous things there doctors aren't allowed to do in our slow, but civilized countries. He needs the very best, something experimental."

My head is still reeling. It takes me a full minute with

him hovering over me, eyeballing me, before I can bring myself to speak.

"And that's what you'll give me if I…marry you?" God. It scorches my tongue just to say it.

"Certainly, that's the major benefit. I'm also offering you a two million dollar stipend and all expenses paid for, while we're together. Far more than any glorified actress has ever earned. You'll sign a prenup overseen by the best lawyers in the kingdom, of course, and I may ask you to do something when our time comes to an end that turns your name in this country to fucking mud."

"Oh." My hands clench the edges of the chair, tightening in disbelief. "So, not only am I supposed to marry you, but you're asking me to piss off several million people?"

"Only for the tabloids." Prince Silas frowns, waves his hand, as if it's no worse than asking me to do the dishes. "I can't have you going down like my late mother, you see. The people would never understand that divorce, if they love you. Especially after all the years my father had his flings behind her beloved back."

It makes a sick kind of sense, knowing the history I've read about his family.

Jesus, though. I'm not really considering this…am I?

"I still don't understand why you want this, Your Highness. There must be something very important on the line for you to go to these extremes…"

"Our kingdom's entire future hangs on it. My family line continuing to rule, anyway. I have a certain...obligation." The word sounds poisonous. He turns away from me, his hands behind his back, staring across the high rising tops of the capital below like a god.

Up here, I suppose he is, in all but name only. His head turns, and he stares at me coolly.

"Believe me, this is the last thing in the world I ever wanted to consider. You've read the trash on the internet and on the supermarket shelves. I'm not the kind of man who's content to pair up with a plain, inbred princess several countries over. I'm not ready to settle down. Not now. Maybe not ever."

This isn't making sense. I don't understand how he's going to sell this fake marriage to the media, even if I decide to go along with this temporary insanity to save dad's life.

Dad. He's the only thing that gives me pause. If it were just money, I'd already be gone, on the fastest plane home to LA.

"I don't understand, Prince. I can't."

"Let me break it down for you," he says, coming closer, sitting on the edge of the chaise next to me. "I need a wife to smile and look pretty for the cameras. You're beautiful enough to be a princess, love."

Bastard. He tells me with all his infinite charm, like it's really true. My face instantly overheats, and I wish I had one of those big, round ice cubes to calm the flush.

Worse, he isn't done talking.

"You're also a foreigner, without any investment in landing me for real, or ruining a royal name you don't own by taking my ring in all my infamy. You, Erin, won't make a fuss. You'll turn the other cheek when I stagger in from the club with too many drinks in my blood. Leave me to my parties. Look away when I disappear with other girls to fuck. You're a living, breathing gag for the playboy bullshit that's followed me like a plague. You'll be my human shield when I live like the man I am, and pretend I'm someone I'm not. Hell, we both will. That's all this is, Erin. Make believe."

"Insane," I tell him again, shaking my head. "*This* is nuts, and so are you. Everything about it."

"It's perfect, love. And so are you. My pretend princess. The American girl who came stumbling into my arms. Love at first sight. Those fucking jackals in the press will be so busy dogging their new Cinderella, they won't look at me when I'm balls deep in my next mistress, doing what I do best."

I'm not going to call him insane for the hundredth time. Doesn't change the fact that he is.

"Can I go? I need time to think about this."

"Of course. Take the whole day. My valet, Victor, will help you find your room and unwind. It's not quite as nice as mine up here, but it's still a damned good view."

I stand up, making sure I'm able to walk without having a relapse into unconsciousness. Thankfully, I can. Once I'm steady on my legs, I beat it, running back inside his castle penthouse and heading for the gold trim door as fast as my heels will carry me.

I'm supposed to be rushing home to comfort dad.

Instead, I might be taking the biggest risk ever, one I couldn't have imagined just a few hours ago. *Whatever it takes to save him.*

There's a sickly feeling in the pit of my stomach as the tall, older man in the neat suit takes me several rooms down the long hallway.

I can't avoid what's coming next. I'm going to have to sit down and think.

Think hard and serious about staying in this crazy place, with Prince Asshole, a lot longer than I'd ever imagined.

* * * *

I'm dialing the number I've been given to reach my dad. The long table in my ridiculously oversized dining room looks like something from a mafia film.

Sitting at the edge, I rest my hands on the tabloids I've asked for. Reams upon reams of them, every issue about Prince Silas Bearington and his disgusting, unbelievable, sexist antics.

Prince Scandal. Prince Hung. The Prince I'm about to marry, if I stomach going through with this.

"It's me. How're you feeling?" I say over the line, as soon as I hear him grunt a hello.

"Better. Whatever they've got here to take the edge off the pain, it's better than the crap on that damned island." Dad pauses. "Always wanted to vacation Mexico, you know. Just didn't think it'd happen like this."

"You're in good hands," I tell him, unsure if I really believe it.

"Yeah, I am. They've got a lot of high tech stuff here. It's a classy place. The doctors talk like they know exactly what they're doing. Remember that story I did a few years back about the rich and powerful going abroad for special treatments? Really hits home now."

I smile. It's the first time I've heard him talk about work since the nightmare started.

"I remember, dad. Maybe you'll do a follow-up when all this is over."

"Maybe." He doesn't say it very enthusiastically.

Still, it's more than enough to make me beam, the very idea that he's thinking about something besides death and early retirement.

"Turns out I got more than the scoop I came to Saint Moore for," he says quietly. "The Prince is pretty decent after all. I regret hammering him before I had my fit."

Ugh. This isn't what I'd expected to hear.

He doesn't have a clue how wrong he is. If he knew anything about the crude, calculating proposal Prince Asshole just dropped in my lap, he'd know *decent* ought to be last on the list of words to describe him.

I don't have the heart to say anything about it. Besides dad thinking I'd gone crazy myself, I'd risk ruining his brightening spirits, and that could easily be deadly.

"So, you're happy with your care so far? I know it was all kind of sudden."

"Right. You'll see for yourself when you show up here. Or are you still planning on jetting back to LA? It'd be nice to have somebody checking in on the condo besides Wilson across the hall."

Shit. I haven't begun to think about how I'm going to tell him I'm not coming back to North America anytime soon if I sign onto this ludicrous proposal.

"I think I'm going to be staying here on the island just a little while longer," I say cautiously, wracking my brain.

"Huh? Whoa, honey, wait a minute...I see what's going on here."

Does he? I hold my breath, feeling my eyelids flutter as they pinch shut.

"That meeting with the Prince, you staying behind, sending me here alone on a private goddamned jet...congratulations, Erin. Seriously."

"What?"

"Congrats. You must've landed something amazing over there with the palace. I know, I know, you're too modest. Only have myself to blame for bringing you up that way. You don't have to tell me the little details until you're ready. I'm so happy for you, honey. You're gonna leave me in the dust before you're thirty. Everybody'll be tuning in to see the Erin Warwick report."

I'm laughing. He thinks it's because I've been caught red handed, bursting with pride.

I wish. Laughing is the only thing I can do to avoid crying hysterically.

"Let's leave off here. Lord knows we can both use some good news after everything that's gone down."

"You're right," I say, grabbing my belly. It won't stop twitching, heavy with the guilt and ten ton stress my father has no clue about, pressing down on me.

"I've got to go. They want to run a few more tests this afternoon. I'll check in again when I know something more,

Erin. You take some time to settle in. If you wind up meeting with the Prince or the Queen, I want to hear *everything*."

"You will," I promise. Another sharp pang stabs me below the breast because I honestly don't know what I'm promising anymore.

I don't even believe myself.

"Love you, baby."

The line goes dead. I hang up, throwing my phone across the table. My elbows hit the dirty tabloids laid out beneath me, wrinkling Prince Sicko's smug, sexy face.

God. Before I'd picked up the phone, I'd secretly hoped for a small miracle.

Dad could've said something to make me re-think this. Anything to put the brakes on this twisted ride I'm about to sign up for to save his life.

If the universe were kind, he would've already had his tests, and the doctors would've told us his cancer had mysteriously gone into remission.

But that isn't going to happen. Not unless I marry – yes, *marry* – the playboy Prince, the tease, the last man on Earth who should've been born to royal blood.

Running my hands over my face, I wait for my temples to stop throbbing. After another minute, they do.

The weight inside me shifts, settles. I'm making peace.

I think I'm ready.

I'm going to do this. I just need to swallow my pride, pretend it's just another job, and brace myself for the public eye.

It's worth dad's life. I'll humiliate myself a thousand times over to keep him from dying young.

Though in this case, I doubt I'll ever get the chance to do it alone. Prince Silas will be more than happy to embarrass both of us if he doesn't give me a heat stroke first from all the blushing, teasing, red hot agony he's bound to bring, too.

When I stand up and press the intercom on the wall to his valet, asking for an audience with the Prince, I want to believe I'm doing something noble.

Noble. Ha! Ha ha.

No, not this time. It feels like I just told my warden I'm ready for my execution, and now I'm just waiting for him to lead me down the long walk to my doom.

IV: Terms (Silas)

She's standing in front of me on the balcony, holding her hands in front of her like I'm her priest at confession, and she's about to tell me something filthy.

I wish. I'd love to know all her dirty little secrets, but I want her agreement more.

"I'll do it, Your Highness. But I have terms." Erin looks up, her soft brown eyes glowing in the moonlight, the wind flipping that chestnut hair I want to pull so fucking hard over her shoulder.

"Terms?" I look into my glass of scotch and give the melting ice a shake. "Let's hear them."

Her mouth is moving, but I'm barely comprehending what she's saying. I'm only on my second drink of the evening, so it isn't the booze.

It's that dress. She's wearing the first thing that isn't some mass produced casual horseshit, one of many fine pieces I had left in her room, and she looks gorgeous. The lily white evening dress clings to her skin, accents her curves, makes my cock stir like a hungry animal in my trousers.

"...and yes, I need everything in writing. We can keep

it between you and me, I don't care, but I want something solid. Trust, but verify, you understand." My eyes are on her lips the whole time while she's yammering on. I wonder how they'd twitch if I sunk my teeth in. "And one more thing, Your Highness…no sex. I mean, you said this was all make believe, so I'm guessing that's a given. I wanted to get it out there, anyway."

"No sex?" I repeat numbly, feeling my cock pulse harder. "Half the women in this kingdom would jump at the chance to have a Prince with benefits. You know that, don't you?"

She makes a face. Probably hiding the flush, the heat that makes her want to take it back. I know a woman when she's playing coy, and when her mind is far from made up.

"Of course I know," she says, staring me dead in the eyes. "No sex. I'm not one of your admirers."

Goddamn, this is going to be a challenge. In principle, I agree.

Fucking her would only make this harder, a hell of a lot more complicated than it needs to be.

Too bad she's just taunted me. There are *very* few things in this world I can't have by virtue of money and power. I can't even remember the last time I've met a pussy I want that's telling me 'no.'

"Is any of this going to be a problem?" she asks, nervously twisting her hands when I wait too long to answer.

"No. Everything you've said is more than reasonable. I'll have my lawyer draw up a prenup tomorrow and a separate document with the terms you mentioned. I have a man who isn't connected to the palace just for these sorts of things, so we can keep this out of grandmom's prying eyes."

"And the last part?" she whispers, fighting to keep her eyes locked with mine.

I take a step closer, polishing off my scotch, setting the glass down on the little table. "No sex?"

"Yeah."

"It's a deal." I wait until we're barely a couple inches apart before I say anything more. "You're a special woman, Miss Warwick. I think you have the honor of being the first woman I've met to make me promise *not* to fuck her brains out."

There's a tick in her lips. Quick, fiery, almost imperceptible. I can smell every molecule rolling off her, a scent my cock knows, pheromones so electric they tell me this is going to be the hardest fucking promise I've ever had to keep.

"I'm glad we can keep this...professional," she says, finally snatching her eyes away, looking over my shoulder at the capital gleaming in the distance.

"So am I. You've got a very bright future ahead when this is through. Believe me, I'm glad I can do this with a woman who's close to my level. Intellectually, at least."

She looks at me like I've just insulted her. What can I say?

Mentally, we're partners in crime.

As for the money, class, ambition? We're worlds apart.

My brain doesn't let go of its old habits so easily. I'm

still in hunt mode, eager to wrap this minx around every inch of me, put my mouth on hers, feel her tight little cunt dripping all over my balls.

Everything I want. Everything I can't have. Not unless I want to ruin this before I've even given it a chance.

"I hope you'll try to be a little more tactful when we're married," she says. "I'm going to be your wife. A...a Princess, I guess. God."

"You guess?" I raise an eyebrow. "That's exactly the title that comes with this job. Princess of Sealesland, Saint Moore, and All Her Tributaries. The next living, beautiful, royal vessel to continue the family line."

I reach for her. She's burning up when I touch her, gently sliding my hands up over her arms, a slow moving embrace that causes my cock to leak like a melting candle in my pants.

"No sex!" she whimpers, sucking her bottom lip.

"No sex. I'm a man of my word, Erin," I growl, bringing my face to hers, close enough to let her smell the liquor on my breath. "But we have to get used to more tender forms of contact, of course. What would an engagement, a wedding be, without a kiss?"

Her eyes go wide. She's trembling in my arms, but it isn't just nerves talking.

I know this heat, this waver, this fire in the blood. She wants me. I want her.

No, I want to be inside her.

We're both prisoners here, holding back on our natural instincts for a greater purpose, the way it has to be. We can only graze, but never gorge.

We can't rip off each other's clothes. We can't try every position I know, and invent several new ones. We can't fuck, and it kills me, the part deep down inside that loves a good conquest.

Fuck.

"It's too soon for that," she tells me, nearly breathless. Her sweet, plump tits wedge against my chest, and I swear I can feel her nipples through several layers. "I need some time to adjust to all this. Please, Your Highness."

"Fine." I tear myself away from her, pulling her with me by one hand, to the balcony's stone edge. "You should really start calling me Silas behind closed doors."

She looks at me, and blinks. I don't say a word, just run one hand up across her shoulder, cup her cheek, and gently tilt her face to the scenery.

"Take a good, long look at all that. It's the very reason you're here. You're doing this with me to save your father's life. For me, this is about a family, a kingdom. All the people down there in that glittering city, and the thousand other villages and towns beyond that make up this island."

"How noble." Sarcasm drips from those little lips I want to bury in mine. "It's not that I don't believe you. It just seems…so unlike you, Silas."

"What do you know?" I growl. "We barely know each other. To be fair, that's the way it ought to be. There's more to this life than fucking and partying. They're simply the fine perks I allow myself, something to keep myself sane when I have to face who I am, and what I've been destined to do since the day I was born."

She stares at me a lot more seriously now. Just like I expect.

This is all too familiar. I've brought dozens of women up here before, and sometimes I launch into this bullshit, after one too many drinks. I haven't had that tonight, but everything's creeping up, slowly strangling me.

The impending engagement. The wedding. The ridiculous marriage I'm going to have to pretend to be enjoy for the next three years, and the divorce that will come next.

Then there's the possibility Her Majesty could drop dead any time. Fuck, I haven't thought about what I'd do if I have to take the crown while I'm still married to this woman.

For a split second, doubt courses through me, deflating my erection. It doesn't go further than that.

I wouldn't be alive today if I let second guesses rule me. I take her hand in mine, squeeze it, and we stare across the capital together, my eyes focused on the palace in the distance.

"Let me tell you a secret," I whisper, wondering why I'm trying to convince her. "I'm not the bastard you think I am. If you'd come up here tonight and told me you wanted nothing to do with this proposal, I'd have let your father stay in Mexico anyway. I won't turn away a dying man from the treatment he needs. I'm not a monster."

Her eyes soften. She shifts, resting one arm against the high stone banister, just as the wind kicks up, ruffling her skirt. The wedding dress illusion to the damned thing makes my cock throb again, though this is far more casual than the long, ornate getup she'll be forced to wear at the actual wedding.

"That's good to know, but it doesn't change my mind. I'm not backing out of anything. I told you I'd marry you, go through with what we need to do. It's only right that we live up to both ends of our bargain. I don't need to know who I'm marrying. I don't care. I just want to get this over with. It's all make believe, like you said, right?"

She studies me closely. Of course, she's right. I give her hand one more fierce squeeze before I draw away from her, slumping against the balcony's edge, allowing my turquoise tie to hang in the breeze.

"Absolutely right." I turn my head, taking her in, trying not to let my eyes roam her curves for too long. "We can both be very fair. Strange bedfellows, as they say, except we won't really be bedfellows at all."

"No sex," she says sweetly, smiling. "Remember?"

"Like I have any reason to forget. Luckily for me, I've got pussy chasing this dick all the time. They don't call me Prince Hung for nothing. I can have my pick, Erin, night after night after night. I'll bring you to the club downstairs sometime so you can see for yourself. You're more than welcome to share the facilities now that we're going to be married."

"Gross." She makes a face, sticking out her tongue. "I don't need to. What you do on your own time, in private…well, that's your business. Just like we agreed."

There's some hesitation in her voice. A noticeable two

second delay that makes me want to rip that thin ivory dress off, lay her down out here, and fuck her until sunrise. Against the better judgment I'm barely holding onto, of course.

"What about me?" she asks, sizing me up. "I'm going to need to see the final draft of this agreement. Need to know you're not going to put me in a chastity belt or something weird in the clause about sex."

I'm rolling my eyes. "Please. They went out of style about two hundred years ago, love. There's a couple of the fucking things hanging up at the royal museum. I'd be happy to take you down there sometime for a tour, just to see them, if you're really so interested."

"Please!" She's laughing, but it doesn't hide the rosy red blush on her cheeks.

"You're free to make your own arrangements with men, so long as you're careful."

Naturally, she's free. I'm not really her husband, her Prince, or her lover.

Why do the words taste so sour when I say them, then? I shouldn't feel my muscles angrily tensing, the way they used to before going on patrol outside Kandahar, when I think about that perfectly slappable ass she's hiding grinding against another man's cock.

"I will be. I've always been extremely careful with that part of my life, Silas. God." She pauses, closing her eyes. "It's going to take me awhile to get used to calling you by your first time."

"Save the Your Highness crap for the press, and formal

audiences. After the wedding, you're free to talk to me as your friend in the open, anywhere except the most rigid, stuffy, and fucking stupid royal functions."

She smiles. "Friends. I think we can do that."

"I hope so," I say, clenching my teeth because my cock keeps hounding me to make her a whole lot more. My dick won't let up on that *Prince with benefits* idea. "Let's go over more in the morning. I'll bring Vic and Serena in for a full briefing."

Christ, Serena. I wonder how the hell she'll react to my abrupt engagement. One more problem I'll have to deal with tomorrow, hoping the warning has sunk into my lovestruck press secretary.

"Yeah? What's on the agenda?"

"First thing's first," I say, running through the long list of things to do to make this fake marriage happen. "We'll have to tell grandmom, after my closest aides. She'll need an audience with both of us."

"Grandmom? You mean...the Queen?" Her eyes glisten, big and dark and beautiful. Swept up in what must be an outrageous fairy tale to this American girl without an ounce of royal blood in her veins.

"Yes, Her Majesty, in the flesh." I'm going to need a few more drinks to get through the shock and awe tomorrow.

"Get some rest," I tell her, wrapping an arm around her shoulder and leading her back inside my suite. "I'll make sure you get your own aides assigned tomorrow, too, so you'll have some help settling in. After grandmom receives the news, we'll have a press conference. I leave you to decide what you want to tell your father."

"Damn, don't remind me! It's going to be difficult." She drifts out of my embrace near the door leading out, rubbing her temples. "Jesus. This is happening so fast. Whatever, we'll figure it out. I'm in this with you, Silas. I won't let you down."

"No, you won't. I always make the right choice. You're going to be the best goddamned plastic Princess a future King could hope for. If anything comes up, I'll be here, right down the hall. Starting tomorrow, you don't need to check with Vic to request my presence. If anything comes up, you know where to find me."

"Okay. Goodnight," she says, shooting me one more look with those chocolate eyes I want to lose myself in.

Smiling, we leave off there, and I shut the door.

I'm alone, left to wonder what the fuck I've done. The most restless night of my life since my father died on that damned yacht begins.

Flipping through my phone, I look through the numbers of men I served with, and stop just short of dialing them. I haven't talked to most of them since I got discharged, even the ones who were like brothers in arms.

They're good men. They held my life in their hands, like I kept theirs, and that will never, ever change.

But they're commoners. Happily married, some with families, without crowns to worry about.

They can't understand this shit. They can't help me with this, like they could with Taliban sentries. Nobody can.

I'm too fucked up to go to the club. So, I break out a

fresh bottle of scotch, settle into my granite bathtub with the waterfalls running out of the wall, and drink.

My cock stays hard as a stone when whiskey dick sets in. I can't get her off my mind, Little Miss Warwick the pure, begging to be corrupted.

I think about tearing that white dress off, down in the country mud, somewhere up in the highlands where you can walk the beaches nude for miles.

I don't want to kiss my new wife. It's not enough.

I want to bite her, slap her, fuck her. Bind her hands together at the wrists with my finest ties, over her head. Hear her whimper while I tease her nipples between my teeth. I want – no, *need* – to rub the full length of my raging cock across her slit, let it soak me with her cream before I finally plunge in and take her the fuck over, one hungry inch at a time.

Every atom in my body howls to fuck this girl, purely because I've told her I won't. What better way to realize my own depravity?

I'm burning up. My hand drifts underneath the water, grasping my cock, pulling off all ten inches with rough, angry strokes.

"Princess – fuck!" My eyes are closed, and I'm jerking off harder.

"Erin…" Her name growls through my throat like lava when I shoot my load in the water. "Fuck. You."

No, fuck me. I'm the whole reason she's about to be a piece of royal meat for my designs.

My huge, fit chest swells underneath the water, sucking

in oxygen to replenish the life that's been sucked out of me.

I can't screw this up. I need to keep this promise. I'll do it, no matter what happens.

Even if I have to spend the next three years kicking, screaming, boozing, and fucking everything in sight to keep my dick away from her.

I meant what I told her. Whatever else I am, I'm a man of my word, and I'll keep the promise I've made that's about to be backed up by a legal contract.

I'll switch to ice baths tomorrow if it'll help keep my cock away from my make believe Princess.

* * * *

I wake up late, sometime after eleven, and summon Vic immediately. I'll deal with Serena and figure out whether I need to fire her and find a new press secretary later.

He's in my room while I'm eating breakfast when I break the news. "I got engaged last night, and I need to take my girl down to the palace today to fill in grandmom."

"Engaged?!" He practically chokes. "You're getting…married, sire? Forgive me, but this comes as a great surprise."

"No shit. It happened very fast. It's the American girl, Erin Warwick. We've been spending a lot of time together since she fell into my arms. I've never thought real seriously about that love at first sight nonsense, but there's something about her. I've been converted. I'm a believer, Vic. Nailed in the ass by cupid's arrow. This is the woman I want to spend the rest of my life with, as ludicrous as that sounds."

His expression makes it look like he's been to hell and back.

It takes a huge sip of strong black tea not to burst out laughing. When he reaches for his elbow and pinches himself, I have to flex every muscle not to spit my drink all over the room.

"You're certain about this, Your Highness?" he asks.

I can't blame him. But I've been preparing for this, expecting it, even when I opened my eyes and felt the hangover pulling at my skull. I'm ready.

"Damned right, I am. This is more than just another slut, Victor. I've met the woman I'm going to marry, the girl who's going to serve the whole kingdom when she shares my throne one day."

I smile. Victor looks completely pale.

Shit. Trying not to laugh in his face just got ten times harder.

"Entirely your decision, as is your right, my Prince. If it's all right with you, I'll request an audience with Her Majesty this instant so she can meet the future Princess."

"Do it," I tell him, taking a long pull from my cup. "And make sure Erin's got something stunning to wear to the palace. Get the ladies up here who handle fashion at the royal bashes. We need to make the best first impression we can."

"Certainly, sire." He tips his head respectfully and I watch him head out the door.

I stand up, wash, and then get dressed in my finest suit. Amazingly, my latest hangover is already a distant memory.

If that's a side benefit from all this marriage bullshit, then I'm becoming a believer.

Vic sends me a text, letting me know everything should be ready in two hours. I step out into the morning light, feeling the warm sun on my skin, looking down on my kingdom while I fix my tie.

Erin can't comprehend what's at stake. It doesn't matter that I tried to show her, to explain it, to give her some small insight into the crushing, constant duties being born a Prince brings.

Too bad. She doesn't need to understand a damned thing to take my ring.

I need a toy. An actress. Someone to get the bastards in the media to drool all over her instead of my latest scandals.

Someone to make the future King look like one.

Someone to make everyone down there believe that I'm worthy, that I can actually fill grandmom's shoes. Or at least know that I won't ruin Saint Moore forever.

Someone to give me a second chance, for fuck's sake. To let me prove myself.

I'm better than my parties, my drinks, my pussy. Leaning over the edge of the balcony, my fists tighten. I see the kingdom's flags fluttering on the high towers in the distance, the black double-headed eagle grasping the crown in its talons.

That bird isn't ever letting go. Neither am I.

"You're going to find out how wrong you are," I whisper. "Every last one of you. This girl's my chance to show you that I'm going to be the best fucking King this island ever had."

Yeah, she is. And if she gets me harder than a rock in the process every time I think about her, much less see her, just like I am now, who am I to complain?

V: Her Majesty (Erin)

I'm barely out of bed, processing the insane thing I agreed to the night before, when I'm picked up by a whirlwind. Rather, three middle aged women.

Two of them lift me off my bed, gently shaking me awake, while another stands next to a rack of clothing that's materialized out of nowhere.

"Hurry, Marissa, she's only got an hour! We'll get her washed up."

"Whoa, whoa, whoa! I think I can wash myself!" They don't listen. They've pulled off my robe and carried me halfway to the bathroom before I'm able to speak.

"Nonsense," the oldest one snaps. "It'll be much faster, more efficient, if you'll allow us, madame."

Jesus, no. This is happening too fast. These manic aides or royal valets or whatever they are will strip me naked in a matter of seconds if I don't say something.

"Stop! I order you. I'm engaged to Prince Silas Bearington himself, and that means you're supposed to do anything I say."

Does it? I have no clue. I *hope* it does.

The women take their hands off me, the three of us standing in the bathroom, staring dumbly at one another.

"Engaged?!" The dark haired one looks at her companion. "Mary, I thought she was just a guest. I didn't know we were dealing with the future...Princess."

She blinks her eyes, totally shocked. Part of me regrets letting the news slip so easily – but not if it means I'm going to get a chance to bathe myself.

"As you wish," the redhead named Mary says. "But please, madame, you need to finish quickly. Marissa's waiting outside with your clothes and breakfast. You need to be downstairs with his Highness by noon."

I nod, tapping my foot impatiently. They're out in a few more seconds, and I let my robe drop.

It's been a rough night. I don't bother using the gorgeous bathtub with the gold trim and the waterfalls flowing from the slots in the wall. I hop in the shower and stand underneath what's probably a thousand dollar shower head, beaming me with jets.

The pressure massages me. It feels good, especially after last night.

It hasn't been easy getting used to this.

I'm surprised I managed to get any sleep. No sooner than I got back to my room and laid down, I spent several hours tossing and turning.

Thinking about this role I've agreed to play. All but whoring myself out to a man who's using me to lie to millions of people.

Thinking about dad. Thousands of miles away, battling

for his life, and getting a fighting chance at it only because the same asshole who thought nothing of using me as a prop stepped in to help him.

Thinking about the Prince. Everything he's gotten me to agree to should worry me.

But my mind goes somewhere else whenever I think about Silas.

His heat, burning beneath his skin each time he touches me, his breath drifting across me like smoke.

His power, his strength, the arrogance in every movement. He's grabbed me more times than I can count, something no man ever did before.

Always without asking. Always with superhuman confidence, like he already owns me, and we haven't even signed this stupid contract. Always with the glint in his ocean blue eyes that says everything I fear most about this insane arrangement.

I can fuck you, love. Anytime. Any place. Any way I want.

And you'll love it, Erin. Fuck yeah, you will.

You won't stop me. You'll beg because it's that good.

And once we get started, we won't be stopping until you've soaked the sheets.

"Madame?" A loud, desperate knock at the door breaks me from my filthy daydreams.

I look down at the aching, wet mess between my thighs. My hand went there without me even realizing it, my fingers drifting over my clit, stroking it while I imagine what would happen if the Prince and I threw that 'no sex' rule to the seven winds.

"Coming! Hold on, just a second," I grunt, standing up straight, flattening myself against the wall.

I don't know if she backs away from the door. I don't care.

It's dirty and depraved, but it's the release I need. It's the tension Prince Hung is strangling me with.

Is he really as *hung* as his nickname implies? Or is it one more lie he's fed to the media to make himself seem like a god?

I want to believe. I want to think about how huge he is because I *need* my release if I'm going to survive today.

The kind of sweet release I've never, ever gotten as a sheltered virgin, who always thought she'd save herself for her husband. For a good man, a noble man, someone closer to my level, sexually and otherwise.

Not the Playboy Prince, who's probably fucked hundreds, the one who doesn't even want me for real, the man who makes me want to tear out the 'no sex' clause in our non-existent contract with my bare teeth.

Oh, God. Oh, fuck.

Silas!

My thoughts are off the chain, surrendering to the filthy hulk I want bending me over, fisting my hair, slamming into me so hard I can feel my hips shaking my shoulders. He really is Prince Hung and so much more in this fantasy. He's about to push me over.

"Madame? Are you all right?" Mary sounds extra nervous in that not-quite-English accent. She jiggles the doorknob, but I can't stop now.

"Coming!" I scream again, this time a little more breathless.

Yes, *coming*.

Coming for the bastard, the player, the Prince. Coming so hard I feel myself gush all over my hand, something that rarely happens. Grinding my teeth, heaving my lungs, pushing myself up into the jet stream so the waves lap at my nipples like tongues.

I'm coming the way I've wanted to since I climbed into bed last night.

Coming, coming, coming while I think about him grabbing my wrists the next time we're face-to-face, pushing me against the nearest wall, and ripping off my panties...

My knees are shaking when I finally pull my hand away and turn the water off. By now, two of the women are in a full blown panic. I hear one slamming herself into the door like a battering ram.

"Jesus Christ. I'll be out in just a minute – I'm drying myself now!"

The commotion stops. I hear them angrily chattering away behind the door while I rip the Egyptian cotton towel off its golden clip.

Recent pleasure aside, I'm hating Silas even more. His lies are rubbing off on me, and so is his dirty, evil charm.

This has to be some kind of black magic. Saint Moore, like any other European country, has its legends about sorcerers, witches, and other crazy things. I think I'm cursed. The fact that I'm pulling on fresh underwear after masturbating to a man I hate makes me wonder if all the myths are true.

"Okay. Sorry about that, ladies, I sometimes have allergies and like to breathe the steam to clean my sinuses." Another lie.

Mary and Charlotte glare at me. Fortunately, the more chipper Marissa steps between them, yanks me forward, and sits me down in front of three huge mirrors. She blow dries and combs my hair, humming an odd sounding tune.

I'm allowed to gulp down a thermos of strong black tea and something that tastes like waffles stacked high with a fantastic spread of fruit and cream drizzled over it. Delightful.

It takes me a minute to recognize the tune. It's *King of All Things,* the elegant overture Saint Moore adopted as its national anthem. It's also the song that plays every time one of the royals steps into a public setting.

It's about a great King, Queen Marina's grandfather, I think. Of course, it's loud, arrogant, and probably caused a few composers to wag their fingers angrily when it was written about a hundred and fifty years ago.

Yeah, the longer I'm here, the easier it is to see why such cocky, manipulative crap runs in Silas' blue blood.

"Stand up, please, madame! We're on a very tight schedule, you understand. Pardon the hurry." Marissa beams me a tense smile.

No sooner than I'm on my feet, she's wrapping me in several layers of the softest, most expensive clothes I've ever worn on my body. It's a long, flowing, very traditional dress. Very red – blood red. Complete with a sweet smelling flower she tucks into my hair, giving it a final push in the mirror.

"There, there. You look just lovely. What do *you* think?" She puts her hand on my back and spins me around.

It takes me a second to recognize myself. *God.*

I've been transformed. Completely. Unrecognizably.

Even in my best formalwear, I never looked like anything more than a smart, savvy student from a very American college. Now, I look like I belong on a theater stage, re-enacting some play from a hundred years ago.

Or else in the royal palace on this insane island. The place I'm supposed to wind up in less than thirty minutes.

"It's good, I guess," I tell her. "Uh...shoes?"

"Of course!" She snaps her fingers and dives down on the floor, grabbing my feet and stuffing them into wooden clogs with gold and rubies.

The heels are surprisingly high. I hope I can actually walk in this getup without tripping all over myself. I don't stop to think about what a pain it's going to be if I have to use the bathroom.

"Just perfect, madame! Your Prince is waiting downstairs. Shall we go?"

"We shall," I say, leading them out the room, straight to the elevator.

When we're on the first floor, the boys take over. Silas' valet, Victor, nods respectfully and walks me out to the waiting SUV tucked into its motorcade.

"His Highness is already waiting for you in the rear, madame. Please don't be afraid to grab my arm if you need some help on these stairs."

I thank him, but intend to take them myself. I could use

the practice. I manage, slowly and haltingly, careful not to go tumbling down in a flash of reds.

The SUV's door opens. I slide in next to Silas, or that's what I mean to do, except suddenly I'm stuck.

"Jesus. Look at you," he says, lowering the expensive shades he's wearing.

It's a look that's way too similar to the imaginary smile Prince Hung just gave me in the shower.

I'm embarrassed. Victor comes running up to save my skirt from tearing on the metal. I swear, if Silas is about to hit me with some snotty remark, I won't hesitate to give him the slapping he deserves. Prince or not.

"What?" I say, narrowing my eyes.

Finally. The skirt comes free and I clamber up on the seat next to him, grabbing my seat belt.

"You're gorgeous, love. Looks like it was made for you."

Surprise. Compliments aren't what I expect.

I bat my eyes a couple times and turn away from him, trying not to think about what he made me do in the shower this morning.

"Well, I think this would be much easier if that were the case."

"I'd say you'll get plenty of practice, but you'll be happy to hear occasions this formal tend to be rare. You can go back to your thongs and yoga pants when we're done. Just be sure you wear something halfway decent when we're in front of grandmom."

Thongs and yoga pants? *Thanks, asshole.*

Without thinking, I reach over and sock him on the

arm. He laughs, grabs my wrist, and brings my hand to his lips.

I hadn't noticed how insanely hot it is underneath all this. Naturally, I do when he kisses my skin for the first time. It only lasts a second, more than a gentle peck. It's forceful, a little wet, and haughty as everything else about him.

"If you really want to cause damage, you'll have to punch me a whole lot harder next time. That swing just turns me on. You get rough with me, I'll eat it up and spit it back ten times harder." He brings his mouth to my hand again, this time sinking his teeth in, a gentle bite igniting a flash fire in my body.

Bastard! I can't let him play with me like this. I won't, I tell myself.

He's never polite, even when he says nice things. He just wants me to let my guard down.

"No sex," I tell him, jerking my hand away.

"Please. I haven't forgotten," he says, pushing his shades back over his beautiful eyes. "I'm practicing my most gentlemanly kiss. We can't be like ice, Erin. You'd better believe the tabloids will pick up a frigid marriage if they get so much as a breeze."

"Really? Is that why you're hiding behind those sunglasses?" I stick out my tongue.

"This is pure style for a bright day, love." He grins. "Same brand the late dictator Mesaru wore in North Africa. I've heard his collection of designer shades is the only thing that survived when they ransacked his palace and stabbed him a hundred times a few years back."

"I know all about the Arab Spring," I said, confident I knew a lot more than him. "Didn't know you took fashion tips from dead tyrants."

"Hey, the man was a sick fuck, no doubt about it. Sometimes even the assholes know how to look good." He lifts his eyebrows, a gesture that lets me know he's practically eye fucking me behind his lenses. "We need to be in our Sunday best, and on our best behavior, too. You've only got one chance to make a first impression on Her Majesty."

Damn it, he's right. I tense up, folding my hands in my lap, very conscious that I'm about to meet a Queen, a ruler, a billionaire, and one of the most beloved elder stateswomen in the world.

"Love, don't spill your spaghetti now," he says, barely hiding the amusement in his voice. "It's going to be fine. Trust me, I've visited her before with enough mud dripping off me for the both of us. Unless you drop the dress and prance in naked or something, nothing you do will ever one up me in the scandal department."

He's right, of course. So, why the hell isn't that any consolation?

The worst part is, he senses my nerves coming undone. That's probably why he reaches over, clasps my hand, and holds it like he cares.

We share a slow, tense look. Then he cocks his head, looks at me over the tops of those shades, and says something that makes me believe he isn't just an asshole for about a minute.

"You can do this, Erin. You've got family, life and death on the line. That's as valuable as an entire kingdom."

"I'll do my best," I say softly, promising both of us that I will.

"Yeah, you will, Princess. I wouldn't take on anybody who half-asses it. Not even a pretend bride." That smile on his face erupts into a full panty-melting grin. "Half-assing anything isn't in your nature. I know because every inch of what you're sitting on is too fucking fine for half measures."

Oh. My. God.

Here I am, decked out in this dress that's worth more than the luxury vehicle we're riding in, and he's commenting on my ass. I can't take it anymore.

I lean in, let my hand fly, and give him what he deserves. Silas' royal stubble burns my palm when it explodes across his cheek.

Pulling back, my fingers are trembling, wondering if I've just blown the whole thing.

No, he's still smiling. I should've known, after what he said about liking it rough. The idiot on top of the world next to me *likes* this.

"Hope you're feeling better," he says, as if I just sneezed. "I'll take a blow like that anytime if that's the price to pay for complimenting one of the finest asses I've ever seen."

I don't say another word until we're at the palace. He takes off his shades, steps out before me, and comes to my side to help me out. I take his hand angrily, catching his dizzying blue eyes for a second before I look away.

I can't let him get to me again. This is too important.

I'm already feeling light headed by the pomp and glamor adorning every inch of this incredible building. It's only my second time here since the disastrous interview, since the unthinkable became my reality.

Silas stops in front of a regal looking man in a suit that's almost as nice as his. "Where is she?" he asks.

"Throne room, my Prince. She's waiting for you, having finished with the Belgian trade minister a few minutes ago."

"Damn," he says, turning to me as he leads us on, his personal entourage trailing behind us. "I'd have hoped for some place more casual for an introduction. Whatever, it's a test. If you can get through this when she's there, perched in all her splendor, you can get through anything, love."

My heart starts hammering in my chest. Thank God corsets aren't a thing in royal fashion anymore, or else I'd be screwed.

It takes several minutes to travel through the palace, taking in more history, wealth, and power than I can fully absorb. Hell, I think I'll need several lifetimes to do that. Every wall, every ceiling, every chandelier oozes class.

The very highest, most exclusive class a human being can belong to. These royals make billionaires and celebrities back home look like posers.

I'm walking into the home of living, breathing people who think they're gods, put here to shape this island and the broader world as they please. It's their destiny, the one they're told to fulfill from the day they're born.

Besides being alien to everything I know, I can't lie about what it means. It's fucking *terrifying*.

The door to the throne room – if I can even call it that – is huge. Scenes of battle, triumph, and dragons are carved into every inch, stretching from floor to ceiling. Two men in traditional navy blue uniforms with rifles slung over their shoulders bow their heads as soon as they see us.

"I'm here to meet with Her Majesty," Silas tells them. "Let us in."

The men move like clockwork. They march several long strides to the center, and grasp the huge silver handles. The door creaks open like it's hiding Aladdin's long lost treasure – what else? – and I'm staring into a scene from another century.

Inside, Queen Marina Bearington sits on her high throne, a tiara like crystal on her head. I've seen it in the pictures. She's like a living ornament on a Christmas tree turned into a room, decked in jewels, metals, and silk robes. It's hard to believe she's human, much less standing in front of me.

Yes, *standing*, rising to her royal feet. Waiting for us.

"Come on. Just follow my lead," Silas whispers under his breath. A move that teaches me *everything* echoes in this monstrous, awesome chamber, however subtle.

He steps forward, and I'm at his side. When he bows – much more deeply than the shallow head nods I've seen in the kingdom before – I do it, too. Then I curtsy, careful not to catch my dress on my heels, embarrassing myself forever.

"Your Majesty. It's my great honor to present my fiancee, and future Princess, Erin Warwick from the United States."

My head stays dipped too low to see the Queen, but I can feel her eyes. They're focused on me like a hawk's, wondering where the hell I came from, and why.

"Rise." She speaks one word.

Silas takes my hand and helps me up. We're standing beneath her elevated throne, just several feet away from a woman who's ruled over millions long before I was born.

I can't make out any of Silas' facial features in hers, but they share the same eyes.

Deep, dark, royal blue, unchanged by age.

"You're the girl whose father collapsed on television, interviewing my grandson, aren't you?" she says, slowly scanning me with her gaze.

"Guilty as charged, Your Majesty." I want to kick myself as soon as it's out of my mouth. Jesus, what was I thinking – *guilty?*

The Queen turns to Silas, her tiara catching the light, sparkling brilliantly like stars in her head. "What's the real meaning of this, Silas? Tell me the truth."

He looks taken aback, and his fingers tighten in mine. "The meaning? I've found the love of my life, and I'm claiming her. You always said I ought to find a good girl to settle down with. Someone to calm me, bring balance. Well, Your Majesty, I have."

The Queen looks incredulous. "So, you've done exactly what I suggested in a matter of days? You couldn't have possibly known Miss Warwick much longer than that, all things considered."

"You're right," he says. "We've barely known each other

a week, if you want the full truth. This woman, she's different than all the others I've ever been with. She isn't just another fling. When you meet the love of your life, you just know. I used to laugh at that, but now? I get it. Hell, yeah, I do."

He pulls my hand up, brings it to his mouth the same way he did yesterday on the balcony, and puts it against his lips.

The floor drops out beneath me.

I can't believe I'm standing here, having my hand kissed by a Prince who doesn't believe a word of anything he's just said, all in front of Queen Marina Bearington.

"You're lying," she says, turning her angry eyes to me, making my heart sputter. "You're either lying, or you've lost your mind, son. When I said you should find a woman, I meant it should happen slowly…naturally. Just as these things are meant to. You can't possibly think I meant for you to find a wife in less than a week. What I don't know is *why* you're doing this. Regardless, it isn't going to work, Silas. I see through it, and I'm going to instruct the royal chapel not to approve any weddings with this woman."

"No!" Dad flashes in my brain, and I step forward, speaking my objection like a bullet. "I know what this looks like. It seems insane, Your Majesty, like something from a dream. That's been my last few days with the Prince, exactly. The truth is…we're in love. We want to move this forward. But I can't do that unless he gives me a place in the kingdom so I don't have to go back to LA."

Her gaze picks me up and throws me down again. I feel

like I'm disembodied, watching myself plead this crazy case, telling the biggest lie I ever have in my life to a famous person I never imagined talking to.

"You don't have to believe it, but I'm giving you the truth. And the truth is…I've never met a man more kind, more noble, more handsome than your grandson." I pause, feeling his smile burn when I call the bastard handsome. *Damn him.* "I want to have a life with Silas. I'll do anything to make that happen."

"Certainly, you will," she snaps. "It isn't every day a commoner has the prospect of becoming a Princess staring her in the face."

"No," I agree softly. "Believe me, that isn't what I'm after. I'll do whatever I need to convince you I'm sincere. I'm not looking to get rich or have a title behind my name."

Except…that's exactly what I'm hoping to get from this.

"Nonsense. You'll acquire both those things, no question about it, if you two go through with this madness. Technically, there's no law restricting marriage outside the family to royal blood, so I can't oppose you on those grounds. There is, however, more than ample reason to stop this when I believe my son's judgment has been compromised. It's ludicrous!"

That last word rings off the gold walls like a cannon blast. She's rattled, for good reason, but it's disturbing as hell to hear the Queen get so emotional.

"My judgment?" he says, sharp sarcasm in his voice.

Great. They're about to argue, and I'm going to be sick. My stomach flips itself over several times. I'm almost grateful when Silas steps in front of me, closer to the throne.

The Queen nods. "You can't be in your right mind. I want her gone, Silas, and then I'm going to ensure you get a full evaluation at the royal hospital."

Silas snorts, shakes his head, and points a finger up at her.

"You've got to be fucking shitting me, Your Majesty, if you think this makes me mad. Where were you, questioning my judgment, when I decided to be the first royal since World War II going into battle? I'm pushing thirty soon. I've led men in war and saved lives, foreigners and our own subjects alike. I've watched my parents live and die. I've seen their mistakes and their triumphs. No, I haven't been perfect, but I'm trying like hell to be better, and Erin's the best chance I have to do that. Knew it the second I laid eyes on her, when she fell into my arms. You want to question my judgment? Then start by asking why the *fuck* you never did it sooner."

The Queen doesn't flinch at his rough language, which surprises me. Probably a sign she's heard it all before. She's used to Silas' outbursts by now.

She lets out a long, tense sigh. "I'm too old for this. If I wasn't bound to wear this crown on my head to the grave, or I had someone worth handing it to, I'd give it up tomorrow. Silas, you're right, for once in your outrageous life."

He blinks, his face softening. "I am?"

"I'm going to allow this, with a few very strict conditions." She steps down, her robes flowing over the short golden stairs leading to the floor like she's hovering. "Number one, Miss Warwick will be thoroughly vetted, trained, and assessed for the duties she's bound to take on as your wife."

Nod at her, damn it. It takes every muscle in my body to move my head.

Suddenly, now that she's on our level, Queen Marina is coming toward us. It seems like she's shrunk at least a foot, but she's no less imposing, decked out in her royal wears like a ghost from a lost time.

"Your Majesty, I –"

"Quiet." She cuts him off, turning away from us, slowly pacing on the floor. "Second condition, this wedding won't happen for at least six months. That's more than enough time for you, Silas, to decide if you've made a terrible mistake, given your track record with women in the past."

"If you're saying I'll get bored of her, you're out of your damned –"

She holds up a finger. "Third and last, you'll announce this news to the kingdom. Both of you. Should you decide it's off sometime in the future, then that will fall on you, as well. I won't keep this a secret and risk sensationalism running wild."

"Very fair, Your Majesty." I tell her it is, anyway, even though thinking about the inevitable appearance in front of millions is turning every muscle in my body to stone.

"Silas?" She stops in front of her grandson, face-to-face, a royal challenge across generations.

"Whatever. I can live with it," he says. "It's going to be

my pleasure to show you how wrong you've been, grandmom."

Queen Marina doesn't say anything. She simply turns, moving back to her throne, a force of nature.

"I don't want to hear about it until we're closer to the date, unless I change my mind," she says, once she's perched in place again. "I'll hear everything I need to from Mister Mead, my chief of information. You're both dismissed."

Silas looks like he's about to make his handsome face crack when he dips his head again. I mimic the gesture, watching him the whole time.

God, he's so wound up. Tighter than a spring.

Hard. Angry. Did I say *hard?*

My eyes tick over to his crotch for a split second before I jerk them away, remembering where I am.

Holy hell, what's wrong with me? I can't risk another scene.

I have to get out of here. Before we both drown in the thick, smoky tension curdling the air.

I hear the doors creak open behind us. Silas and I both rise. He snatches my hand, leading me out, and doesn't say a word as we take the long, dream-like path through the palace.

"What do you think? Was that her taking it well?" Truthfully, it seems like a disaster, but I'm new to all this and I don't know the Queen's attitude like he does.

"Well enough. She didn't outright forbid it," he says, helping me down the stairs. We take a turn toward a new section of the palace, and I realize it's adjacent to the huge, semi-public entrance that leads to the big conference room where I fell into his arms.

"You were very well spoken back there, swearing aside." I mean it, too.

"Yeah, well, I know how to pull her strings. I've been doing that damned near twenty years by now. Anything about God and country, about my service…it really gets to her, love. Reaches her on a primal fucking level."

Ouch. I cringe, suddenly wondering if he rehearsed everything about her questioning his judgment. That would be so Prince Playboy, wouldn't it?

I have to remember who I'm dealing with.

Silas, the manipulator.

Silas, the most immature war hero in the world.

Silas, the lying, faking, self-absorbed bastard.

"What's next?" I ask, trying not to dread it.

"We're going to have some tea and lunch. Then, a quick meeting with Serena, my press secretary. You've met her once with the whole press corps, under very different circumstances."

"Oh, we're being prepped already to talk to the media?"

He flashes me that wicked, teasing smile. "Babe, we've got ourselves a press conference this afternoon. Just you and me, in front of the entire kingdom. Grandmom wants me to show I'm serious? I'll make her believe in this fake marriage more than we do."

Crap! I don't say anything. I just hope there's something stronger than tea up ahead.

* * * *

We don't say much through our snack. We have the fanciest pot pies I've ever eaten, stuffed with something that tastes like duck, veggies, and wine sauce, plus spring salads, and plenty of that dark, coffee-like tea that's a standard in the kingdom.

It's just me and the Prince. Victor stands quietly in the corner like a loyal dog.

A servant comes in, takes our plates away, and awkward silence returns. The Prince leans back in his chair, eyeing me.

"It'll all be over soon. I promise. You're doing a damned good job for your first day, I have to say." He leans forward, clasps my hand in both of his, stroking the back of my skin way more seductively than he should. "You're going to make a beautiful bride. Absolutely fucking beautiful, Princess."

"Don't call me that until it's official. I'm not anybody's princess yet, I mean. It's strange enough." I smile uneasily, wondering what happens later, when a short-lived princess divorces her prince.

Victor turns our way. He's frowning.

Has he figured out it's all just an act? I don't know, but it doesn't help the butterflies in my stomach.

I'm nervous. Cameras are nothing new to me. I did plenty of journalism in high school, and video blogs in college for my projects, but I never imagined I'd be addressing an entire nation.

"What?" I ask Silas, noticing he hasn't taken his eyes off me.

"You're mine," Prince Silas says, smothering me in those intense blue eyes. "Mine."

"Your what?" I'm trying not to completely lose it.

"My Princess. I don't give a damn if it isn't official yet. We're in love, right?" He cocks his head and winks, urging me to play along. "Doesn't take a royal crest on your clothes to remind me you're my one and only. The one I chose. The one I'll keep. The one I'll bind forever. By blood, by marriage, by kiss."

"S-sure. Of course, you are. We're going to be a great. The two of us. Together."

God. I'm clucking like a total idiot, and I'm sure Victor catches every awkward word. It doesn't help that he's staring at me like it's all true.

How can he do that? It's like he's had years posing as an actor, instead of a spoiled Prince. His charms are so powerful, so real, they're dangerous in the moment.

Then I feel my hand moving through the air, going to his lips yet again.

Instant heat flows down from my belly, settling between my legs.

I can't do this right now. Jerking my hand away, I fold it on my lap, hoping Victor doesn't see. Whatever, I'd rather have him see the serious lengths I'll go to avoid physical contact.

That's better than *anyone* realizing how hot, how wet, how much I want when Silas lies to me like a champ.

A knock at the door breaks my confused haze. Victor strides across the room, opens it, and nods.

"Miss Hastings, sire. Punctual, as usual."

Prince Silas' evil, teasing expression goes flat. He stands as the familiar blonde steps in, wearing heels that put anything of mine to shame. There's something odd about the way she looks at him.

It's more like an old friend than a servant. Like a woman who's seen past the royal mask he wears, down to who he truly is.

"Serena." That's his greeting when they're face-to-face.

She looks over, noticing me for the first time. Tension lines her face the second she takes in my dress, my place at the table with the Prince. I'm used to his entourage and the Queen herself being horrified by this fake engagement by now, but with her, it seems like something more.

"Hello, again." I smile politely because I don't know what else to do.

"I think I'm going to need a quick briefing," Serena says to the Prince, flipping her blonde hair. "There wasn't a formal email or anything. I'm…surprised to see her here again, Your Highness. With you, in private, that is."

He looks at her sternly. "That's because I need you to help introduce Erin as my fiancee. Future Princess of Saint Moore, Sealesland, and all her tributaries. You know, the usual. There wasn't time to write. This all came together fast."

"Fiancee?" It's like a rasp coming out of her throat. Her hand touches the corner of the table, as if she needs to steady herself, but she doesn't crack.

I stand up. Whatever's going on here, I want to show him that I'm useful, that I can help diffuse yet another crisis.

"It's a pleasure to see you again," I lie. My limited experience with this woman tells me she doesn't do courtesy, much less smile at strangers. "We're grateful for your help."

"It seems to me you already have a plan to handle this without consulting my expertise," she says to Silas, without even acknowledging me.

"You're right, I've been through the ropes before. This time, my image issues are bound to control themselves. Everybody loves a big, beautiful wedding, right?" He gives her a second, but she doesn't answer. "Whatever. I'm not the one who needs a fucking primer on how to talk to the kingdom. Erin does."

I watch the bitch swallow. She looks at me with the slowest glance in the world, eyeballing me like I'm something rotten she's just found on her plate.

"How long do we have?"

"An hour and a half. That's when the press conference is scheduled. Full house." Prince Silas folds his arms, giving her no mercy.

"Jesus," she sputters, looking back at him. "You expect me to give her a whole course on royal protocol and media pitfalls, just like that?"

Serena snaps her fingers. Way too close to the Prince's face. Victor cuts in just then, getting between us, gesturing for me to walk next to him.

"Miss Hastings, you know your duties here are whatever His Highness tells you. Please, let me escort you ladies to a private room, where you can get to work without any further interruptions. With your permission, of course, my Prince."

"Do it." Silas nods, giving me one last look. "Just do what she says, as long as it's reasonable. I'll meet you on the stage in a couple hours before all the jackals file in to pick at our bones."

It's a joke, but I'm not smiling. Victor leads me out with this woman who despises me for reasons I don't understand, into a small sitting room across the hall.

"I'll be right outside if either of you need anything," he says. "Expect a knock when the time draws near."

"Christ, Victor. Time management is part of my job, remember?" Serena says, practically spitting in his face.

We step in, and he closes the door behind us without another word.

"Let's get this over with." She finally looks at me, drinking me in. "You look like you're having a terrible enough time wearing that ridiculous thing. Lucky you, if everything else is equal, the tabloids will be talking about your fashion sense once they've finished squawking about the main announcement."

"It wasn't really my choice," I tell her, taking a leather seat across from hers, next to another fireplace with a hand carved mantel. I've seen more art in this palace than I've seen in my life, I swear.

"No, of course not. First things first, you let him do the

talking. Whatever he says, whatever questions may come up – you take your cue from His Highness. He's done it before, and he should know what to say. Lord knows I've tried to teach him, anyway."

I can't believe her tone. It doesn't brighten up through the whole lecture. She's wearing a trim skirt, her legs crossed, one foot angrily bobbing her black heel.

I've had enough. "I'm sorry, is there something I've done to offend you?"

"Only by coming out of nowhere. Winning yourself a man, a kingdom, you know you don't deserve. You're not even a citizen of Saint Moore's for God's sake." She stops there, her raging green eyes telling the full story. "No, it's not my place to criticize. I'll never understand *why* Silas picked you, but I'll *try* to respect it."

"Silas," I repeat.

It's just Silas. No Prince in front of it. Yeah, these two definitely have history.

"His Highness." She corrects herself, almost as an afterthought. "I'm sorry for acting like a royal bitch this evening. It's very frustrating to have something like this dropped in my lap without notice, you understand. I don't know how to explain everything in under an hour. The best advice I can give is what I've already said – smile, look pretty, and keep your mouth shut. The tabloids and blogs snatch anything you feed them. Any misplaced word, any screwed up gesture, anything scandalous. The more boring you are, the better."

"Good advice." I honestly don't know if it is, but her

crazy eyes aren't making me comfortable.

I want this to end. I'd rather have the press conference now than go over every movement and word with this envious bitch.

"Let me ask you this, Miss Warwick, what experience have you had on camera?"

Smiling awkwardly, I shrug my shoulders. Her eyes get wider and meaner.

"Just knock me out already. Please, for fuck's sake," she mutters to herself, running a hand across her face. "Okay. I'm going to do my best…"

And she does, for the next hour. She's cold, detached, more like someone giving a job interview than a woman I've personally upset.

She tells me who to watch out for, all the names of the biggest muckrakers in the kingdom, and several who will be flying in from Europe. I'm briefed on where Silas has gone wrong before, though a lot of his mistakes were completely off the record. Playing bad boy and getting caught gave journalists plenty of fodder, attracting them like flies.

After what seems like half an hour, the biggest takeaway I've got is what she said before.

Shut up. Look pretty. Let him lead.

That's what I've signed onto with this whole stupid thing, isn't it? I'm not really his wife.

Not really a Princess. I'm nothing more than another stage prop in Prince Asshole's life, no matter how good my motive. I've signed on to being used, and I ought to be conscious of it.

At some point, Victor knocks. "Ten minutes, ladies. Please finish up as soon as you're able."

"You seem like an intelligent girl, if a bit naive. I wish you the best of luck, Erin, and I hope you understand what you've gotten yourself into."

Holy shit. I've been holding my tongue through this entire miserable experience. I look at her, straightening up in my chair.

"You seem very smart, too, but you're kind of a bitch."

"Touche." Serena gives me a nasty smile and stands up. "I'll leave you to straighten that thing so it doesn't get caught. I don't think either of us need a cat fight to ruin that pretty dress right now. Good luck, Princess. You're going to need it."

She's out the door before I can follow up with another insult. *Infuriating.*

I can't let her drag me down now, though. As soon as she's gone, Victor steps in. I'm starting to get annoyed with his constant chaperoning.

This isn't the way I imagined royal life. The servants are supposed to help, to wait on us hand and foot. I guess they do plenty of that. But they're also *everywhere,* never more than several feet away. I'm craving my long lost privacy like never before.

"Straight through there, madame. His Highness is waiting for you on stage, near the podium."

I follow through the backstage door, to the place where he's pointing. I've forgotten how open and spacious it is in this huge, imposing medieval hall.

Yeah, privacy is the last thing I'm getting for the next few hours.

I'll be lucky if I ever find it again once the kingdom sees my face.

"Finally," Silas says, when I take a seat next to him. "Did she do her job? I'm going to jettison that woman if she's giving you any trouble. I've warned her before about setting her personal shit aside."

I have a chance to get Serena fired, and that gives me more than a little pleasure. But I don't have the heart to do it just yet. I decide to lie – what's one more on top of the untruths I've built up with just a couple days close to the Prince?

"It was fine. She could be a bit more personable, I guess, but what she said was useful."

He hesitates for a moment. "Okay. That'll do until this is over. Then we'll go back to my place and get you out of that damned thing."

He sounds like he's almost as tired of the stifling, formal dress as I am. Small relief.

It doesn't last long. About five minutes later, the main door across the room swings open. A large gaggle of reporters files in and takes their seats while Silas' royal guards swarm in the room, checking their earpieces, always looking for nonexistent threats to the Prince.

I can't imagine he has any real enemies. Maybe a lone nut, looking to write their name in blood on history, or a few of the extremists I've heard about who believe a republic without a hereditary monarchy is long overdue.

"Ready?" He grabs my hand where they can't see it, looks at me, and smiles.

"As much as I'll ever be," I say, sighing.

The butterflies in my stomach are making tornadoes. My public jitters have gotten a lot better since I started taking journalism seriously, but I've never given a speech in front of a crowd like this.

My knees wobble when we finally stand up, right after Victor announces a special Q and A session from His Highness, and a guest. *King of All Things* plays, a shortened version of the anthem, and then it's go time.

We're hit with what seems like a hundred different cameras when we stand up. Flashing. Beaming. Blinding.

All of them wanting answers.

There's no going back. I'm about to introduce myself to a few million people I know next to nothing about.

And then, once it's over, I'm going to shut myself up and scream, as long and as loudly as I can.

VI: Once in a Lifetime (Silas)

It's our time to shine, and I'm getting pissed.

Maybe it's the frustration that sets in every time I have to face these gutter feeding reporters, drooling over their next slice of red meat.

Or maybe it's the fact that I know she's brushing off Serena's bitchiness. I fucking knew my press secretary would make this harder the second she stepped in, and looked at me like I'd lost my damned mind for introducing my pretend fiancee.

Mostly, I'm fuming because I can barely see Erin's ass underneath that hundred year old thing she's wearing, and that's a brutal shame. She's in front of me, at the podium, trying her damnedest to follow my lead.

I want to take my bare hands and start tearing through every layer, then lay her out in front of me, naked as the day she was born.

Christ. I need to fuck this girl. However wrong, however complicated, however self-destructive, I don't care. My cock can't even try to give a shit.

I look into the closest camera and smile, calm and cool

as I humanly can. "Ladies, gentleman, and friends of the kingdom. This is a very special day for our people, our family, and for me, especially. You'll recognize the special guest at my side as Erin Warwick, daughter of Tom, the journalist from the United States. We're not up here to discuss her dad's health, or book a follow-up, so don't get any crazy ideas."

A couple laughs ripple through the crowd. I'm going to tease the assholes as long as I can, before I hit them between the eyes, and leave them running around like headless hens.

"Those of you who've followed me for years know I'm all about the unexpected. Miss Warwick tumbling into my arms is the happiest surprise I've ever had the pleasure of receiving." I pause, wanting to snort at my own prim and proper bullshit.

The press laps it up, of course. They love the Jekyll and Hyde split in my ego. One more contrast between buttoned up heir to the throne in public and the shameless playboy who gives them infinite drama when his private life leaks.

"Sire?" Vic mouths it from the side of the room, letting me know I've let my mind wander too long.

"Yes, well, this world's full of shocks. Some of them very ugly, like the time I found out my father had gone down with his yacht, lost to the sea forever. Some surprises, however, are quite beautiful. I walked into that interview with the Warwick Report expecting a slew of pointed questions. I didn't expect him to collapse on this very stage, and wind up leaving our kingdom for the best care a man can receive for his condition. I'm pleased to be a part of that treatment, whatever it takes to save the life of a world renowned journalist."

Next to me, Erin's face has turned visibly somber. I've said enough to play the kind, charitable Prince. I'm not going to dwell on her dear old dad's health a second longer than I need to.

"What I didn't expect, ladies and gentleman, was to find something wonderful in that public tragedy. You're all wondering why she's here, at my side, today. I won't leave you in suspense any longer. I've gotten to know her better than I ever imagined since the last day the cameras landed on us. Erin?" I turn to her, pull her closer, taking her hand.

She's squeezing me tight, but we can do better than that. I lace my fingers through hers and take her tighter, owning her fingers the way I want to claim the rest of her body.

"I wasn't looking at the time, but I can't deny what's right in front of me, precious and pure. I'm pleased to announce I've found my future wife, and the kingdom's next Princess." I wait for stunned murmurs to whisper through the crowd before I continue. "Erin Warwick and I are engaged. We're due to be wed this winter, shortly before Christmas."

I see Erin in my peripheral vision. Her eyes are huge.

We are? She knows I've just taken a piss on grandmom's conditions, setting a firm date nobody else knows about.

The room explodes. Every reporter jumps up, going completely apeshit. The next time I speak into the mic, I have to raise my voice, watching as Serena scrambles desperately through the rows of press, trying to restore some order with threats about throwing them out.

My guards have closed in, prepped for trouble, however unlikely.

"I'll be taking your questions for the next few minutes, once you're ready to quiet down."

That does it. Slowly, haltingly, the wild animals get back in their seats and shut the fuck up. That is, until the first one stands up, practically jumping out of her heels to flag me down.

"Your Highness! Isn't this happening very fast? How could you decide to marry her after only knowing her for a few days?"

"Prince Silas – over here! Does the Queen know and approve? What's she said about all this?"

"Prince, Prince, Prince! Does Miss Warwick know the first thing about this kingdom, or what she's getting herself into? She's barely been here a week, for Christ's sake!"

"Please, please. One at a time." I hold my hands up patiently like I'm talking to excitable children. "It's true this is happening very fast. There's no good explanation, except for the fact that faith and love move in mysterious ways. I've had a better kindred spirit in Erin this past week than I've ever had in anyone else. There's only one answer I can give. When a man meets his soulmate, he just knows."

I look at her. She's red as a damned beet from all the attention. Seeing her nervous expression, the way she sucks her little lip, douses the fire in my dick with kerosene.

I can't hold back. I snatch her hand, bring it to my lips, and kiss it like I'm sucking her face.

A couple dozen phones and cameras fire like machine guns for the next thirty seconds. When I finally pull away, she's shaking. I put one arm around her, bringing her closer, steadying her.

"Erin? Why don't you take the next question, love? The one about the Queen…"

She shakes her head, but I push her toward the mic. Time to do her part, and show me I haven't made a giant mistake.

My hand drifts down her back, trying to calm her, stopping just shy of that sweet, round ass hiding beneath the dress.

"The Queen knows, and she agrees, ladies and gentleman," she says very softly.

"Louder." I whisper in her ear, letting my lips graze her skin when I pull back.

Fuck, she's burning up. Like a fever. Tempting me to make her body blaze a hundred degrees hotter.

"Her Majesty approves!" she says, this time louder, shouting over the commotion. "And I think I deserve a little more credit than you're giving me. It's true that I'm not a subject of Saint Moore's by birth, but I've been reading about this island and the royal family for years. Coming here was a dream, whatever else happened with my father. It's been a bigger dream than anything I could've imagined, meeting my future husband, the love of my life. I'm going to marry this man next to me, His Royal Highness, and I don't care if anybody wants to question it. They'll see the truth, in time."

"Very bold." I whisper in her ear again, this time more loudly, while the journalists break into another mad bout of jeering questions and cheers.

This time, the guards move in. A reporter from outside the capital shoves a man wearing a French tricolor on his press badge, and all hell starts breaking loose.

It only takes one brief flash of a taser to make the rest of them settle the fuck down. All eight guards in my personal entourage, plus several more palace security members, patrol each row like sheepdogs, herding the journalists into their seats.

"This is what you wanted a career in?" I ask, quirking an eyebrow.

"Oh, shut up." She's careful to lean away from the mic, elbowing me in the stomach softly.

I'm so ripped I barely even feel it. Technically, she's just committed assault on her royal fiance, and I don't even care.

It just makes my dick throb harder. I lean in, wrapping one arm around her waist, bringing her into me.

I see her reflection in the teleprompter next to us. I never even use the fucking thing, but it's there for notes when formal speeches happen up here.

Right now, it gives me a perfect view of her face.

She's smiling through her nervousness. The redness has settled into her cheeks, painting them with a rosy hue – the kind I imagine she wears after she's come herself breathless.

"Miss Warwick! Prince Silas!" A bitch I recognize stands up. It's Eva Patina, an award winning shit stirrer from Ireland, notorious for giving celebrities hell across the continent. "I want to know one thing – what's *really* going on here? You can't expect the whole world to believe in this love at first sight charade. She looks like she's barely into this – barely into *you*, Your Highness. How much did you pay her?"

Fuck. Eva smiles her world eating grin, flashing her overly perfect teeth, framed in expensive ruby lipstick. She has an uncanny knack for seeing right through me, and everybody else unlucky enough to take her stupid questions.

"How much?" I step up to the mic, tightening my hold on Erin. "How about this much?"

Time to fight fire with fire, and give my own dick a little relief before it burns through my pants.

Erin gasps a little as I tip her back, grab her neck, and bring her into my kiss. Feeling her lips on mine makes me see white.

Goddamn, she tastes good. Everything I've imagined is there, tasting her. They're naked, raw, and perfect. She isn't wearing anything over them, a refreshing change from the glammed up whores and low swinging royalty I've had since my balls dropped.

This kiss is pure.

This kiss tastes like sugar and whiskey begging to slide down my throat.

This kiss slams my cock into a whole new universe of desire.

Here, now, there's just Erin and me. All the screaming, frenzied fights in the press corps, people climbing over each other like cats, fighting for the best angle to get our kiss on film forever fades away.

Three seconds in, she moans into my mouth. Her lips go slack, and she stops fighting.

She's giving in, surrendering her mouth to mine, giving into me. My hands roam up her back, while the digits on my other hand squeeze her neck gently. Every cell in my body wants to show her what's coming if she just opens up, surrenders a little more.

And fuck, she does. Her lips part, perfectly and irresistibly for my tongue.

Her tits crush flush against my chest. I can practically feel her nipples there behind the fabric, hard as stones, begging to be sucked soft.

I wonder what it'd feel like to slide my oiled cock between her tits and shoot off in her mouth.

The same warm, sweet mouth that's pulsing underneath mine. My tongue sinks past her lips, anchors against hers, and takes control. Both our bodies twitch when the intimate kiss deepens, sending lightning through us.

I don't know how long we're up there, in front of the entire kingdom. Lips and tongues locked and moving like two horny teenagers. I don't know, and I don't fucking care.

All I'm thinking about is moving my hand down to her breast, and putting the other on her ass, squeezing them both at once.

I'm going to, when the earpiece I'm wearing chirps loudly.

Vic cuts in, ruining our first kiss. "Sire! The situation has become too unruly out here. The full security apparatus is coming to reinforce us, but we can't guarantee your safety. We have to move."

Damn it. I'm growling as I break away, catching Erin's soft eyes, suddenly as surprised as mine.

I'm holding her as I take a good, long look around.

Fucking hell. The press conference has collapsed into complete chaos. Half my entourage is on the floor, wrestling with reporters, while several angry bastards hurl loud insults at each other. A couple pick up the closest chairs, and let them fly.

I turn my back, using my body to shield Erin, in case anyone loses their mind and starts throwing shit at the stage. "Come on. Victor isn't kidding about this situation. Let's move."

It's a complete shit show on the way out. Several reporters have broken rank in the commotion, climbed over the ropes they're never supposed to cross. Somewhere behind me, I hear Serena arguing loudly with a woman.

Three crazed reporters stand between us and the door. I stop and stand up, looking them dead in the eye.

"Move, or I'm going to flatten all your asses."

"Your Highness, please, just a few more questions!"

They can't be fucking serious. They're all foreigners, wearing flags from other countries on their badges, so my royal aura has little effect on them.

I don't know where Victor or any of my guards have gone. I tell Erin to hold on tight while I charge through the three greedy bastards blocking our exit, standing in front of the door backstage, their arms out.

My body blows them down like bowling pins. Erin's racing behind me, doing her best not to trip in those clogs, looking desperately over her shoulder. Several more assholes are chasing us.

She stops, spins around, and slams the door shut as hard as she can. I look back and nod, motioning with my hand.

"Can you run?" I yell.

"In this thing? Are you *kidding* me?" she looks down, eyes big and scared. The outfit has become a damned prison.

Without saying anything, I rush over, scoop her up in my arms, and go. Behind us, there's something huge and heavy hitting the metal door.

They're using a goddamned battering ram.

It's only going to be a matter of time until they break through.

I'm transported back to the fields outside Kandahar. I remember my last mission, when three good men got themselves killed. They started shelling us as soon as we landed, destroying our transport chopper.

We were stranded. Pinned down. Running on nothing except the basest survival instinct.

The very same instinct kicks in now. Except, this is different because I'm carrying a woman who's clinging to me, a woman I want to fuck, seed, and own in the most carnal ways.

Charging through the nearest exit outside, I hope to find more guards waiting with our SUV down below. I see it – only, it's hiding behind a huge throng of assholes pouring in from downtown.

They've seen the commotion by now on social media. I

won't be surprised to see #palaceriot trending all over the damned place, assuming I get out of this alive.

The crowd sees us, recognizes us, and starts moving in. Erin turns her head, takes one look, and screams.

"Silas! We need to get out of here!"

"Tell me something I don't already know, Princess." I need a second to think. "Hold on to me as tight as you can. It might be hell getting out of here."

Might? I know it's going to be.

I only see one weakness – a thin gap between two bigger, older men filming with their phones as they close in. Several older women surround them. It's a group I know I can push through if I really need to.

Yeah, I do. I give it everything I've got, shoving our way through them.

Wrapping my arms around Erin as tight as I can, I ignore the jeers exploding around us.

"Prince! Prince Silas! We looooove you!"

That's about the nicest thing I hear. Several angry protesters are in the mix, assholes who want to overturn the monarchy. They won't think twice about grabbing us, humiliating us, or worse.

"There's the fucking bastard! Spending even more of our hard earned money on his engagement – as if his parties and booze aren't enough! You going to let him, lads?"

"No! No, no, no!"

Shit's about to get serious. I take off, heading for the weakness I saw, away from the dangerous assholes calling for my head.

I may have fucked off half my history classes, but I know damned well what happens to Kings, Queens, and Princes when would-be revolutionaries smell blood. I'm not dying out here, ripped apart by an angry mob, while poor Erin gets caught in the middle.

The need to protect her supercharges my blood. I feel like I'm on fire as I crash through several skinny arms, bowling over several people, and then I keep going.

I don't let up. Not even when I realize I'm running straight into gunfire.

Shit, shit, shit. Things are really fucking bad out here, if they've brought out the guns.

How the hell did this ridiculous press conference lead to the opening shots in a civil war? At this rate, I'll be lucky to flee the country before they stick my head through the guillotine.

People start fleeing, blurring by us. Erin has her little face buried in my chest, but she's screaming just the same. Can't blame her, hearing the world fall apart around us, shattered in a hail of screams and bullets.

"Prince Silas, sir!" A loud voice screams out ahead, just as I'm starting to lose my sight. We're almost to the curb. "Down here!"

Several soldiers have set up a protective ring around what's left of our motorcade. The motorcycles have been knocked over, replaced by Humvees and armored cars. Vic looks up behind the troops, relief spreading across his face when he sees me.

About half a dozen soldiers shove the crowd, opening a space just wide enough for us to jump through, closing it the instant we're climbing inside the SUV. I hear them start shooting.

Our SUV takes off, flanked by the military vehicles. I'm wondering if I'm about to the see the beginning of the end of my kingdom. Except the rioters wouldn't fall down so unnaturally like that, without a drop of blood spilling out.

Smoke rises around the palace. It's tear gas, rubber bullets, and water cannons.

Standard riot control stuff.

Not live bullets after all, thank God.

"Jesus." She slumps back in her seat when we're finally freed from the danger zone, racing across town. "Did you have any idea this was going to happen?"

"No." I'm telling her the truth. "It's gotten heated a few times before at the palace, but it's never devolved into a full scale riot. There's something else going on here, and I'm going to find out what."

"I can't believe you're shooting them…"

"They're damned lucky it's not real ammunition," I tell her, wondering why she's defending these animals.

The people are one thing. I'd never want shots going into innocent bystanders, even the curious ones who should know better than to be there. But the protesters…the Republic fucking Firsters…they don't care who they hurt. Why should I mind if they catch lead between the eyes?

"Look, they're breaking up the riot with all the non-lethal force the kingdom has to muster. Every man in uniform knows there's going to be hell to pay if they reach the Queen's doorstep."

Fuck, grandmom. For the first time since we got into the vehicle, I'm worried.

"Surely, they're as surprised as you, Silas. I don't think anybody can be blamed for this insanity."

I ignore her. Instead, I tap the glass separating us from the driver. A second later, it goes down, and I see the man looking at us in the mirror.

"Your Highness?"

"What's the situation at the palace? I want constant updates."

Victor sits in the passenger seat up front. "I'm receiving them now. Secondary blockades are closing off the nearest streets, and the crowd is slowly dispersing. Rest assured that all the rioters with press badges will have them permanently stripped. They'll be blacklisted, Your Highness. I'm deeply sorry for this, we should've vetted *everyone* who stepped into the event, short notice or not."

I look at Erin. There's something about her sweet, pure face that actually causes my anger to weaken.

"Don't be sorry," I growl through the opening. "You couldn't have known, Vic. None of us did. It's got to be the damned Republic Firsters. A rat on the inside. Probably that Patina bitch. They'll do anything to make the family look bad, even when we're bringing the kingdom good news."

"Rest assured there'll be a full investigation, my Prince, as soon as the situation is under control." Vic bows his head.

I don't say another word. The glass panel rises, and we're left alone.

If I've ever needed a drink, it's now. Next to me, Erin

looks like she's losing it, her face criss-crossed with a thousand kinds of confusion.

She flinches when I reach over, grabbing her hand. "Do you think we've made a mistake?"

"Mistake? Bullshit." I shake my head. "It won't happen again, love. I don't give a shit if we have to flee to the mountains and have our wedding there. Nobody's unwinding this clock. I wanted you before, for all the reasons we've discussed, and now I want you at the altar a hundred times more."

Her big brown eyes light up when they widen. Rich, electric, and fuckable. My cock stirs to life, wanting to make them roll back in her head, and feel those scared little lips on mine again.

"What now? We both know it's going to be a disaster in the media. Probably an international one."

"Yeah, it will be. They can fucking suck it," I growl. "Don't worry. A stern word from Her Majesty will put the kingdom right. She always comes on TV when it gets bad enough, and I'd say this warrants it. She'll put the Republic assholes in their place, and then some. They're used to beating up on me and my dad, when he was still around, but this is different. *Nobody* insults Her Royal Majesty. Next time we talk to the press, they'll be lucky if they aren't wearing handcuffs, looking at us through bullet proof glass with their beady little eyes…"

She laughs. I can tell she isn't sure if I'm serious or not. Hell, I don't know if I am.

"What's so funny – the handcuffs? Didn't know you

were that sort of girl, love. For the record, I'd enjoy seeing you with your hands cuffed to the nearest bed, a pair of gold clamps softening up your nipples for my tongue."

I fucking mean it, too. Can't resist telling her. It earns me another slap, clean across the face, and I'm smiling at her through the blistering burn spreading across my cheek.

"Glad I can help you work it out of your system, beautiful."

"You're ridiculous." She rolls her eyes sourly, too tired for another hit. "Just tell me where we're going? I can't imagine there's any place that'll be safe for us in the whole city."

"No, you're right. We're heading for the summer palace. That's the protocol when a shitstorm blows in. The Queen, she won't leave for nothing short of a nuclear war. You and me? We're going to the country while things calm down. We can deal with the fallout there."

"Okay," she says quietly.

Just okay? *Fuck me.*

Nothing's okay at the moment.

For the first time since we got our pretend engagement on, I'm feeling a pang of guilt. A normal person would let it take over, making them wonder if they've fumbled something terrible, dragging a down-on-her-luck foreign girl into this royal mess.

Not me. Prince Silas Bearington the Third doesn't make mistakes.

We're going to the summer palace, and we're going to unwind. We'll write up our statements while the wedding planning gets underway. We'll let grandmom, her courtesans, and bitchy Serena deal with the press nightmare.

More importantly, I'll have plenty of peace and quiet to explore my new wife. Find out what buttons to press to make her relax. And I'll put a fucking stake through the hearts of every evil doubt she's got running through her right now.

I'm going to have my wife, my Princess, come hell or high water. This *will* work the way it should.

If the stars align, I'm going to fuck her, too. No bullshit. I'll seduce this girl, and she'll learn to love it.

Yes, it's insane, it's suicidal, it's a thousand mistakes rolled into one, but I'm going to try.

I'm convincing myself this mad thing between us is real so no one will doubt it again, much less those jackoff reporters.

Believe. Straight down to the taste of her pussy while her legs are tossed over my shoulders. Just thinking about that warmth and wetness trembling beneath my tongue makes my cock want to spit fire.

I'm going to know every single inch of her. Whatever it takes to throw this clusterfuck of an engagement back in grandmom's face, and then I'll do the same with the other 4,999,999 people in the kingdom doubting us.

This is my once in a lifetime chance to prove myself, to save our kingdom, and show this woman that I will never, ever let a disaster come down on her head.

She won't walk away from me, disgraced and disappointed. Erin Warwick isn't going anywhere until I've fucked her senseless first.

VII: Royal Pain (Erin)

I don't see much of Silas for the next few days after we're settled in the highlands. My orders.

There's a knock at my door several times that I'm sure isn't the guards. Then whispers, what sounds like his soft, feral voice arguing with my keepers.

From the second we stepped into the summer palace, which feels like the world's most expensive lodge, I've told my handlers I want complete, perfect, unobstructed privacy. God himself isn't going to interrupt me for the next forty-eight hours, and that extends to his royal jackass, too.

I need time to process. To think about the fact that I've narrowly survived being ripped apart by an angry mob.

Yes, I've signed the contract, presented to me this morning. Slipped it under the door without a word, triple checking to make sure our 'no sex' clause had plenty of legalese behind it.

I'm surrounded by his men in this place, the security entourage assigned to me.

I'm worried Silas can overrule the guards. He's the second most important person in this whole country, after all. But for some reason, he doesn't, and I hear him slip away while I'm laying in bed, or lounging on the ivory white chaise with my phone resting on my belly.

Incredibly, the bastard respects my privacy for once in his life. It's a life where he's had everything handed to him on demand, which makes it more amazing.

It isn't much consolation. Locked away in here, I feel like I've entered another kind of fairy tale. I wonder if Rapunzel or Sleeping Beauty ever faced their own demons the way I'm staring mine down now.

The world goes on, even if I'm hidden behind the most luxurious wall on the planet.

Dad tries to call at least three times over the next few days.

It's no surprise, having a father as an award winning journalist means his eyes are glued to the news. By now, he's seen the craziness at the palace unfold a hundred times over on social media, from every single angle.

His dear naive daughter, up there on the stage, engaged to a Prince. All hell breaking loose around us.

They still don't know what caused the riot. At least, the palace isn't saying whether it was troublemakers who want to see the monarchy abolished, or just a wild energy that took on a life of its own.

I can't say I care. I'm too busy being terrified for the future, for what I'm going to tell my father.

There's no combination of words that can soften the blow. He's a smart man, no matter how sick and scared he is. He'll put the pieces together, if he hasn't already. And then he'll know I've basically whored myself out to the biggest player in the world for a chance to save him.

Only, I've sold everything except my body. The 'no sex' clause in our contract feels like the only smart thing I've done in this situation. It also might be the dumbest, because right now, I'm so miserable I'd love to lose my virginity to blow off some steam.

Even to Prince Silas. Hell, *especially* to Silas.

I can't stop thinking about him. The way his lips roamed mine...

He kissed like an animal. His lips are always so aggressive, so controlling, moving like they're entitled to mine. No different than the way a summer storm sweeps the countryside with its raw power. If I give him a chance, that same wicked energy will go straight to his hands, moving across my breasts, my ass, between my legs...

God. I run my hands across my face, just as my phone pings me again.

My stomach growls. They've been bringing me food at my request pretty regularly. It must be late evening now, close to when I should be asking for dinner, but I've lost track.

My heartbeat quickens as I look at the screen, cringing. It's another voice mail from a number in Mexico.

I can't live like this. I need to come clean.

Frustrated, I sit up. I shouldn't be so horny when there are about a dozen other emotions boiling away beneath the surface.

I just want to get this over with. All of it.

Like the brutal conversation with dad, or the wedding, and the riot that'll probably follow it. Even fucking the Prince, if I'm going to, so he'll finally have what he wants and leave me with some peace and quiet.

I want my money. I want dad to get better. And I want to go home to our boring middle class condo in boring old LA, where Kings and Queens are just something you see in movies or read about in trashy blogs.

Only one way to make that happen, to speed things along to their inevitable, probably catastrophic conclusion.

I dial dad without listening to the voice mail. "Hello?"

"It's me," I say, hearing a strange machine whirring loudly in the background. "What's that noise?"

"Fluids cycling. It's a kind of chemotherapy, my dear. I'm sitting up right now, trying to distract myself while they pump this poison through my veins."

"They're doing their best to heal you, dad," I whisper, hating the tension in his voice. "How're you feeling?"

"Very restless the last few days," he says slowly. "It's not the treatment. That's going fine, and I'm taking it as well as I should be. Rather, I'm having a hard time because my own fucking daughter decided to marry a goddamned Prince without saying a word about it."

Shit. My stomach does a nosedive. I'm speechless for at least thirty seconds, trying to pull out of it, and keep myself from running to the bathroom to vomit.

"It's not like that."

What am I saying? It's *exactly* like that.

"Bullshit. Erin, I don't know what he's offered you, but

you don't have to do this. Don't do it for my sake. I raised you better than selling yourself out for anything, including me. I'd rather die than be a bargaining chip."

"Daddy, it's not like that! Silas is a good man, when he wants to be. He would've flown you there anyway and given you treatment. That's exactly what he did, before I agreed to anything."

"Silas?" I can hear him smirking over the phone. "You're on a first name basis with the Prince? Jesus Christ, Erin. Guess it makes sense, seeing how you're going to get hitched."

He's got me by the throat. I want to lie, tell him that we're truly in love, and he'll see how wrong he is very, very soon.

But it's such a load that even I don't believe it. Neither will he.

"You need to get better," I say, the only thing I really can. "You'll understand someday. Just trust me, daddy. Please."

"Don't worry. I'm going to try to kick this thing, whatever happens. If I live, I'm going to figure out how to get you off that damned island before I wind up dead from disappointment. There isn't a cure for that."

Disappointment? It hurts, but I can't blame him. I still can't believe I'm doing this.

Is it too late to walk away? To take a car without Silas chasing me, and hop the first plane to Mexico City so I can apologize up and down to my father in person?

No. I'm all in, and it's already too late.

"I'll find my way, dad. Don't waste any energy on me. Get better."

He doesn't say anything. When I look at my phone, it's blank, the call terminated without a last goodbye.

There's a terrible urge to hurl the damned thing across the room. Before I can, there's a loud tap at the door.

Horrific timing. I creep up to it and put my ear close, yelling through the thick, ornately carved wood. "What?"

"His Highness has requested an audience tonight, madame. Seven o'clock, and strictly voluntary." It's Dean, a voice I vaguely recognize belonging to the man who's been assigned to me personally, posted outside.

"Tell His Highness that I'm resting again tonight. I don't want to be disturbed unless there's food involved." Fuming, I do a full 360 degree turn, realizing I've forgotten one thing. "Make sure I get a bottle of wine, too. I could use it tonight."

"Of course, Miss Warwick. I'll relay the message to Prince Silas and the staff. If you need anything else, I'll be here until at least nine, before the shift change, and –"

I stop listening. I'm heading for the bathroom where I can soak for a long bath.

Maybe it'll help drown my inner bitch for the time being. Or if it doesn't, then it should at least tide me over until the wine comes. Tonight, I'm going to forget my father, my predicament, and the persistent asshole who's sucked me into all this.

* * * *

I'm half asleep, surrounded by soft, cloud-like foam in the steamy bath when there's another knock at my door.

"Yeah, who's there?"

"Dean, madame. I have dinner and a gift for you."

Gift? From who?

I don't even need to ask. I have an ugly feeling I already know.

My nose wrinkles, and I stand up, stretching while my naked skin drips fresh glacier water and thousand dollar soap.

"Leave it on the table outside, please!"

"As you wish."

I step out of the huge tub and start drying myself off while I hear him enter with a cart on wheels. It only takes him a few seconds to lay out the dishes and whatever my – ugh – *gift* is on the table outside.

By the time he leaves my room and I hear the lock click into place behind him, a heavenly smell punches me in the nose.

Dinner. My gently growling belly becomes an earthquake.

Slipping into a fresh silk robe, I don't bother drying my hair, heading out to where my precious food awaits.

It's absolutely perfect, of course. There's a nice sized steak slathered in buttery goodness, just the way I want it, with citrus glazed vegetables and roasted marrow off the side, still in the bone. I don't even need to cut it to see that it's medium rare, just the way I like, cooked to perfection by chefs who are probably imported from the finest schools in Paris.

They've remembered the wine. Except, instead of a cork, there's some weird metal object stuffed into the top. A small card hangs off it, hooked to the loop with the diamond in the middle. It's a little tag, with a man's thick, black ink scrawled on it.

I'm going to help you unwind, one way or another, Princess. Look in the box of chocolates, too. - HRH

Rolling my eyes, I grab the bottle and pull out the stopper. It's got to be a joke that he's using the His Royal Highness abbreviation in his note to me.

But when the strange, heavy stopper comes out with a loud *pop,* what I'm looking at isn't a joke at all.

It's a vibrator. Gold plated with stripes of silver running through it, or maybe even platinum. What else from his royally ridiculous and filthy highness?

I slam it down on the table, clenching my teeth. Of course, it accidentally triggers the switch, that diamond on the end of the ring. It buzzes and jerks until I cover it with my hands, struggling to turn it off.

My eyes dart around nervously. I used to have one of these back home, before the noise became a huge liability. First with dad, and then with my roommates.

Suddenly, I'm not as hungry. I don't even want to look in the box of chocolates. I'll probably find a huge dildo, or something even nastier.

Pulling my chair roughly across the Turkish rug, I sit, pouring my wine glass so full it almost overflows.

I need to eat. Need to distract myself from the fact that Prince Asshole thinks he can send me sex toys.

I'm not stupid. Everything he does is painfully obvious. He's rubbing the no sex rule right in my face by trying to get me to rub something else.

All horror aside, the wine tastes good. The food, magnificent.

Silas' insanity won't ruin a meal like this. I dig in with a hungry, American etiquette that would probably leave the chef who prepared it shaking his head.

The only thing I'm craving by the end is something sweet. I can't remember the last time I had a piece of chocolate. Not since coming to Saint Moore, certainly.

I'm looking at the rectangular gold box like a fish stares at bait on a hook. Yes, it's a trap.

I just *know* I'm going to find something worse than the stupidly expensive vibrating bullet inside. Is the chocolate worth the price?

Reaching out nervously, I drag the box toward me and pull the little red bow wrapped around it loose. The package falls open. About a dozen of the most divine truffles I've ever laid eyes on surround a little compartment in the middle, housing something that looks like a small gold necklace.

I pop the first truffle in my mouth and let myself melt from the fireworks dancing on my taste buds before I pull the gold chain out. When I see the two little pinchers hanging on the ends, I gasp.

The clamps slip out of my hand and clatter gently on the table. Jesus.

I remember back to the conversation in the car, just a

couple days ago, when he joked about seeing me naked, handcuffed, and locked up in these.

What kind of girl does Silas think I am?

It's like he doesn't know that he's dealing with a virgin who's never felt comfortable enough with a man to let her inner freak out. Or maybe he knows exactly what I am, and that's what gives him the eerily accurate insight about what turns me on.

Tight, wet, and very taboo desire burns between my legs. I pinch my thighs together, chewing another truffle, unsure whether I should be more disgusted at him or myself for taking a second look at these terrible gifts.

Oh, and there's another little notecard tucked into the empty shell I pulled the clamps from.

In case you wondered, I'm not breaking our agreement, it says in his all too familiar bold, angry script. *No sex means you and me going skin on skin. I'm perfectly entitled to send you fuck toys, and you're more than welcome to send me pictures of you using them, love.*

I don't read it a second time. I'm standing up, ripping up the card, and that's when I realize how fucking wet I am.

The bastard has a scary way of feeding on my frustrations. Turning the grossest things into things I crave like magic.

Maybe I should do the unthinkable – get this *out* of my system.

I drain the tall glass of wine while the fiery, insistent tingle coursing through my body deepens. My robe falls off before I'm heading for my room, grabbing my glass, the bottle, and the two illicit gifts on the way.

Fine, I'll let myself explore if that's what it takes to scratch this itch. Alone.

Hell no, I won't send him pictures. I won't be caught dead with him knowing I've ever touched his filthy offerings.

This is for me, myself, and I. My pleasure, not *his.*

The canopy bed I've been sleeping in must have a two hundred year old frame. Each night, I'm half expecting a dashing vampire to come flying in through the glass doors leading to the balcony, making my trip back to romantic Victorian times complete.

Only, tonight there's no vampire fantasy. There's nobody on my mind except Silas as I lay down, completely naked, and tease the golden bullet against my clit.

I'm way past sopping wet. My hot, aching pussy leaks all over the thousand stitch sheets, freakishly horny in this strange, infuriating place that's beyond my class and everything I ever thought I'd be.

I hate him for putting me in this situation. I hate his toys, his presence, the very air he breathes.

But he's all I'm thinking about as I move the humming metal through my folds, focusing its energy on the little bud that won't stop pulsing, burning, begging for Silas.

My clit is a traitor. It doesn't see Prince Asshole, Prince Playboy, Prince Fuck Off Forever.

It only sees Prince Hung and his ridiculous gifts. It wants to feel him, too.

Oh, shit. Holy hell.

I'm going to come soon, thinking about his tongue, his fingers, his big and legendary cock shaking me to my core.

First, I ease up, gripping the golden clamps tightly in my hand. They're easier to attach than I expected. The hard, angry bite sinking deep into each tender nipple right now is exactly what I need.

Pleasure hits my brain, rougher than before.

So real, so precise, it scares me out of my wits. I'm going, going, *gone.*

Given over to the need for a hate fuck overwhelming my body, making me grit my teeth and pant his name through my teeth.

"Silas, you asshole. No pictures. I can't believe *this*. Can't believe you're in my head, making me —"*Oh, God.* My hips start to tremble and I can't hold back the fireball building in my womb.

"Fuck you, Prince! I'm coming."

And I do.

So hard it's blinding. My whole messed up world disappears in a hot flash of red and white explosions rippling over my rolling eyes for what feels like forever.

His wicked, royal face is the last thing I see before I come up from the deep, deep ecstasy he's thrust me into. I imagine him whispering in my ear, his fingers tangled in my hair, jerking my head back, growling with that low, sexy voice that's naturally tuned to make any woman helpless.

You like that, love? Yeah, fuck yeah, you do. We can throw this no sex rule out any second.

You can feel my mouth, my fingers, all over your sweet little body. You can feel me inside you.

Coming hard. Coming deep. Coming together, just like we're meant to.

I lose myself in the toys for hours. Lost in the rage, the need, the wine, and all the shades of wrong coloring my attraction to the world's nastiest high class bad boy.

I'm drunk, sweating and exhausted. I barely remember to pull the clamps off before I pass out. I should feel ashamed, or guilty, like I have every other time I've ever stroked my body in the past.

No, not now. Something's changed.

I want to believe it's my situation, the deal with the devil I've made to save my father, and possibly myself, if I've ruined my career prospects with this crazy engagement.

But it's not any of that. Not really.

It's Prince Asshole. Silas.

The man who won't leave my head when he's the last person I want to see.

I can't stop thinking about his kiss, or the tight, possessive grip he had on me as he carried me out of the palace, protecting me with his very life.

No one's ever fought for me like that before. And I won't forget it, however badly I want to.

I won't stop thinking about his gorgeous, smug, and sinfully dirty highness. I won't do it for all the pain, love, and money in the world.

Even if I wanted to erase him from my mind, I can't. He's in too deep. He's marked me psychically, emotionally, and if I give him a ghost of a chance, he'll mark me physically, too.

And that scares the crap out of me.

* * * *

"Holy shit. Somebody's been busy."

My eyes pop open. It's morning, probably early, judging by the golden light streaming into my room through the lovely glass panes leading to my private balcony.

It's Silas. In my room. Hovering over me while I'm wearing nothing but a sheet, dangling the nipple clamps by the chain above his face until they reflect the brilliant light.

Jerking up, I'm careful to keep the sheet wrapped around my breasts. "What the *fuck* are you doing in here?! Give them back!"

"Checking on what's mine, Princess."

"Oh? I had a feeling that package was meant for somebody else. Guess those are *your* nipple clamps." I stop just short of sticking my tongue out.

He grins and his fist tightens around the little gold chain. I won't let myself look below his waist. I know he'll be hard, imagining what went on here last night.

"Nah. They're custom made to match that little bullet, and it looks like it's gotten one hell of a workout." He gestures.

My horrified eyes move to my glass nightstand. The tiny ornate vibrator I had between my legs for at least an hour last night sits there, taunting me.

It's already too late, but I snatch it anyway, tucking it

beneath the covers. He waits until I'm glaring at him with new hatred to start laughing.

"Get. Out!" I'm so pissed my voice cracks.

"Fuck, love, you really crack me up. I'm just screwing with you because I'd really like to get you to drop that sheet, but I'll take the laughs, too." He pauses, his smile disappearing, looking me up and down like a hungry tiger. "Seriously, it's going on noon. I thought you were a Type A, up early and often, always put together?"

"No. I'm the type of girl who's going to jump out of bed and scratch your eyes out if you don't get leave, Silas."

"Whatever, I'll give you some space to get dressed. Hurry up. We've got a date today."

Great, I think, gritting my teeth. It isn't much consolation watching him turn his back and step out the door, into the other room, waiting for me.

I take my sweet time with a shower and a fresh set of clothes. The whole time, I'm trying not to wonder exactly what he's got in store for me, for us. After surviving the palace riot and another brutal conversation with dad, a new media shit show is the last thing I need.

If it's another press event, I'm saying no. We can do the damned thing another time.

By the time I come out, he's sitting by the fireplace, toying with a tiny antique tiger statue he's swiped from the mantle. Silas looks up, extinguishing more of my anger than he has any business doing with those damnably deep, beautiful blue eyes.

"I saw these in Pakistan when I served. Almost identical.

We'd go out on the town, me and my men, whenever we stopped off at the allied base before heading back to hell. Hard to pull local pussy, but damn if the scenery and the food wasn't out of this world. Lots more of these little icons where this one came from."

I'm folding my arms and rolling my eyes. Simultaneously.

Has he lived a day on this Earth when he isn't totally full of himself?

"I'd love to show you sometime, Erin," he says, a sly smile on his lips. "Today, I'm more interested in getting the hell out of here. Let's get out, clear our heads, pretend the last week was nothing but a bad dream."

"So, wait, you're telling me there isn't a formal meeting with the royal whatever?" He shakes his head, gently setting the tiger statue back down on the stone. "You want to – what? – have a freaking picnic?"

"More like a night of camping, down by the beaches. The bluffs up here are pretty goddamned gorgeous. Don't look at me like I've lost my mind," he growls. I'm seriously wondering if he has, thinking I'd volunteer to go anywhere with him alone. "You're going to be my Princess, Erin. It only makes sense that you explore more of the island."

I can't take this. He's acting like nothing happened. I step up and ask him point blank, ready to walk back into my bedroom and lock the door if he gives me any crap.

"Is this marriage thing still on after what happened the other day? Be honest."

"Please," he snorts. "If anything, we've got a better

chance than we had before at bringing grandmom on board. Her Royal Majestic Pain in the Ass doesn't buckle to terrorist riots, much less on her own doorstep. I talked to her this morning. We're speeding up the wedding, love."

My eyes go huge. It's not what I expected to hear.

Smiling, he steps up, and wraps his arms around me, holding me like we're really lovers. I hate the electric heat that spreads through my body when we touch. Hate that it makes me feel so good, so hungry for more, when everything about Silas is royally bad.

"That's right. Forty days. We've got another week up here, and then we're going to get our asses back to the capital for planning. It's going to be locked down tight, everything carefully choreographed. We're all going to be wearing smiles constantly. Hope you're able to pin those pretty lips, love. This goes beyond you, me, and our silly little deal. We're getting hitched to help stop this whole fucking kingdom from going tits up."

He reaches up, slowly moving a finger to my mouth, pressing it gently against the center of my lips. It takes me about ten seconds before I jerk away, stumbling out of his arms.

"You're insane! This whole thing is nuts. Psycho!"

"Yeah, yeah, you've said it so many times I've lost track." He has a terrible knack for acting like everybody else is crazy, while he stands there with his calm, collected, pompous mask. "So, are we just going to mope around the summer palace all day, or are we going to have some fun?"

I don't say anything. I won't look at him with the panic

setting in, twisting my heart around in mad, dizzying circles.

I'm scared my father might be right. This isn't me.

Oh, my God. What have I done?

I'm still wondering when he comes up and puts his hands on my shoulders. He holds them there gently, the only reason I don't scream, spin around, and spit in his face.

"You're going through some shit. You're entitled to, love," he whispers in my ear. "I'm trying to help. I realize everything here hasn't gone according to plan. You can believe me or not, but I feel bad about that. I'm a man of my word. Right now, I'm extremely pissed that outside circumstances are fraying my promises. Let me undo the damage. I'll take you out for some fresh air, show you the highlands, just you and me. Without any guards or tourists or fucking cameras."

A retreat in nature actually sounds good, even if it involves Silas. He flexes his muscles a little firmer when he feels me sigh. Rolling my shoulders, I let his hands slide off, and turn back to face him.

"Just give me a few minutes to pack."

"Awesome. I'll wait outside." He's smiling, practically beaming because I've folded without putting up another fight. "You won't regret this, babe. You'll have more fun with me in a day than you've had in ten years."

Ugh. There's that attitude again, erasing every trace of the man I'd felt a few seconds ago, the one who made me wonder if he might be able to care about more than just himself. I shouldn't even wonder.

I've seen everything I need to know exactly what kind of 'fun' I'm going to have with Europe's most spoiled playboy.

VIII: Fire in the Night (Silas)

We're about fifteen kilometers down the road in my brand new Maserati when I pop the bottle and pour myself a glass of wine. Erin does a slow turn, her eyes bugging out, and gives me that look like the stick up her ass has just wedged in deeper.

"What? This thing has all the stabilizing mods in the world. I'm not going to spill a single drop on the seats."

"I don't know much about the laws here, but I'm certain every civilized country in the world has a very *big* problem with drinking and driving!" She stops, hissing pure frustration out her nostrils. "Jesus Christ, Silas. You really are insane."

"Whatever." I sip my wine gingerly, tapping the accelerator while I take my hands off the wheel.

"Silas!"

I'm laughing. I can barely even choke down the fucking wine when I see the look on her face.

We're heading right for a cliff. Her boring old life in the States is probably flashing before her eyes. It makes me smile because I know she's reliving our kiss, the one time I got my lips on hers, before all hell broke loose in the palace.

I never touch the wheel. The car jerks back to the road automatically and slows before we fly to our deaths.

She blinks, stunned for a moment. Then she shows her teeth and punches me in the bicep.

"What the hell?"

"The new model's self-driving, love. Isn't technology amazing? Won't be available for the other millionaire jackoffs who drive these things until next year. For me, they've made an early bird exception."

She's shaking her head, relieved and awestruck as the car's steering wheel tilts in front of me, bending us around another hook in the road. We've got a ways to go, before we're heading straight down to the beach.

"The only rich jackoff I know is the one sitting next to me," she says. "Jesus. You scared me shitless."

"Sure did. Here, have some wine, I brought a couple extra glasses." I turn around and fish into the little case next to me, producing a new crystal glass.

She doesn't protest while I pour her a glass, passing it over. She looks at it glumly before taking a sip.

"It's okay, Erin. Really. You won't find any traffic cops here on royal land, but if there were, I'd offer them a drink, too. The police love me. Grandmom's always pushing parliament to shore up their pensions."

My perfectly uptight Princess rolls her eyes and sucks down half the glass. Finally.

I smile, relishing my triumph. It makes the rest of my glass taste even sweeter.

Erin is practically begging for a refill by the time the car begins its glide down to the beach. My finger taps the switch for the windows, pulling them down a few notches. The soft, rhythmic slap of the sea comes through, almost as comforting as hearing her purr.

Fuck. I've got to stop thinking like that.

It isn't easy when I've gotten her out here. Alone. My dick hammers in my jeans, emboldened by the fifty year old wine, thinking about all the places I want to lay her down out along the rocks and sands.

I won't return to the palace until I've fucked this girl. Or at least gotten her to laugh.

"You look very different today," she says, her eyes rolling up my body.

Different? Has she noticed the hard-on about to rip through my fly? Is she thinking about how good it'll feel deep inside, stretching her pussy with royal cock, right this very second?

"Different how?" I ask, ignoring the hum of sex and the pleasant buzz building in my blood.

"So casual."

I shrug. "It's the beach and the bluffs, babe. Do you expect me to show up there in a tux, wearing my royal medallion?"

She blushes. "No, of course not. You just look so...normal."

"Newsflash – normal is my middle name when I'm having fun. You'd be shocked how many more scandals the tabloids have missed because they don't recognize me when

I'm out in jeans and a t-shirt."

"Oh?" Erin quirks an eyebrow.

Shit. I shouldn't have reminded her.

"In case you hadn't noticed, I don't enjoy the stuffy royal protocol and palace shit. I'll tolerate it because it's what I was born into. On my own time, I like loosening the fuck up, living my life to its fullest. I learned how to play hard years ago, and I can teach it, too."

"Like I need a lesson from you." That little motion when her big, brown eyes roll around in her head would be annoying by now, if it didn't make my cock throb harder. "Whatever. I'll try to have fun today, just for you, Your Royal Highness."

Grabbing her hand, I refill our glasses, stopping to clink mine on hers. "Yeah, you will. There's no point in being Princess if you can't enjoy it."

* * * *

A couple hours later, we're back on the beach after a long hike up the tallest bluffs. Erin's tank top is practically soaked in sweat, giving me a fantastic view of those tits she carries around like the world's sweetest melons.

We don't talk much. I shut up for once and let her take in the scenery. And fuck, what a view it is up here, right by the abandoned lighthouse. My great grandfather personally broke a bottle of champagne across the walls as King, about a hundred years ago.

Erin and me, we do wine instead, a fresh bottle from the fifties I pulled from the palace's wine cellar before heading out. We talk history. I answer her questions, like why the island still has royalty when most of Europe shrugged theirs off before I was born, and why I'm adamant that I'm going to be King someday instead of a powerless pretender to the throne.

Now, I'm gathering wood for a fire on a nice flat spot on the beach. There's an overgrown fire pit that hasn't been used by the royal family since grandmom was my age.

Erin watches, chugging water from a bottle, splashing more wetness over her chest every few sips. Like I need another jolt to the dick.

I'm hotter than hell once the wood is stacked up, searching for a light. I kneel down near the bag next to her, peeling off my shirt. I hear her gasp.

"See something you like? Or did you just spot a Moorish beach skunk?" I growl, pulling out the lighter, without hiding how much I love her enjoying my body.

"No, no," she stutters. Always so damned modest. "It's just…your tattoos. I've seen them before on the blogs, a few old photos taken from a distance. They're a lot more detailed in person, up close."

"Yeah, they should be. This Russian guy I paid a small fortune to for my ink's supposed to be the best on the continent. Here, have a closer look."

I step right in front of her. At first, she tries to hide how much she loves it, but her eyes betray her.

Sweet, wet, fuckable Erin looks at me like I just stepped out of her dreams.

"See this big one in the middle? The artist pulled it right

off an old royal flag that's been in our palace since the Great War. We weren't so neutral in that war, just like the second, and everybody paid the price. Even my family. My uncles served. One died in a shelling, a hundred years ago. They used the flag to try to stem the bleeding." I shift the lighter to one hand, banging my ribs with one fist. "Didn't work. That's why you're seeing red and black, love. The thorns going around the whole design were my idea."

"That's surprisingly deep for you, Silas." She's trying to stay sarcastic, but I can tell she wants to drag her little tongue all over the tapestry on my chest. "I didn't know you had it in you."

Plenty of women have.

I want to pull her hair while she's doing it. Have her on her knees, face gliding down to my cock, both hands tied behind her back.

Fucking hell. No, control yourself.

"What do you know about *deep*, love? I'm not talking about the English literature you studied for your minor." Her eyes pop angrily when I remind her how much I know about her. "I'm talking about fucking. How long has it been?"

I point the end of the lighter right at her pussy. She stands up, pressing her legs together, making a face like she's disgusted.

"Creep! Do you really think I'd tell you something so personal?"

"Well, obviously. We're going to be hitched, you know. Husband and wife. King and Queen."

She does a double-take, and I stop myself from doing it too.

Fuck me. What did I just say? King and Queen implies we'll be spending a lot more time together than three years worth of sham marriage. It says I'll keep her until I'm wearing the crown myself, leading this nation into a brand new age.

"You know what I meant," I growl, hating that I even have to acknowledge the slip.

"No sex," she says, tucking loose chestnut hair back behind her shoulders. "I'm here to hang out and help you start a fire. We are *not* getting more drunk than we already are, and we're definitely not discussing my sex life."

"So, it's been eons, right? Hell, you must've gotten laid last around the time the lighthouse opened up." Smiling, I gesture toward the tall stone citadel towering above us, several cliffs over.

"Come on, Silas, that's enough. I'm hungry."

She looks down like she's defeated. Christ, it was just a joke. More of the banter I've been laying on her since the day she tumbled into my arms, and I decided if I can't rip off this girl's panties, I'm damned sure going to tease them until they melt into a puddle at her feet.

I watch her grab her water bottle and head toward the firewood. It takes me a minute to join her, wondering why the fuck she's acting so wounded.

Surely, it isn't true? All the crap I've given her about not getting fucked?

Doesn't add up. I've had my fill from out-of-control

college girls before. Never met one who wasn't wild, who hadn't bedded at least ten guys by the time she hit her junior year.

Erin can't be a virgin. She fucking can't.

Because if she is, I think my dick is going to explode in my Egyptian silk boxers.

We stack up the last wooden beams in silence. Then I pour on a little kerosene and give it a light. Doesn't take much longer to get the grill arranged, just a big slab of metal I brought up here years ago, balanced in the middle over the flame.

A couple minutes later, I'm pulling the steaks and boar sausages from the ice chest, plus a few big slices of squash and mushrooms. We'll do s'mores later for dessert, or whenever I think I can handle seeing her get sticky without having to run to the nearest bushes and empty my balls before I explode.

"Damn, that smells good," she says, inhaling deeply behind me. "I've been starting to get sick of all the rich foods lately. It's nice to have something simple."

"Simple? We've got nothing less than finest grass fed lowland beef and boar meat from Africa. My men used to flip when I got this stuff shipped in special to base. Only thing that kept us sane sometimes with the Taliban waiting to strike us from the hills, every damned night."

I wait until dinner's half done before I reach for a new bottle. This time, it's rum, imported to the palace from the finest distillery in Martinique. Even after hundreds of years, the French are still trying to kiss our asses, especially when it involves access to our fishing waters and the new tech development we've got springing up in the capital. The palace gets about a hundred of these every year, with a personal note from the French President.

"It's almost ready. Here, have a shot."

She cocks her head. "Uh, we don't have any glasses, and I'm not pouring that stuff in my wine glass. We're royals, remember? We're supposed to have standards."

I laugh. She watches as I tip the bottle and pour the amber liquid straight into my crystal stem glass. Grandmom would probably have a stroke if she could see me now, and so would the elderly royal etiquette tutor who drilled me like a beast when I turned five.

Sweet, fiery warmth floods by throat and goes off like a bomb when it hits my empty stomach. I tip my head up, suck in the fresh ocean air, and start peeling down my jeans.

Won't make hiding the raging hard-on any easier, but fuck if I care.

"Hey, hey, I don't need to see that. Is it really that hot out here?" She's protesting like crazy, holding a hand over her face, but I can see her looking at the bulge in my shorts through the gaps in her fingers.

"Give it up and join me. I've got a feeling you're wearing a bikini under that thing. Don't tell me you're a commando kinda gal."

"Am not!" She clucks her tongue, one more sign that she might be.

Fuck it, I'm going to find out.

I take the risk of burning the meat to walk over and grab

her. Screaming, slapping at my hands, she squirms in my arms. Music to my ears, her loud yelling echoing on the cliffs, turning into nothing but giddy laughter by the time I get her tank off.

"Ha, am I ever wrong? You're yellow like a goddamned hornet."

"Fuck you! I wish I could sting. I'd do it in a heartbeat – anything to get you off me." Lies, every single word coming out of her mouth.

It's no joke, the yellow bikini. I'm impressed.

I expected something less bright and flashy from Little Miss Modest. Maybe she's got a few surprises left, a couple mysteries I'd love to unravel, sure as I'd love to get her naked.

Erin keeps wriggling in my arms while I grab the bottle. I pop the cap, take a big swig, and pass it to her, running the rim dangerously close to her lips. I have to keep my hips off her ass, or she'll feel how hard I am, fighting the urge to grind my hard-on right into her lush skin.

"What's the problem, love? Don't I taste good?"

She takes a mouthful before I step away, laughing as she spits it out, fuming. "I'll never understand how you're going to be king someday! You're less mature than a twelve year old, Silas. God!"

"Funny. I remember being that age. Never hung out with any boys packing anything like this." I grab my cock through my shorts, twisting the fabric around it in my fist, letting her see the full, magnificent outline. "They don't call me Prince Hung for nothing."

I'm ten inches, and proud of it. I've had my share of models who laugh about my big dick when I hint about it. Plenty of jealous little bastards have raged from the sidelines when they hear the rumors.

By the end of the night, nobody's laughing, because their girls are on my arm and they want to fuck.

God gave me a winning lottery ticket. Every woman I've ever bedded knows the numbers after it's been inside them. They learn to count their lucky stars fast for a chance to ride this royal scepter.

They scream. They worship. They beg for a third, a fourth, a fifth lay, when I just want to get the fuck away the next morning.

I want to do it all with Erin, except for the morning part.

Yes, the urge to fuck and *stay*, that's new.

It scares me. More than the expression on her face when she takes a good, long look at this dick. She wants me bad, but she doesn't want to cross the line because she's wondering what that means.

Unfortunately, so am I. *Why?*

"Gross! You'd better not let that thing out, or I'm going to scream," she says, shaking her head, lying her sweet ass off.

"Suit yourself, Princess," I tell her.

For once, I'm going to take her advice. Truth is, I'm half-freaked out by the time I turn around, walk back to the grill, and tend the meat, letting the rampaging hard-on die between my legs.

She's putting on a front. It's as weak as it is needy. I

know how to deal with that, but everything storming up inside me, I'm clueless.

No, it won't take much to have my way. One more little push and I'll be between my fake fiancee's legs all night.

Why the hell does that have me so worried now? It's everything I've wanted for days.

Shit, I've never backed off pussy before, much less one that puts up a fight and makes me chase it.

I focus on dinner, pushing the thoughts away, plating up the steaks, sausages, and veggies. When I pass her plate, she's sitting on a rock, half a wine glass filled with rum in her hand.

"You finally cracked." Smiling, I join her on the little boulder nearby, my own plate in hand.

Erin shrugs, forcing me to look at her cleavage again. "When in Rome…or Saint Moore, I guess. Besides, I've all but given up hope I'm going to survive the night without something strong enough to handle your antics."

"No more bullshit. You're enjoying yourself," I tell her, stabbing into my boar sausage and taking a big bite. It's good on its own. Better because I made it. "Admit it, love."

"I'm enjoying this dinner. I wish I could say the same for the company, but, you know…we couldn't be more different, Silas."

"That's what makes it so exciting. I'd have never asked a girl I found boring to marry me."

"No? I thought you wanted one who would just lay down and accept all the teenage crap that seems to be your specialty."

"Try the steak," I tell her, pointing with my fork.

She blinks in surprise. I wait until she listens before I say anything else. Her face lights up when she tastes the garlic rub. My cock stirs for the hundredth time since we got here, imagining the same expression on her face when she takes every inch of me.

"That's my specialty, beautiful. I've got a few more to my name, but you'll have to wait until later tonight to find out."

Her fork crashes on her plate. "When are you going to stop? No sex."

Who knew I could hate two short, simple words so fucking much?

I glare at her, chewing my food. Okay, I'm back to wanting to close her sassy little mouth with every stroke of my dick.

"Soon as you learn to have some fun, Princess. You were doing great earlier this evening. Now, you've pushed that stick back in, deeper than before. I should've brought more rum for this job…"

"Yeah, that's exactly what we need. More booze, so you can act out even more, and I can be a babysitter instead of your wife."

My gaze on her tightens. Her cheeks go brilliant red, and it's not just the fire. It's the only thing that tells me she really just said what she did.

Looks like I'm not the only one slipping on rum tonight.

"My wife," I say softly. "That's what this is all about, isn't it? Look, I know what you think about me from the tabloids. You think there's no depth, nothing past the parties and the sluts I take to bed. You're worried you've agreed to a pretend marriage with a boy – not a man."

"Have I?" She's asking honestly. No sarcasm this time.

"I never told you why I signed up for the Royal Marines, did I?" She shakes her head while I grab a stick near my feet, tracing lines in the sand in front of me. "I wanted an adventure, sure, same as every other red blooded kid does once his balls drop. But I wanted to give back, too. It was a trip to Africa that did it, this little war-torn country run into anarchy…I must've been seven or eight."

Erin's watching me intently now. "Dad was there on charity, and he let me come along. Said it would be good to see what a future King handles beyond the stuffy bullshit back home.

"He spent about an hour talking to the elders in this village before security hauled us back to our luxury compound in the hills. I watched my father and his latest side bitch stuff themselves on caviar, expensive wine, and then head off to bed early. They slept in a handcrafted bed from the old colonial days. Me, I barely ate. I couldn't stop thinking about those people in the village. Their pain, their horror. Too many human skeletons missing limbs. Landmines did the damage, or so I'm told, and the chemical waste left by the war did the deformities. Hell's got nothing on what they went through. Just dragged through shit I couldn't even imagine, especially with my wealth and fame."

I don't say anything until she nudges me. Everything's

gone silent around us except for the distant, peaceful churn of the ocean and my stick skimming the sands. "Well, what happened?"

"Next day, we had to go through the village again, on our way to the landing strip to get back home. Our motorcade stopped a little ways outside it. At first, nobody knew what was going on, until the UN soldiers showed up with the Royal Marines. They said we'd have a bigger escort because the whole fucking village had been raided, burned to the ground, and every last person executed overnight by a few rebels who hadn't agreed to the truce."

"Jesus." Erin looks at me, her eyes big and wide, like she might be seeing something different for the first time.

Fuck, what am I doing? I've never opened up like this to anyone, much less a girl I want. Whatever the reason, I'd might as well finish the story.

"We made it home, obviously, without any further hitches. But we drove through the village. I'll never forget the burned out homes and the smoking piles of what must've been the poor, miserable people we'd visited the day before. They'd gone down easy after suffering so much. They were defenseless. I never forgave those rebels – I had Royal Intelligence hire hit men to murder what was left of them a few years ago. They hunted them down in the jungles like dogs, and they deserved every goddamned bullet."

Erin's eyes are flickering now, and I watch the fire, letting the flames feast on my anger. "It wasn't just the rebels, though. I also never forgot what my father did – he covered up his bawling mistress' eyes and turned the fuck away."

My muscles twitch. The stick snaps in my hand. Clenching my jaw, I lift it from the sand and fling it toward the fire, listening to the crackle and pop.

Even after all these years, I'm pissed. I'm not sure why I decided to tell her this shit, but it's definitely a bad idea.

Only thing that calms me down is when I feel her little hand on my shoulder.

She's comforting me. Erin, my Princess, the girl who's been looking at me all day like I'm something she found stuck to her damned shoe. I might as well double-down because this story is doing something.

"Yeah, so after all his lectures about royal duty, charity, and shit, he can't be bothered to look at what's happened to the people he's been pretending to give a damn about for a day. I realized speeches and lofty promises in front of the cameras won't solve shit. That's why I signed up to serve in the Marines. It wasn't about Queen and country, or some medieval fantasy about leading my boys into battle like my ancestors did. I had to do *something*, however small, to prevent a massacre like that from happening again. Nobody deserves to be defenseless, or stamped out like fucking ants. I'd like to believe we stopped a few executions in Afghanistan, but some days, I just don't know…"

"Wow." Erin whispers softly, giving me the most predictable look in the world. "Well, you did everything you could, Silas. Don't beat yourself up."

I ought to roll my eyes at this fairy tale fucking ending.

I've just spilled my guts, one of my deepest, darkest secrets, and now she's seeing beauty behind the beast.

Beauty. Do I even have that?

Does it get any more cliché than this? Fuck, I don't care.

I won't tell her the rest. There's another reason I paid my dues to the crown in my uniform.

That's because I'm scared shitless of ending up like my father, who took his scandalous life one step too far. He paid with his life and died with nothing to show for it. Nothing but a drink in his hand and another nameless slut on his arm when his party ship sank.

I can't end up like him. *I won't.*

"My life's a lot of fun and games, but that's not all it is. I don't care what the tabloids say, what grandmom thinks, or what you see, Princess," I whisper. "There's more to me than fucking, drinking, and fast cars. I've done my time in the service, but damn if I'm going to stop doing whatever I can to help the people so far down on their luck they don't have any. I'm giving back to my kingdom and the world. It's the only thing I think about when I'm not drinking or screwing."

"Giving back," she repeats, looking past me in the fire. "I think I see now. That's why you chose me, isn't it? You could've had anyone, but you picked a girl who doesn't have wealth or fame or royal blood."

Has she lost her damned mind? She couldn't be more wrong. I reach for her hand and pull her up, refusing to say anything until we're both standing in front of the fire.

"This isn't charity, love. You're as crazy as you are

gorgeous, if you believe that." She can't hold my gaze. Doesn't stop me from setting her on fire with my eyes. "This isn't real, we both know it. Doesn't change the fact that I'm a picky son of a bitch. I want a Princess who isn't afraid to sling it back at me. A woman who does more than just strike my cock like lightning every time I'm looking at her, feeling her, thinking about how hot and wet and sweet her lips taste on mine."

Goddamn, I'm going to lose it. I can't stop myself anymore. Erin trembles in my arms, and I jerk her closer, holding her against my chest while I reach up with one hand, and cup her chin.

"Silas…"

"Enough. I don't want to hear my name coming out of your mouth again unless you're screaming it," I growl, moving my lips to hers.

Fuck, fuck. She tastes incredible – better than the day I kissed her with the cameras watching.

It's not just the ridiculous, romantic setting out here, with the sea, the fire, and the sun sinking below the horizon, surrendering to the rising moon. It's her.

It's Erin. She *wants* this. I feel it in her kiss, the way she moves her tongue against mine when I take control of her mouth.

My dick turns to steel, ready for conquest, hungry to be in her. I won't let the greedy bastard rule me.

I'm taking this slow, savoring it, relishing her in a sweeping, slow moving conquest like a fire sweeping through the forests.

"No, Silas. No sex," she whimpers, one last gasp from the rational, scared side of her I'm about to fuck into oblivion. "The ink's barely dry on what we signed…"

"Contracts change, love," I whisper, closing my fist behind her head, taking those long, silky brown locks I've been dreaming about fisting for a solid week. "We can fuck. We both want this, we're alone, and there's nothing in the world that's going to stop us."

"Yeah, there is." She looks at me with those soft, dark eyes, so scared and so horny all at once. "If we do this…it won't be pretend anymore."

"Bullshit," I say, smiling. I'm going to kiss her again in about five seconds, whether she fights it or not. "Time for an amendment to the deal, effective immediately. Let's do this like adults, like lovers, and then go our separate ways when the time comes. It's just sex, love. There's nothing saying you can't be my fake wife and a fuck buddy simultaneously. I'm your Prince with benefits, starting now, and you're going to love it."

She doesn't have an argument because I've already won. So has lust.

Our mouths do the talking when I crush my lips down on hers again. Then I reach for that little bikini strap behind her back, my cock throbbing ten beats a second, craving what I've been denied.

I'm owning every last inch of Erin Warwick tonight, and as long as she's wearing my royal ring, I'm not stopping.

IX: Like a Dream (Erin)

I never, ever imagined this.

There I am, standing on the beach, face-to-face with the dirtiest playboy in the world. No, *closer.*

He's kissing me with a heat and intensity no woman could resist. He's already popped off my bra, taking one aching breast in his thick, strong hand. His fingers move with the same grace as his mouth – hungry, but ready to tease.

Silas looks at me, swallowing me up in those big, blue eyes, just as his fingers roll my nipple.

"God!" I sputter, pressing into his grip, wishing he'd pinch, suck, and fuck me harder.

"You're beautiful when you're on fire. Fuck, Erin, Time to feel mine. All of it. I want to light you up like Christmas and see how hot you get."

My knees go weak. I can't tell if I'm pressing my hips into his because I need the support, or because my pussy keeps going against the rock hard, insanely huge outline of his cock like a magnet.

A very wet, persistent magnet that's put me completely under its control.

I can't think anymore. I can't protest. I can't even imagine it with him slipping down my body, sliding his rough dark stubble against my throat, kissing my cleavage as he pulls me down.

When I open my eyes, we're in the sand. Just two moaning shadows, delighting in ourselves with the heat warming us, a delicious contrast with the cool, clean earth underneath our skin.

He's going lower. My fingers grip his shoulders tight, pressing my nails into his skin. Oh, God, he's really going there. He's going to –

"Fuck!" I curse like mad.

That's all I can do when Silas reaches out, grabbing my breasts, plumping them so sweetly in his palm. He's tugging at my bottoms, dragging them down my legs.

I realize a second later he's got them in his teeth. And he's growling, just like a wild animal, a predator who's going to eat me alive.

My ass rises instinctively. He squeezes my breasts tighter, tighter, taking me halfway to the low, full moon hanging over us while my bikini bottom disappears around my ankles.

"Christ, you're wet," he growls, kissing up my thighs, stopping to inhale my scent. "Can't believe you've waited this long to get licked and sucked. I promise, love, it's all been worth it."

And it is. The instant I feel his hot breath over my pussy, right before puts his mouth against it, I know it's true.

At first, he's teasing me. Teasing until I'm soaked,

dripping, shaking next to his lips. My fingers push into the sand at my sides, searching for something to hold onto.

But there's nothing except my own ecstasy and the dear, sweet earth once his tongue rolls across my opening.

Holy, holy fuck.

Silas!

There are no words. No expression adequate for the rough, prickly heat coursing through my blood. One of his hands leaves my breast, sinks down, and opens my lower lips. So much better for him to suck, tongue, and fuck me deeper.

He's in my pussy, in my head, maybe even in my heart.

Prince Asshole has become Prince Charming the second the pleasure sets in. Soon, I guess I'll meet Prince Hung, too.

Every lick takes me a little higher. The bastard growls, his animal energy sweeping through me, a feral warning before he finds my clit.

I was on the verge of completely giving it up when he thrust his tongue inside me. Now, I have no choice, not when he sucks my burning nub between his teeth and lashes it a dozen times.

Oh. My. God.

"Silas, no." I hate myself for giving him what he wants – me, writhing, screaming his name on the beach. "Don't. Stop."

Trouble is, I love myself, too. Love it for giving in, for letting him push me over the edge, for giving everything over to his mouth. Just the way I imagined last night, when

I held his filthy gift between my thighs and came so hard I saw red.

Tonight, I'm blind.

I'm coming so hard I can't breathe, can't move, can't think. The roar of the ocean and the light of the fire, the moon...it's all gone.

There's just me and the Prince. His fingers are in me, stroking away, hitting some spot that makes me feel like I'm gushing all over his chin. He won't stop licking me, even when it's too much, and my body tries to squirm away.

He growls louder. He holds me down, shoving both hands on my thighs, pushing me deeper into the floury beach. He treats me like what I've become – his Princess with benefits. His wife, his woman, quintessentially and completely *his* to own any way he wants.

It's scary as hell. Scary, and exciting.

It also makes me come even harder, knowing I'm under his thumb, and loving it. Or is it under his tongue?

I feel like I've been picked up by a tsunami wave and thrown back down again when it's over. He's hovering over me when I open my eyes. I take in his huge, handsome, viciously tattooed chest, rising in falling in shallow, hungry breaths.

"We can fuck, or you can get on your knees and suck my cock. Only reason I'm giving you a choice is because you're a virgin. A fucking virgin." He growls the last sentence like he can't believe it.

I'm flushed, naked, ready to give it up. My feet dig into the sand and push my hips up into his, feeling his erection.

There. It's true, isn't it?

The interviews I've read with his one night stands weren't lying about his size. I've never been with a man, but I don't need to be to know he's huge.

Ridiculously big. How fitting for a man who walks like he has the biggest, meanest dick in the world to actually have one.

My hand reaches down, trembling as my fingers stop at his trunks. I feel his outline, press my palm against it, and squeeze.

"Fuck! Yeah, love, yeah. Touch it all you want. We can take this slow, let you show me what you've got…"

I don't want him to accommodate me, just because I'm inexperienced. He's been talking about giving back all evening. Maybe it's time for me to do the same.

The fact that he's not a total asshole makes me want to. My spine keeps tingling while I sit up, let him flop back onto the sand, and hold myself over his thighs. He fists his trunks in one hand, jerks them down, and I run my hands along his six pack abs.

Hell, I think I need to. I'm about to topple over without the support when I finally *see* what he's been hiding.

It's as long as I thought, and even wider. It's so thick, so angry, so alive, pulsing when he grabs my hand, pulls it down, and wraps my fingers around the throbbing root.

"Feel that? It's yours, babe. Every fucking heartbeat. You suck me right now, I think I'll be the happiest man on earth."

His dirty promise makes me want to smile. I think I

would, if I was anywhere but next to his impossibly huge, eager cock.

My eyes close and every nerve in my body tingles when I squeeze him gently, rolling my hand up and down his length. Growling, he drops back, giving me the space I need to work.

It's the first cock I've ever had my hand around, but I'm not totally clueless. I've talked to my friends about boys, and read my share of books about billionaires, bikers, and kings fucking the ever living hell out of damsels in distress.

Maybe those stories and talks have prepared me for this moment. I want to please him, to show His Royally Hung Highness that I'm worthy of being on my knees, in front of his naked body.

Surprisingly, it doesn't take much to hear thunder on his lips. Pleasure, given voice, coursing through his body.

Is it all psychological – or does he truly like me this much?

"Fuck," he growls. "Fuck! Faster, Princess, stroke me, suck me, just like that."

Over and over and over, he curses, guttural and lost in his pleasure. I haven't started sucking him yet.

It looks like he'll barely fit in my mouth. Only one way to truly find out...

My lips part, and I run my tongue across them. We lock eyes before I take his swollen head in my mouth. He's leaking something warm, clear, and oily all over my fingers while I quicken my strokes.

His head slides in easier than expected. I keep going,

pushing my lips wider, but I still can't make it halfway down his massive shaft.

He's looking at me with his eyelids half drawn. Slowly, I start moving up and down, watching his deep blue eyes disappear behind his lids.

"Fuck, love, don't fucking stop!" His palm moves against the back of my head, urging me on.

He tastes masculine. Like earth and salt and raw, royal power in one.

My pussy tingles, enjoying what I'm doing to him. I shouldn't like serving him so much. But I can't fight what feels good, what's natural, and this is *magnificent.*

It's only nature. His power, his arrogance, and what I think must be his heart of gold makes me enjoy prostrating myself to Prince Playboy, sucking and stroking his cock like my life depends on it.

No, maybe not my life, but definitely my next orgasm.

He's growling now, grinding in my mouth. His heavy balls swing up, clapping against the base of my hand.

"Shit, that's good. Too fucking good. You've got no business sucking like this when you're new."

No business, huh? I answer him by moving my lips faster. I'm ready for anything, ready for him to explode in my mouth. He'll probably spill more come than I could ever hope to swallow inside, leaving it spilling on my breasts.

Filthy. Wrong. Yet, so, so predictably hot.

He's thrusting in my mouth, moving to match my strokes. I push my tongue up underneath his thick head, tasting more warm pre-come drooling into my mouth.

Every time I touch that spot with my tongue, below his crown, his hips jerk.

He's holding back. Trying not to hurt me by ramming his cock down my throat like I know he wants to.

Jesus, what's happening? Am I really thinking like this with my mouth full of him? Imagining how hard he'll fuck me if he's between my legs, unimpeded, punching my V-card like he's been waiting to half his life?

"Fuck, fuck! No." Growling, he pushes me away, pulling my face off his cock by the hair.

For a second, I'm worried I've done something wrong. But he rises, takes me in his arms, and flips me over. Silas pushes me into the sand, flat on my back, grinding his bare, slick cock against my slit.

"I'm not wasting this nut down your throat, much as I fucking want to. You'll taste my come later," he growls, his fingers pressing into my chin, craning my face to meet his. "Right now, we're fucking, Princess. Fucking all damned night in front of this fire. I'm going to leave you so sore we'll need Vic and the boys to come tomorrow and carry us home."

The idea fills me with horror. But I forget all about it a second later, when he moves his cock against my slit, pushing his fullness dangerously close to my entrance.

He barely remembers to stop, pull away, and reach into the bag behind him. I watch as he returns, tearing the condom wrapper with his teeth, then sliding the rubber over his length in one stroke.

It has to be extra large to fit him.

I want to tell him how much this means to me. How I'm still not sure what's happening, but I'm going to enjoy it, and trust him for this beautiful, furious moment. For one night, I belong to Prince Hung, and I'll take every one of those benefits he's offered me.

"Silas...I'm yours," I say, grabbing him by the shoulders. "Take me. Take my pussy. Any way you want."

God. It sounds like something from a bad romance novel.

Is this how people talk dirty, or am I totally blowing it?

He smiles, slides his fingers through my hair again, and jerks my head back. "Love, I want this pussy so many ways I couldn't do them in a thousand nights. We can get started, though. We can see what it's like when your hot little cunt sucks the life from my balls when I'm coming inside you."

Yes, please!

My legs hook to his, trembling, begging to do everything he just said. Maybe I've screwed up this dirty talk because I can't form words at all, overwhelmed with the need to have him inside me, to feel his cock pulsing.

"Please," I whimper. Yes, *whimper.*

No more delay. He locks eyes and pushes into me, filling my virgin hole with everything he has.

It's incredible. It hurts a little bit at first.

Mostly, it feels so fucking good, stretching to fit him, my body shifting at a physiological level to fit Prince Silas like a silk glove.

Nothing's stopping this. I'd probably die on the spot if it did after feeling my wet, craving pussy gliding around his cock, his fullness, his essence.

Silas fucks me slowly. He's careful, still holding back, even though the animal energy rolling off him doesn't feel like it understands what careful even means.

His thrusts dig deep. Mining for pleasure, marking me from the inside-out, reminding me in every single stroke who owns me now.

And I'm okay with it. Really, *really* okay with everything he's doing.

My feet hook to the backs of his legs. He grabs my wrists with his free hand, pinning them above my head, pressing his mouth down on mine while the other hand pulls my hair.

The first time I come on his cock, I'm squealing into his mouth. He drowns my moans, my screams in his groaning, growling pleasure.

I think he's about to join me, adding his convulsions to mine, especially because his infuriating royal smirk has become a caveman's smile of teeth and lust.

No. Hell, no.

He fucks me right through my first orgasm, and doesn't let up. He's going faster, shaking my body like we're suddenly riding an earthquake.

Every curve ripples. Every drop of blood in my veins becomes fire, lapping at my veins. The ocean's roar behind us merges with our pleasure, our desire. Just one strange, inseparable fusion of earth and sex, sweat and muscle, bound to this cock that's filled me up to my womb.

"Never had anything this tight," he snarls, when I'm on

the verge of coming again. "Take it, Erin. Every fucking inch. Every thrust. Every way I want, when I want. I'm ruining you for taking any cock that isn't mine again. Oh, fuck!"

Everything I've feared is happening. The words coming out of his mouth while his defenses are down don't sound like pretend anymore. Not like something a Prince with benefits would say.

We're more than just two crazy people who've struck an unthinkable deal when he's balls deep inside me. More than just fiances playing a game.

We're lovers. Losing our hearts and minds in the ecstasy igniting our bodies.

I'm helpless, scared, and more confused than I've ever been in my life. But I'm also buried in pleasure when Silas rears up, slams his hips into mine, and swells deep inside me.

He's coming through his condom. I'm coming apart.

For the next five minutes, my brain loses the ability to dwell on any higher thoughts than *yes, yes, fuck me! Fuck me more! Silas, fill me.*

His royal seed nearly does. He explodes in the condom, growling louder than ever before. His fingers jerk my hair so hard it nearly hurts, but it tips my head back to the moon, and I scream.

My pussy won't ever be the same after tonight, if he's serious. I know he is.

We're just getting started. He's going to keep fucking me, coming in me, spilling everything he's got until he's empty, and I'm so spent I'll be lucky to walk tomorrow.

Tomorrow. That's a scary thought after the mindless, screaming, skin soaking sex we're having tonight.

I don't know what we'll be when we wake up. I'm not sure if we'll be royals with benefits, or totally ruined.

I'll be lucky to keep my own sanity after tonight.

"Damn it, love, you're going to kill me before we're through," he growls, pulling out of me and tossing the condom aside.

We kiss. That's when I put my hands around his neck, scratching my nails against his skin, and deepen our tongues moving against one another. They're searching, tangled, and still so hungry.

Nothing else matters tonight except the flesh. I'm going to force myself to live in the sex, the pleasure, even if it means our dream is about to become a royal nightmare.

* * * *

We don't get much sleep. Sometime near dawn, he wakes, nudging me out of our rum and sex fueled frolic.

My head hurts. My pussy aches so good, after taking him two more times, the last time bent over in the sand while he slammed into me from behind.

Silas passes me a water bottle. I drink it down like it's ambrosia, straight from heaven, groaning angrily when he tries to get me to walk.

"Come on, love. You'll catch cold out here in the morning. Can't risk you getting pneumonia – how're we going to fuck then?"

Jerk. It gets a smile, though.

I watch him get dressed, summoning just enough energy to gather up my own clothes and slip into them. When I delay moving too long, Prince Silas the soldier emerges. He picks me up, takes me in his arms, and carries me up the steps to his high tech car.

Before I know it, I'm slumped in the leather passenger seat, watching as he starts the engine and puts it on auto-pilot. The car drives us back to civilization and the summer palace.

His guards nod politely on our way inside.

If any of them think our relationship is a sham, they don't show any signs. Or maybe they're just smart enough never to question their boss.

Soon, we're upstairs, skipping my room entirely and heading for his. He's got another one of those big, warm, and incredibly overbearing canopy beds like something shipped direct from 1820.

It doesn't matter. I crash on it like it's a silk cloud, safe in his arms, and sleep like the dead.

Silas' heartbeat guides me to my dreams.

If this is what being a Princess with benefits is like, count me in. It's a comforting thought, one that hangs with me through the sleepy morning, until I wake up.

Silas sits on the bed's edge, a phone in his hand, muttering angrily to someone on the line.

"Fuck. *Fuck!* It's a goddamned disaster, is what it is. Okay, okay, just give me a couple hours. Yes, we'll take the damned helicopter. We'll be back in the capital as soon as we can. You tell them to do every fucking thing they can to save her!"

Forget dreams. I just woke up into a royal nightmare.

X: With Bated Breath (Silas)

"What? What is it?" Erin sits up, the silk sheet wrapped around her, threatening to tease my cock awake after it's fucked itself into a coma for several hours.

Any other time, I'd be ripping that thing off, throwing her on her back, and having my way.

But after the asshole from the palace gets off the phone, sex is the last thing on my mind. First time that's ever happened, and I hate it. Almost as much as I hate having to tell her the news.

"Her Majesty's in the royal hospital. They think it's a stroke," I say, feeling another blow to my guts when I repeat what I heard. "Those fucking muck raking, gutter swiping plebes…they must've pushed her over the edge. She's eighty years old, for Christ's sake – too old for the media's shit."

"Don't worry about the why," Erin says, laying her hands on my shoulders, rubbing them gently. "We just need to get back there, like you say. We'll have time to sort out everything else later."

"We need to get our shit together. *Now.*" I'm growling every other word, and I can't stop myself.

I yank her up from the bed so hard she drops the sheet. "Let's shower and get dressed."

"Shower? Together?"

No shit. Normally, it'd be the perfect opportunity to bend her over in the wet, balmy bath, hands against the wall, and fuck her pussy until I can't think straight.

Today, it's just a time saver. We step into the huge marble shower stall together, and I slam the glass door shut.

Just seeing her naked has a calming effect. Thank fuck.

I need it right now, anything that prevents me from thinking about the thousand and one hells waiting if grandmom doesn't pull through.

I've got my Princess, but it doesn't mean the island will accept me as king. The jackals in the media will have a field day. The Republic First assholes will raise holy hell, circulate a million petitions calling for my crown, and they'll probably get it after the nastiest referendum campaign this country's ever seen.

Hell, I'll have to address the bigger, uglier jackals in parliament. One wrong move there, and the populists will pounce for political points, ending our fifteen hundred year old crown forever.

"Silas...relax." She's lathered up, smiling softly, running her hands up and down my chest.

I've never let a woman touch me like this before. Erin looks like an angel, and I can't refuse, even though she's seeing more cracks in my armor than any girl has business seeing.

I let her little hands glide down my body. She lathers me up, giving me a questioning, hungry look when her palms graze my thighs, next to the hard-on raging between my legs.

"Later, love," I tell her, cupping her ass with my hands. "Turn around."

She listens. I squeeze out a dab of thick, fragrant shampoo and lather it through her hair.

She's perfect. She's real. She's magnificent – even when I'm keeping myself from fucking her like I want to.

Erin backs into me, letting the water roll over us from the spigot above while I rinse her hair. It's strangely soothing, like some zen meditation I've been waiting half my life to discover.

I hate it like hell when I have to shut the water off. We step out together, ignoring the rock hard cock I've still got swinging near my belly button, and start toweling off.

Whatever happens, I *will* take care of myself later, and Erin, too. These royal distractions, this is the part of being a Prince I really fucking hate.

When we're back in my private suite to dress, the balcony door is cracked, letting in the fresh breeze. That's when we hear the thunder coming from one more floor above us. Erin turns around, her eyes wide, fixing the summer dress she's wearing.

"Jesus. You weren't kidding about the helicopter, were you?"

"Do I ever kid about anything?"

She sticks her tongue out. Something that makes me want to smile. Too bad the shitshow waiting for us across the country doesn't let me.

Victor joins us near the exit upstairs. We all climb aboard the huge converted military chopper. It's all mine, complete with the double-headed black eagle on the side.

It's too loud to speak until the doors are sealed shut. Even when they are, I don't say anything, lost in all the dark possibilities waiting at the palace.

We're leaving paradise. We're only in the air for a few tense minutes when I feel her hand on mine. Grabbing her fingers, I squeeze them tight, telling myself this isn't going to be the end.

I don't give a damn how fucked up things get with the kingdom. Nothing's changing my mind about my woman.

* * * *

Soon as we're on the palace's landing pad, Vic and I slip off. I kiss Erin goodbye, and straighten my tie, ready to take on everything that's keeping me from her.

A long walk down the hall and several flights of stairs later, we're in the throne room. It's weird as hell to see it empty. Unoccupied.

That chair has never looked so imposing because I might be in it sooner than I ever expected. Worse, it could up a museum piece, never to house a royal ass in it again.

"How is she?" I ask sharply, seeing Patricia waiting for us by the window.

The Queen's valet is there, along with her personal emissary to parliament, a big man named George. There's also Serena – the last bitch in the world I want to see right now. She flashes me a huge, man eating smile. I don't even acknowledge her, focusing on Patricia instead.

"Stable, Your Highness. The symptoms began this morning. She woke in a state of confusion, and had great difficulty sitting up. We had her rushed to the hospital immediately. The medical team says she's in good spirits, resting, while they wait for a few more scans."

"My God. What if there's brain damage?" One sentence from George gets everybody's nerves going. "I'm sorry, that was rude. I'm worried about the inquiries from parliament, Your Highness, nothing more. They won't like this uncertainty, particularly after the recent upsets in this very palace."

"Fuck the politicians!" I snarl, pacing in front of the window.

They know to give me my space. All of them except Serena, who creeps up next to me, mustering her most soothing voice.

"My Prince, I'd advise against that kind of tone. We need our PR working to unify the country. The last thing we ought to risk is more division."

"Didn't ask for your advice," I snap, pushing past her. "The country's already divided down to its roots. It's going to take weeding to bring it together again, and everybody in this room knows it."

Vic clears his throat. "Sire, if you'd like us to put a cap on this, and head for the hospital, I'd be more than willing to summon a car." He speaks slowly, trying to diffuse the walking bomb I've become.

"No, we have to talk this out," I mutter, hating what I

have to admit next. "Serena's right, damn it. I'll be there immediately if grandmom's condition changes, for better or worse. It's our job to make sure the whole kingdom doesn't go to hell in the meantime. I want her on black out — anything that isn't absolutely necessary doesn't get through. No politics, no drama, no jackals buzzing around her room. We can't risk upsetting her while she's being treated."

Patricia gives me a sour look. She's never liked me very much. Her first and last duty is to the Queen, sure, but her distaste is personal, too. The prim, proper woman is probably about to lay a load because there's a risk I'm about to become King far sooner than anyone expected.

Including me.

Christ, King. My gaze drifts to the throne.

I can't imagine myself up there, wearing my grandfather's crown, wrapped up in robes made from mountain lions, wild bears, and gold. I see myself surrounded by guards and valets, Victor in Patricia's place, and — of course — Erin at my side.

Then the others vanish. I'm imagining myself on the throne in *just* my robe. Erin is on her knees, her sweet, smooth skin reflecting the fire's glow. Naked for me, ready to sit on my raging cock and take the sovereign's seed, pump my dick with her luscious cunt until we're dripping all over thousand year old gold.

Fuck. Patricia's talking, but I've been too busy thinking about filthy, ridiculous things to listen.

"We'll take it day by day with her condition. That's all I'm asking, Prince. We needn't consider anything rash, much less any assumptions of royal power, unless it's clearly necessary."

"Patricia, you know full well what palace protocol and the kingdom's laws say about this," Victor cuts in. "A country needs a head in the crown. If Her Majesty is incapacitated – briefly, I pray – then all the duties fall on the heir in the interim. His Highness is effectively King, the kingdom's chief representative, and its sole functioning sovereign, until such time as Her Majesty is ready and able to resume her full duties."

They look like they're about to kill each other. Just what we need – another standoff.

"Vic, come on. I'm ready to do anything I need to while she's down and out. But I'm damned sure *not* King unless I'm sitting in that chair. I don't need the extra title to sort this out," I say, nodding to the throne. "George, you tell the assholes in the chamber exactly what I've said. The crown isn't passing to anyone unless my grandmother isn't breathing. God forbid."

"Certainly, Your Highness. They won't like it – politicians thrive on what's clear cut, as you know. However, they'll live with it."

Yeah, they will, I think to myself. *Because if they don't, I'll find some way to have the son of bitches dissolved and call early elections. Even the Republic First rabble rousers would love to see that happen.*

"A sensible choice, Your Highness." Vic nods politely, but I can't tell if he's being honest, or just blowing more smoke up my ass.

Patricia doesn't say anything. She turns, staring sadly at the empty throne.

That fucking chair is going to decide too many people's futures. I'm tired of seeing it. I want to get out of here.

"Update me on Her Majesty's condition, the second there's any change," I tell grandmom's valet.

"Of course, my Prince."

I wave at Victor to follow me, and we're gone, heading into the hallway. We're only a few steps outside the throne room when I hear Serena's heels clicking behind us.

Goddamn. I knew she wouldn't stay muzzled forever.

"Your Highness! Please." I hear her calling, barely slowing down to let her catch up. "We need to schedule a meeting to address the PR problem. I'd like to talk with you and that girl in private. Maybe go over some talking points we can use with the kingdom, in case the situation deteriorates."

"That girl?" I stop and look at her. "Is that what you're going to call my fiancee, potentially your future Queen?"

The color drains from her face. Time seems to stop, turning the whole atmosphere electric like a storm around us. Even Vic looks nervous.

"Silas —"

"Your Highness, Miss Hastings," Vic corrects, glaring at her.

"I'm sorry, of course. It's the stress today, that's all," she lies. I'm about to lose what little patience for her I've got left. "I want to do right by the kingdom. You have to know, I feel *awful* about what happened during the press conference. I should've requested more security when I set it up. Let me make it up to you...to everyone. I'll prep three different speeches. One for every scenario we might have to deal with. You choose whichever you like best."

"How about the one where I throw your ass out and tell you to find a new job?" I growl.

She blinks, surprised. Unfortunately, after fucking me, she's too fearless for her own good.

"That seems...rather uncalled for," she says, choosing her words carefully. "I'm just doing my job, Your Highness. Forgive me if I've offended you or your fiancee."

I study her face when she says the last word. Damn if it doesn't look like she's chewing something rotten.

"It's been a rough day for everyone. I'm more than happy to coach Erin with anything I need to. She's the one you've chosen to marry, after all." Surrender, that's what's coming out of her now.

I've seen that hurt, puppy dog look on women I've fucked a hundred times. This has to be the first where I'm feeling absolutely no remorse.

Victor's looking at me. Waiting. He's got one hand on his phone, ready to call security if I decide to kick her to the curb this very second.

Lucky for her, she's too damned good at what she does. I can't risk an untested specialist working the kingdom's media if grandmom's health goes to complete shit.

"I don't have time for this. Go write." I'm flying down the hall without a second glance behind my shoulder.

Vic trots after me, struggling to keep up. I don't slow down for a damned second.

* * * *

I'm alone for the next few hours, stuck in my office. I've got to make a few more phone calls. Contingencies for the worst clusterfucks I can imagine for myself and the kingdom.

First, I talk to the generals and admirals. Their loyalty to the crown means everything if the kingdom falls into total chaos.

Then I'm on the line with the leaders of both major parties. George has already told them what I said this morning, spelling out my role while my grandmother takes the longest break she's ever had from royal duties.

Fifty fucking years holding the scepter. I can't imagine it, but I'd better start. I'm next in line.

I answer the tense, probing questions from the men who depend on lofty promises to win votes for power.

"Everything is fine," I tell them, over and over, wondering if I'll believe it after I say it enough times.

It's a phrase of the day fit for Robby the Talking Horse to sing a song about, if he could, the main character on the nation's kids' show. I sung with him, once, when I was about nine, and they wanted to bring the Prince on as a special guest.

I mangled the stupid ballad about ten times before I got it right in the last cut. Singing hasn't interested me since.

Whatever mistakes I've made before in my life, there's no room for new ones.

Deflect, spin, and promise. That's what I do with the ministers and party leaders before I get the hell off the line, faking a call coming in from the royal hospital.

I'm not even stretching the truth that much. It's the last and most stressful call of the evening. When I get Her Majesty's physician on the line, I look out the window, and it's dark.

Thousands of little lines glowing across the city's skyline, melded with fuchsia and burgundy. Several hundred royal purple candles sit flaming in windowsills, praying for grandmom's recovery.

"Well, how is she?" I ask, ripping open my drawer. The bottle of scotch I've stashed for emergency situations is still there.

"We have more assessments to finish, Your Highness. Tests so far have been inconclusive."

There's a word I hate. It takes a long, fiery swig of booze to quell my frustration enough to finish this conversation.

"So, what? Is it a stroke, or not?"

"We don't know, sire. We're doing our best. I promise you, we'll know more in the morning. She's being monitored around the clock."

"Give me two scenarios, best and worst." I pop the bottle open and take a long pull while the doctor clears his throat, closing my eyes as sweet, calming fire splashes my stomach.

"Best case? We find the event was limited, hasn't done any lasting damage, and she's discharged within the week. As for the worst, well...she's eighty years old, Your Highness. Worst could mean a lot of things."

He won't tell me she could die. Nobody has the balls to say it, to even think it. Not when this woman has been on the radio and TV since most of the kingdom was in diapers, a comforting presence in the troubling times.

"Call me if anything changes. Don't care if it's the middle of the night. You call, doctor."

"Understood, Prince Silas."

I slam down the phone. There's a schedule in front of me, glowing on the screen, everything the Queen had lined up for the next week.

Tomorrow, there's supposed to be afternoon tea with the Russian ambassador, and then a late dinner with the emissary from the States. Our kingdom's longtime neutrality and grandmom's generosity has put us front and center, mediating a territorial dispute in the Baltic.

I don't know where the negotiations are at. There's a good chance I'm going to turn over the table if we can't get the Russians and NATO to shake hands, accidentally starting World War III.

Fuck.

I stand up, bottle in hand, barreling around the office. I'm looking for a glass so I can really lay down the scotch. When I finally find one, I stop just short of filling it.

My stomach turns, staring at the liquid gold in the glass.

It's…revolting.

Double fuck. The day I've always feared has arrived. Booze won't help me anymore. It won't do anything except cause a disaster if I'm sucking on the bottle as King, and starting tonight.

Growling to myself, I push the cap down on the bottle.

I'm growing up. The fucking, the drinking, the parties with supermodels and spoiled rich kids from across Europe, they're in the past. I can't indulge them anymore. I don't even want to because they're not going to take the edge off.

There's only one thing that's made me feel human since I found out the brutal news this morning.

Erin. My Princess with benefits.

She's waiting for me in her chamber, probably pouring over the news breaking online. Wondering what kind of man she's going to see when I return.

I have a chance to show her it won't be a stumbling, horny drunk. To show myself that I can take the reigns without falling off my horse.

My father would be a drunken, weeping mess right now. Probably running for the nearest bar with another slut at his side.

Never me. I grit my teeth, staring at my reflection in the empty glass. No, fuck, I'm better than that.

If I can fix this kingdom in its darkest hour, then I can damned sure fix myself. And that means this crazy thing I've got with my Princess could be more than pretend.

Am I ready for that? Ready to settle down, to love, to act like a man with his wife-to-be instead of just a carefree fuck with a dick bigger than his crown?

I don't know, but I'm about to find out.

XI: Open Revery (Erin)

It's late.

I haven't seen Silas since we returned to the palace. I've been in his chamber all day, watched around the clock by Dean and several other guards.

They've been whispering into their phones and radios all day.

I hear the same words over and over.

Her Majesty's health. Chaos. Damned rioters.

Silas. Prince. *King.*

Every time I hear that last one, it makes me swoon, and get so lightheaded I want to throw up. I've barely gotten a handle on this Princess thing. I never imagined I'd be a Queen in my wildest dreams – even a pretend one – and I'm scared. I'm in too deep.

The way they say *King Silas* makes me worry, too. It's said with tension and humor, the way a person talks about a silly hypothetical, something that won't *really* happen.

I'm sitting by the window, watching the capital's lights wink on below. It seems like half the windows are filled with royal purple candles lit to pray for Queen Marina's health.

Their glow splashes everything like smooth wine. I wonder if I'm watching the last time the kingdom will know peace.

I'm so lost in my thoughts, I don't hear him come in. There's a hand on my shoulder so thick, firm, and confident it can only belong to one man.

I look up, placing my hand over his. He takes my fingers like he owns them, squeezes, then lifts them to his mouth.

His lips make me feel better instantly. Whatever else is happening out there, I know where we stand in this room.

"Hey," I whisper. "What's the latest?"

"Hell," he says, a one word answer heavy as ice on his tongue. "Nobody knows what's going to happen. We just have to take it day by day, love. Do everything we can to settle the nerves rattling this kingdom. That's what royals do."

I stand up, facing him, sliding my hands over his shoulders. He pulls me into his arms. I'm scanning his eyes, falling deeper into ocean blue. I want to understand how he's so calm with the weight of the world – or at least a whole kingdom – hanging around his neck.

"How can I help?" I ask, running one hand across his cheek.

God, his stubble feels good. He hasn't had time to shave all day. It's rough like rest of him. I'm still discovering what I enjoy in a man, but I love when things match, bound together in a single gorgeous package.

"You really want to know?" he asks, that sly quirk pulling at his lips.

Swallowing the expectation in my throat, I look at him, and nod.

"Don't fight me when I rip off that dress. That's going to help a lot." It's the only warning he gives.

His hands are on me. Moving, tearing, pulling. He's quick, ferocious, a wild animal who needs to get me naked *this fucking second.*

When I'm down to just my panties, I turn toward the hall leading to the bedroom. Big mistake.

Silas jerks me into his arms, slamming me against his chest, resting his forehead on mine.

"No. We'll save the sheets for later. We're going to fuck in front of this glass, beautiful, where anyone can look in and see. I want transparency, love. Let the people see their future King and Queen, in lust, with nothing left to hide."

I'm taken aback. More importantly, both my wrists are in his fists, and he guides me to the huge window pane. My back slides against it, cool as a sheet of ice.

Warmth, fire, and glacial cool collides in my bloodstream. It's strange, conflicted, and oh so wrong.

But I'm getting used to wrong feeling right – especially when he moves his head down my breasts. My nipple disappears into his mouth, and my knees start shaking.

"Oh, God!" I whimper, losing myself in the pleasure when his teeth form a tight little ring.

He eases off after several seconds, just long enough to make the wet spot on my panties three times bigger. Clenching my ass, he pulls me into him, then moves one hand around my thigh, sliding to the middle.

He slips his fingers in me hard, never taking those blue eyes off mine for a second. "Silas," he growls.

"What?" I can barely speak when he starts to move, stroking that spot in my pussy that's going to make me see stars.

"Silas. That's the only thing on your lips when you're coming, love. That's the man who's strumming your whole body, making your wet little cunt sing. That's who wants to own you. Body, mind, and soul."

His thumb finds my clit and brushes against it.

Oh, God. Oh, yes. Oh, Silas.

I'm trembling, putting my hands against the glass, hoping my legs don't completely buckle when he makes me come.

I can't think about the people behind their glass. Hell, I won't let myself wonder what kind of message this is sending either. This manic, animal rush to sex when a whole country is hanging by its nails...

"Move that sweet ass. Fuck my fingers," he growls, pulling them away, making me grind down against his hand.

I'm twisting like a whore. It makes me flush, sweat, and get even wetter. Just standing in this palace, with what looks like a crystal chandelier more expensive than a house hanging over us, its edges reflecting every filthy, desperate face I'm making each time he pleasures me.

How can he stroke so deeply like this? So good? How can he know exactly what gets me off?

It's because he's slept with like half a million women, and I've only had him.

One.

For a second, through my haze of ecstasy, that makes me grit my teeth. I'm jealous, and disappointed with myself for falling so hard, so quickly, to this man who's had a king's feast of pussy. It shouldn't be this hard to imagine myself in another man's arms.

But when Silas lifts his hand away, dragging my panties down my legs, there's nothing I want more than having him inside me again.

Him, and *only* him. My Prince with benefits that make my eyes roll wild.

"Step aside, love, so I can get these fucking things off." I lift my leg, and he swings them around, throwing the sopping wet mess behind his shoulder.

"Turn around," he growls, standing up, towering over me.

The hard-on raging in his pants rubs against my ass through his trousers before he even takes it out. He takes my breast again in his fingers, rolling my nipple gently, a prelude to the crisp pinch that's ten times better than the golden clamps could ever be.

"Beautiful, love. You're going to come so hard tonight. So fucking hard we both forget our own names, much less the hell going on around us."

"Only if you make me," I whisper, spreading my fingers high above my head, flat against the glass.

Every gesture in my body language now says one thing – *please.*

More thunder rumbles through his throat, and this time

it doesn't form words. I hear his belt buckle coming undone.

My bottom lip catches in my teeth. My breath grows tense, ragged. My pussy pulses so hot between my legs I need to pinch my thighs together. I'm going to either come on the spot or die first, if he doesn't fucking touch me right now.

"Please, Silas. Make me come," I whimper.

"Make you?" he growls, slipping his bare, seething cock between my ass cheeks. "Love, I thought you'd give me a challenge. Something to take my mind off the kingdom and it's damned bloody politics tonight. We both know you're going to come like mad the second this king sized dick fills your tight little pussy."

No!

"No!" I shake my head furiously, trying to deny it. Too bad my body won't let me.

"Yeah, yeah, fuck yeah," he says slowly, a hot, low groan in my ear. "You're a good Princess because you're begging to be my royal whore. You'll come for me because I've got the biggest, meanest cock you've ever had. The *only* cock. The first, the last, the best dick. Made for fucking your pussy, love. Made for making you come when I tell you to."

I'm burning up. Sweating, trembling, staring out the glass and trying not to pant like an animal in heat.

Jesus, I'm shaking, desperately grinding my ass on his length, bucking my hips to try to pull him inside me.

I see his reflection behind me, his face hovering over my shoulder. He smiles like a lion looking down at his dinner.

Damn him. God damn him!

He's beautiful, but he's still a royal asshole.

I hate that he's enjoying this, watching me come undone. I absolutely, positive loathe that he's making me enjoy it, too — maybe more than he is.

"You're an asshole, Silas, even when you're sexy," I say, staring out at the city.

I've never been so vulnerable before. Anyone with the right angle or a pair of binoculars can look up here and see my naked body against the glass, my hot, desperate breath fogging it up, hiding my face.

Small consolation. So are having his hands grab my thighs. He digs his fingers into my tender skin, and of course, it heats my blood ten more degrees.

"And you're going to come for me, love. You're going to come so hard half the city thinks a fucking bomb has detonated up here."

He shoves his cock in me.

There isn't time to protest. No time for comebacks or denials or self-conscious doubts.

He thrusts about three times, pulling my hips into his, before I'm losing it. My lips form a ring, I lean on the glass, and I'm gone.

I'm coming. His dick fucks me harder, straight through the clenching, screaming, shaking mess I've become.

My back arches so hard my spine goes stiff. Silas grabs my hair, twirls it around his fingers, and jerks me close enough to hear him growl.

That's when the screaming starts. He's fucking me,

drilling me deep, pounding me until some wild, wicked instinct I don't understand rips lose.

I'm not in his palace anymore. I'm in nirvana, spasming and moaning. Slave to his cock for what feels like forever.

"Fuck," he growls, thrusting his full length into me and holding it there when I'm coming down from it. "That's the way you'll always come on this dick, love. Every damned orgasm you have is beautiful because I made it, and you'd better believe I'm making more tonight."

Shit! He's right. There's no stopping him.

I don't even want to. My body leans into his, knees still trembling, letting his strong, tall weight steady me. His hold on my hair tightens, pulling me in. Silas bites my shoulder, sinks his teeth in, growling until it vibrates through my entire body.

We're lost in our sex. I'm not just drowning in those royal blue eyes anymore, but sinking into him, every single inch.

It's scary. It's insane. It chains me up like I'm losing my mind and releases me again.

I've been starved for so long. And now, I'm finally allowed to feast, as long as I'm joined to his ridiculously perfect cock.

When he holds one hand up to my mouth, I bite it, getting him back for the hickeys he's no doubt left around my throat. I know it drives him wild because he fucks me harder.

Pushing me against the window, he holds me by the throat. Gently, but firmly, he starts fucking harder. Faster.

Slamming his hips into mine until I go over the edge at least two more times, crazy to feel him add his heat to mind.

I don't know if he's stopped to roll on a condom. I'm way past caring.

Thinking about his seed inside me nearly makes me come again. Silas is panting, holding us both against the glass. I'm glad it's industrial strength, or else we'd have broken through it ten minutes ago.

Or is it an hour ago? Time has no more meaning, wrecked in our fucking, groaning, screaming affair.

"Please. Please, Silas," I pant, hissing the words through my teeth. "I can't keep this up...I can't..."

Can a person die from too many orgasms? From being fucked too hard? I don't know, but I'm worried I'm about to find out.

I need a break. Just a few minutes to catch my breath, to let my body settle from its proud, mind blowing storm. My toes will lock if they curl anymore.

"Can't what? Can't wait to feel me come?" He pauses, letting the new inferno rush through my blood, setting me on fire again, when burning into a new orgasm should be impossible. I think he's going to give me a few seconds rest.

"Silas..." I moan.

Then the bastard says it. "Erin, love...I'm coming."

It's like I've been trained. My body seizes up and my head snaps backward against his hand, loving how he makes it burn when he pulls, down to the root.

His cock moves in me like a piston now.

In and out. Deeper, deeper.

Stroking, thrusting, slamming into me until his balls swing up, slapping my clit. His free hand reaches down between my legs, pinches my nub, and frigs it until I'm coming apart.

Coming again. Coming for the King.

"Fucking hell!" Snarling, he explodes, holding his dick in me as it swells, releasing pure fire.

Yes, fucking hell. Fucking Silas. Fucking King.

I don't care that he doesn't officially have the crown. He rules every molecule in my body with an iron first.

We're coming together, harder than two people should.

My fingers scratch the glass helplessly. I'm going to need a chiropractor to unfurl my toes, my fingers. I don't know how I'm going to hide the marks he's left on my neck, my shoulders, especially when all but the most formal dresses I've seen in the wardrobe have so much room for skin.

For the next minute, the longest minute of my life, I don't fucking care.

Nothing else matters except the Prince and I. The man who's spilling every drop of himself into me, and making me feel it.

Making my pussy work for its pleasure by wringing his cock until he's spent. His knuckle slows against my clit, little by little, but he won't pull out.

We're panting, drinking precious oxygen into our lungs, when he finally softens. He slips out with a growl, backing away from me, giving me the space to turn around.

"I want you on the pill, the patch, or whatever suits you tomorrow," he says, rolling the condom off his hardness and tying it at the end before he looks at me.

It should be a relief that he slipped one on without me knowing it. Strangely, it doesn't feel that way.

"Next time we're fucking after tonight, I want to feel what's mine, skin-on-skin. I'm coming in you, love. Spilling every goddamned drop."

Yes. I've been wet all evening, and now I'm even wetter.

I pinch my legs together to hide it, walking over, and taking his hand. He leads me to his bedroom at last, where yet another huge bed with curtains hanging around the edges waits like something from a fairy tale.

No, forget the fairy tales. They aren't this dirty.

Cinderella never let her Prince mount her and deliver too many orgasms to count in front of an entire city.

This is for real, and I'm his.

I'm blushing, picturing how we must've looked behind the glass. I sit on the edge of the bed while he pulls a carafe of water from a small silver fridge.

"You think anybody saw us?" I ask.

"Sure hope so."

I raise an eyebrow and love the coolness against my skin when he pushes a glass of water into my hand. "You've got to be kidding me?"

"No, love. We both know I don't do jokes. I'm dead serious." I'm shaking my head, cursing him under my breath again, when he wraps an arm around my shoulder, pulling me close. "I was afraid how we'd look in front of the kingdom before, back before the stupid press conference and the riot changed everything."

"You? Afraid?" I can't believe it, taking a long, refreshing sip.

"There was always a risk that nobody would believe us, love. That we'd come off stiff. Unnatural." His eyes roam my body, telling me something else will be stiff again really soon. "Far as I'm concerned, that's over. All this time getting up close and personal means we're going to make the kingdom believe we're in love."

I reach out, resting my hands on his bare, beautiful chest. I want to tell him I'm starting to believe it, too.

But a man like this doesn't do love. *One and done*, wasn't that motto in interviews with the playboy blogs? I'm feeling a lot of things, an emotional windstorm that would leave any woman dizzy.

"It's becoming very natural," I say cautiously, refusing to let myself believe anything I know I shouldn't. "What will you do when we're at the altar? That's the kiss we have to get right to make them believe."

My gaze drifts up his body, slowly rising from his magnificent cock to his chiseled chin, his magical eyes. The royal eagle sits in his skin, searching, ready to fly out and tear the world apart if he's ever challenged.

"Obviously," he says, reaching behind my head and pulling my face closer. "No worries, love. We've got several weeks ahead for practice. How about I train you to come every time you touch my tongue?"

"Uh, how about you don't!" Laughing, I slap my hands against his chest. "Jesus. You're not joking about the whole kingdom seeing us, are you?"

"How many times do I have to tell you, Princess? I —"

Rolling my eyes, I finish it for him. "Yeah, yeah. You never kid. You're the most serious man in the world. I'm so lucky."

"Say it like you mean it. Looks like you need to be reminded why." He takes my hand, guides it down between his legs, and wraps my fingers around his swelling cock. "I don't think enough people saw us tonight. Should've gone out on the balcony, bent you the banister, and let your screams blow into the streets."

"You're insane! I'm not doing anything worse than what we've already done."

"No? Guess you'll be seeing less of this, then." He pushes his huge, hard erection through my hand, forcing me to remember how good he feels inside me.

"No more teasing, Silas." I let go, drop back on the bed, and spread my legs. "A Prince just takes what he wants, doesn't he?"

"A Prince takes a lot of things," he growls, rolling on top of me, holding that angry, irresistible hard-on against my opening.

Damn! My body aches to tell him I already have an IUD – something I had put in by the college clinic about two years ago, waiting for Mister Perfect. It's been collecting rust until this past week, when I lost my sanity and my virginity to the cocky, hulking, panty ripping rogue between my legs, kissing his way between my breasts.

"This pussy, love, I'm fucking hooked." He stops between my legs, pushing his face in, running his tongue between my folds before he pulls up. "Can't wait to pump my seed straight up you when I'm coming like no tomorrow. I want you leaking me for hours. Only improvement possible for this pussy."

Royal. Asshole.

If he's going to keep teasing me, then I'll leave him one more thing to discover. I'm not quite ready to ride bareback with Silas unless he's going to start fucking me properly, without this torture disguised as foreplay.

Of course, that's an idle threat. I *love* this torture. Love it so much it's frightening.

His tongue teases my clit until my legs part. Then he holds my thighs, spreading my legs wider, placing them on his shoulders. The pompous bastard makes me bite my lip while I'm waiting for him to sink in.

He reaches behind him, producing a condom from fucking nowhere, ripping the foil with his teeth. My eyes betray me, staring as he rolls it onto his huge length, giving his cock one last pump with his fist. It throbs like mad.

I'm not going to beg, I promise myself. *I don't care how good it feels, how much I want you.*

I'm NOT begging, god damn it.

His eyes narrow, watching me twitch and writhe beneath him. He rubs the tip of his cock against my clit, before he lets me have an inch.

"No, no more teasing. Silas – please!"

Fuck me. I give up. My body's begging, so who cares if my mouth does, too?

"Please what?"

"I need this. I need you. Please, just fuck me."

I need this to be more than just pretend, my racing mind reminds me. I don't dare say that part out loud.

"Why didn't you say so?" He sinks into me with a smile, and I'm clutching the sheets, desperately bucking my hips against the cock inside me. "Since you asked so nicely, we'll do it your way, love. No more teasing tonight. You'll pay me back later."

"Later? What's later?" I ask.

He answers me with a thrust, preventing me from calling him all the names on the tip of my tongue. "You'll see, Princess. You'll find out very fucking soon."

I've had it up to *here* with his strange, cryptic bullshit. But I'm also too busy having him, every glorious inch, and I can't bring myself to care.

He fucks me until I'm screaming myself breathless, slipping into the zone. Here, we're alone with our pleasure.

Our worries, our tensions, they all melt away. There's just Prince Silas Bearington the Royal Fucker and that imperial dick of his, the one that's bringing me off for what feels like the hundredth time tonight.

Right before I'm about to go over, he grabs me, jerks me onto his lap, and rolls underneath me.

I'm suddenly on top, and he's moving my hips, pulling my ass up and down in his hands. He wants me to fuck him, to keep the rhythm. Whenever I slow down, he gives me a sharp swat on the butt, like he's breaking in a pet.

Or another servant.

Fuck you, I want to say.

Fuck you and your overgrown, pussy wetting dick.

Fuck you for making me your wife.

Fuck you for making me want it, and for wanting more.

I'm speechless, lost in my thoughts, and about to come.

Those explosive things I want to tell him? Too fucking bad.

There are no words when I'm riding him like this, letting his pubic bone grind against my clit. He takes my hips, pulls me against him harder. There's no hope of escaping this leverage, this manic thrusting.

Silas bears his teeth, tenses up, and I know he's about to come. "Fuck, love. You feel so goddamned good. Come for me again! Come with me."

It's not a suggestion. It's a command, and I'm completely helpless, especially when his cock balloons and the heat surges through his condom.

"Silas!" *Coming!*

"Erin! Fuck!"

We cry out together. Surrendering to the sweat, the sweetness, and the lightning thrashing through our bodies.

I'm coming so hard on his cock I nearly pass out. Ecstasy blurs to bliss.

Then he's pulling me to his chest, while I gather my breath. Holding me, kissing me, showing me there's a tenderness behind all the arrogant master crap I'm becoming a sucker for.

"Seriously, what did you mean by 'paying you back later?'" I ask him again, now that I can actually think straight. "What are you planning?"

"I don't joke, and I don't ruin promises, Princess. And no, that's not more teasing. I'm a man of my word. I'm –"

"The most upright, honorable, and fucking ridiculous man in the world." I stick my tongue out, giving him a perfect opening to kiss me again. He takes it.

"You forgot biggest dick in there, babe," he says, stopping my little fist in mid-air when I try to punch him. "You manage to hit me, and there's going to be teasing. A fuck of a lot more."

I let go, collapsing against his chest.

The bastard wins. There's no way I'm going to risk more delicious agony tonight, even if I'm dying to know exactly what the hell he's putting together in his devious head.

* * * *

"Look, peach, I've been doing a lot of thinking," dad says over the phone the next day. "Maybe this is good for you. God knows I've made my mistakes with women. Live and learn, I'd say, like everyone has to. Just as long as you're avoiding your old man's mistakes."

I'm standing in the royal gardens, amazed that he's doing this strange about-face on me and Silas. It also worries me.

This better not be his way of making peace before his health takes a turn for the worse.

"It's no mistake, daddy. Silas is a wonderful man. He loves me. He cares about me."

The last part is becoming more true by the day, at least. Too bad that makes me want to believe the big, bad L-word might not be a total lie we're fabricating to save a crown.

"I'm sure he does," dad says grudgingly. "It's your life, Erin. If you want to hang up the journalism plan and become a Princess, who am I to say it's not the right thing? Jesus, I never thought I'd say those words."

That makes me smile. I'm walking over a tiny bridge lined with rocks, cherry blossoms, and little stone statues of frogs and birds. It's very zen, like they had a piece of Japan airlifted halfway around the world to the palace. For all I know, that's what they actually did.

Dad isn't kidding about the strange absurdity hanging over us. Silas is a Prince – I have to keep reminding myself – part of the blue bloods with so much money nothing is off limits. Ever.

"Who says I can't do both?" I tell him. "I don't think you have to shut down and disappear as soon as there's a title in front of your name. Silas was just telling me about his cousin the other day, the Duchess of Southshore. You'd know her face if you saw her. She's been partnered up with fitness guys and New Age gurus for years, helping push health, her passion."

"Your first responsibility is always going to be to that country," dad says. "Don't have to tell you things work different in Europe than they do in the States, peach. Marrying that man means taking on a hell of an obligation – maybe one that prevents you from doing a lot of what you want."

"I know exactly what I'm getting into," I snap, forgetting the fact that I barely have a clue. "Well, the wedding's coming up in about a month. I won't be talked out of it. And, daddy, if you're feeling up to traveling, I'd really love to have you there."

I shouldn't say it, stifling the tremor in my voice, but I do. It's official. I'm inviting my father to my fake marriage with a man who's little more than a fuck buddy with royal blood. A man who's already said he's going to let go at some point, leaving me with these insane memories, along with more money than I can imagine.

"You're right. It's not my place to tell you anything. You're a grown woman, and you can do what you want."

"Exactly. So, maybe I won't be trotting around the globe interviewing celebrities and Presidents like you, daddy. But someday, I'm going to publish an amazing book."

"Yeah, you will." I can practically hear him smiling over the phone, warming my heart.

I have to know how he's really doing. This kind of surrender, acceptance, tolerance just isn't like him.

"How's the treatment, anyway?" I ask. "Have they done more tests since your last round of chemo?"

"It's…inconclusive," he says, choosing his words carefully. "Doesn't mean anything bad. They don't have a lot of experience with what I've got. It's the Big C, yeah, but they all behave a little differently, from what I understand. I'll know more next week."

Next week. It feels like an eternity to me, waiting to find out if he's sitting on a death sentence or not. I can't even imagine what it's like for him, and my stomach twists in knots, weighed down with guilt. I regret being so bitchy about Silas just a minute ago.

"You're going to be *fine,* daddy. You have to believe that. Positive thinking…"

"Peach, with you and Prince Charming pumping the finest drugs money can buy into my veins, I'm bringing the fight. I won't go down without swinging back as hard as I can. Whatever happens, it's been a good life. I'm always going to worry about you, Erin, because you're my daughter. But I'm not worried about you doing the right thing anymore. You've got your head screwed tight and your heart in the right place. I did a good job with that, whatever other mistakes I've made."

"You did." The way he's talking makes me want to cry.

I sit down on a small bamboo bench by the stream, staring through the dense trees, wondering how hot the sun feels on the other side of the world in Mexico.

"I've got another appointment in about ten minutes, so I'd better go. Love you, darling. Always have, always will, and always gonna be –"

"I know, I know," I cut in, finishing the phrase he's said to me since I was as little girl for him. "My daddy."

"Damned straight." My phone goes quiet.

I lower it to my lap, brushing the tears from my eyes. The furious lion that's always been a fixture in the media has turned into a gentle giant. I'm touched and scared for him just the same, and I spend the next few minutes enveloped in my thoughts, a thousand chances at life and death rolling by like clouds taking shape.

"What the hell happened?" I hear Silas growl it before I

look up, feeling his protective hand on my shoulder.

"It's nothing," I lie. "Just worried about my father. We talked. He's doing okay – or so he says – but he doesn't do details. It's almost like he knows he won't be around much longer."

Silas sits next to me, putting his arm around my shoulder, and pulls me in tight. "People change when they're face-to-face with death, love. He's going to make it – none of those doctors would dare to let me down after all the money they've gotten for their research."

"I don't know that cancer cares about your generosity, Your Highness," I say, more sarcastically than I really need to.

I hate it when I'm sad.

I'm the kind of girl who wraps herself up in barbed wire to hide the pain. Anybody coming too close *will* get pricked, and bleed with me.

"No, but the small army I've got working on it are better than any disease. I've always been careful with who I fund. Nobody gets a penny unless they're the best of the best. Mom taught me that lesson."

He squeezes my hand. I look at him slowly, the bitterness fading.

Different doesn't begin to describe the worlds we're from, but here, we're a lot more alike than we should be. His mother, the kingdom's beloved Princess for twenty years, already had her fight with the same thing hammering my dad. She lost hers when he was just a boy.

"I'm sorry," I say, lacing my fingers through his. "I

forgot, you've been through all this before…"

"Not quite. Mom's fight was hopeless. The technology wasn't as good, and she held off too long on treatment. The woman stopped caring about her health after the cheating started. My goddamned father, she never got over it…losing his heart, and his loyalty. Watching him ruin himself on women half his age. Pissing away his life, until the ocean put him out of his misery for good."

I stare at him, not saying much, dragging my heel through the gravel underneath us. "I can't imagine what it's like, losing both parents. I barely talk to mom. She hasn't wanted much to do with either of us since the divorce. She's all work, spending her days and nights at the law firm in New York. Maybe she's trying to forget the life she used to have, including me. It's like addiction comes naturally to people trying to run from something. Like your dad, maybe."

Silas snorts, lifting my hand to his mouth. He stops to kiss the back of my hand before he says anything. Heat blooms inside me, hot and red and wanting.

I still can't figure out how this man is so damned good at turning me on with nothing more than the slightest kiss.

"My father never saw past pussy and drink. Although I've inherited his knack for getting panties wet, I'd like to think I'm more than just another player."

Right now, he's *all* player, and he's won the game. I'm burning up by the time his fingers trace through my hair, and he pulls my face to his, smothering me in another fiery trademark kiss.

"Let's forget all this shit. It's too beautiful a day to dwell on it," he says, gesturing to the green vastness on the path I haven't even explored. "You haven't seen all the gardens yet, have you?'

I shake my head. "No. I might need a tour guide for that, I'm afraid."

"At your service," he stands up and does an exaggerated bow.

It's so ridiculous coming from a real life Prince, especially one as arrogant as Silas, that I burst out laughing. "I don't know if I can handle more of that on the trail."

"Deeply sorry, love, I'm afraid I'm your only choice today," he says, doing his very best to imitate Victor's prim and proper style. "These gardens go on for at least a thousand acres, so you're not going alone. And I'm not turning you over to fuck the gardener."

Sticking out my tongue, I slap his chest. "Like I would ever do that!"

"I don't know, love. I think I've created a monster when I took you to bed. We both know you need it morning, noon, and night."

There's Prince Asshole again, jerking me to his chest, guiding me into his next kiss. Everything says I should fight like hell to push him away, but I don't when I feel him, taste him, lose myself in his infuriating lips.

If this thing is a fairy tale, then it's the most twisted, incredible story a girl can live.

* * * *

We're deep in the gardens, talking about everything and nothing at all. I find out things about Silas I never imagined.

He got suspended from the most prestigious prep school in Europe for sneaking in his childhood bulldog. The animal went on a rampage, chewing up several priceless books in the school library after getting spooked by a violin practice next door.

He likes his coffee strong and black. The only way it should be after a late night with too many drinks.

He remembers the war. Afghanistan follows him, especially when he sneaks away to the royal military cemetery once a year. Always on some dark, cold, rainy day when people hold their umbrellas low, reducing the chances he'll ever be recognized.

He isn't shy about his big, beautiful cock. Well, I knew that before, but he's still stroking his…ego.

At least he says I'm the finest, hottest pussy he's ever had wrapped around it.

I roll my eyes and laugh at his latest crude jests. They do their job, though, making me uncomfortably hot and wet. I'm grateful for the humid, lush forest surrounding us on every side. It's the only thing that distracts me, helps me keep my hands off his big, solid body.

"Since we're playing a thousand questions, there's something I'd like to know," I tell him, holding his hand while we go over yet another beautiful stone bridge that's at least a century old. "What happened with Serena? What's her deal?"

His face darkens. "I made a big fucking mistake with that one. Put my dick somewhere it never should've gone last summer. She hasn't gotten over it."

"Did you lead her on?" I look at him, point blank.

"Hell no. Truthfully, the bitch is psychotic or painfully desperate. Maybe both." He shakes his head so adamantly I have to believe him. "I never promised her a damned thing. She let her Princess fantasies get to her, like some women do. They suck me, fuck me, think it means they're going to wear the royal ring and have Sunday dinners with grandmom. The other girls were easy to brush off. Serena, not so much, because she's too good at her job. I don't want to send her packing unless she crosses the line."

She already has with me. Several times. I keep my thoughts to myself, knowing it isn't my place to decide who he keeps as press secretary.

"You can't take back what happened. I get that."

"Yeah, and we don't need to dwell on it, love. I've taken the liberty of chatting with the bitch myself so you don't have to. We're set for tomorrow."

"Tomorrow? What's happening then?"

"Our second appearance in public." He tightens his hold on my hand when I look at him, my eyes going huge. "We've got ourselves a royal parade scheduled. Show of power, really, to remind the Republic assholes who's still boss. We're going out for a ride with tight security. There'll also be several dignitaries present, paying their respects to Her Majesty while she's ill."

My chest tightens. I have to hold my hand across my

breast. Silas stops when I do, his head cocked, wondering what's wrong.

"You're sure it's safe? It seems so soon, riding out into crowds like that, after what happened at the palace."

I took too many history classes for my own good at college. I'm having brutal flashes of JFK and Arch Duke Ferdinand, both cut down in their prime with their Princesses riding next to them.

"The rabble rousers don't have the balls to do anything except sneer at us from the sidelines with their signs and banners. I've been through this half a dozen times over the years, love. I promise it's safe. Trust me."

He reaches for my hand. I hesitate for several seconds before I let my fingers wind around his. Reassured, for now.

Maybe he's right. Publicity is half of what I signed up for when I agreed to this marriage. I can't be scared.

"Okay. I'll do my best. Will they expect us to speak again?"

"A few words from me in front of the cameras, maybe," he says. "Not like before. This isn't an announcement. We're there for eye candy, moving through the streets like living ornaments. We'll meet some dignitaries at the end of it, but whatever comes after with them will be said behind closed doors. Most of the people love us. We'll make the world see a couple thousand smiling faces, and just a few angry pricks. Believe me, if anything gets out of line, they won't get far with the extra agents stationed in the crowd."

I hope you're right. I hold my tongue, thinking it, without saying anything.

"I haven't gotten a tour of the capital yet. Good way to do that, I suppose," I say.

"It's gorgeous. Lucky for you, I'll also be giving you that surprise tomorrow morning."

Oh, God. I'd almost forgotten it. Now, I can't think of anything else with the sly, mischievous glint beading in his deep blue eyes.

"Tell me, Silas. I don't like surprises."

"You'll love this one. Small disclaimer, I'm not responsible if you accidentally come your brains out."

I don't even have time to gasp, or hit him with a dozen questions. He takes my hand by the wrist and pulls me along, further along the path into the gardens. Deeper into this craziness and mystery, wondering how I'm going to survive.

XII: Public Eye (Silas)

It takes everything I've got not to smile when she opens the platinum box. It's morning, we're due in the car in about an hour, and my Princess is looking at an egg shaped remote-control vibrator custom designed for her pussy.

Her fingers tremble a little when she picks it up. She's eyeballing it like I just presented her with a stick of dynamite.

Hell, maybe I have. My cock certainly feels like it's going to explode in my pants while I'm watching her grasp it, hold it up, and turn that shocked little look on her face into total horror.

"I'm *not* using this in public. You're out of your fucking mind, Silas."

"Yeah? Then why are you holding it like you're already in love?" I smile, sit down on the bed next to her, and put my hand over hers. Our fingers both close around the cool, sterile gold, made to get her hotter than an incoming meteor when I crank it to high.

"No, just – no!" She says it again, shaking her sweet head, desperately trying to push my hand away with the device in it.

I don't let her. "Take a chance on it, love. Let yourself have a little excitement. I saw how nervous you looked yesterday, in the gardens, when I mentioned our outing. Believe me, with this thing in, you'll be too busy coming to think about all the eyes on you."

"Bad idea! All of it." She manages to wrestle out of my grasp, jumping up, pacing around the bedroom. "It really shouldn't surprise me what a crude psycho you can be, but for some reason it does."

I clench the small metal object harder in my hand. Can't stop thinking about it wedged in her sweet cunt, shaking between her legs, making her soak everything she's wearing underneath that fancy formal dress.

It's thinner and more modern than the one she had to wear to meet grandmom. Perfect for hiding what I'm doing to her from everybody with a camera, while it shows me everything.

"Look, if you're dead set against it, I won't make you," I say, standing up.

"Like you could!" Erin sticks her tongue out.

Ah, a challenge. *Fuck me.*

My hand twitches for another reason. I want to spank that ass raw. For a split second, I think about pulling out my phone, calling Vic, and canceling the whole event.

Unfortunately, the interests of the kingdom and my ten inch cock are often quite different. I swear I can hear the world's smallest violin playing a sad song.

"Babe, take it." I step up, pushing it into her hand. I'll risk her throwing it through the wall, or maybe at my head.

"Go. Finish getting dressed. I'll let you decide whether you want to slip that thing in, or leave it on the bathroom counter."

Her cheeks glow rosy. It's a conflicted, reddish flush spreading across her face when she stares at the filthy toy in her hand before she looks up at me, her brows furrowed.

"I can't believe you're thinking about sex again on the day we have a second chance to get this right."

"Funny. I can't believe you think I'd rather be thinking about anything else. Especially when you're folding your arms, pushing your tits in my face, reminding me that I want to shred that fucking dress and have you against the wall."

My dick's doing the talking now. As usual, I'm at a loss to shut him up.

"I have to get ready," she says, briskly spinning around.

As soon as the bathroom door closes, I let myself smile. I'd bet my whole fortune she's wetter than she wants to be.

What are the odds I won't see my gift abandoned on the counter if I look in there before we head out?

I'm still crunching the numbers in my head, trying to distract my rampaging cock, when she finally steps out. The ladies assigned to help her dress this morning are gone at my orders, and I'm relieved to see she can handle the entire outfit herself.

Wait, handle it? No, she looks good. Sexy. Divine.

Good enough to eat my fill. My cock aches in tune with my lips, hungry to get her naked, spread her legs, and lick her hard and deep. I want to make this girl squirt on my face, and taste her own cream on my lips when I fuck her senseless.

"Well? How do I look?" she says, a husky edge in her voice that isn't helping me calm down.

"Like a Princess should," I say, standing.

She smiles, calling me to walk on over and embrace her. There's a knock at our door just then.

"Your Highness, the men are performing the last security check on the motorcade. Everything's ready, at your convenience."

"Thanks. We'll be out in just a minute."

Not enough time to satisfy my evil desires. Just enough to kiss her, grab her ass, and realize there's one more thing I have to do before we leave.

"Go on, love. I'll be out in just a second. Need to make a quick pit stop."

I head for the bathroom. While I'm there, I let my eyes wander to the counter.

No sign of anything there. I'm washing my hands while I let my foot slide to the pedal on the small steel trashcan.

The lid lifts up, and I see the hottest thing in my life after Erin's naked skin.

Nothing. It's empty, which means…fuck.

Fuck yes.

The small, secret remote I've got concealed in my pocket burns like my pistol used to in Afghanistan.

Today just got a lot more exciting, and it's got nothing to do with playing head of state.

* * * *

"Here we go," I say, grabbing her hand as the car slowly rolls forward, perfectly positioned between two jet black SUVs with flashing lights.

She looks at me and smiles. Bashful. She knows that I know what's in her pussy by now, but she doesn't have a clue my words have double meaning.

Here we go, princess. Here we fucking go, and we're not stopping until you've come so hard you won't walk straight.

My thumb burns like mad, hovering over the little wheel that controls the intensity of the earthquake she's about to feel. I've already turned it on, as soon as Victor gave me the thirty second countdown, before our convertible started moving.

He's in the passenger seat next to our driver, eyes roaming like a sheepdog, making sure every little detail goes according to plan. He won't have a spare second to notice what's happening to my Princess in the back seat, next to me.

Seeing the city center with throngs of bystanders is nothing new. Having a woman riding next to me while I own everything that happens between her legs for the next hour or two is.

My finger nudges the switch. Erin's eyelids flutter, and she leans back in her seat, not even noticing the rows of people waving hysterically all around us. We're into the thick of it now. Christ, there must be thousands, all of them here to show their support for the royal family.

The speakers across the city start blasting *King of All Things*. My dick throbs to the heavy drumbeats and clashing cymbals like it's saluting the kingdom's anthem.

"You doing all right, love?" I ask, grasping her hand.

She barely nods. My signal to crank the power higher.

"Oh, God." I can't hear her over the crowd screaming, but I know it's the only thing on her lips when they open up, form a perfect ring, and tell me I'm bringing her O closer.

I have to look away for a few seconds before I shoot off in my pants. Besides, the cameras are rolling. I sit up as tall as I can in the seat, waving to the people, giving them my very best princely salute.

I've watched my grandmom and my great grandfather do it a thousand times in old movies. My hand moves up and waves, every movement carefully choreographed. The people lining the streets swoon with the prince and future king so close.

Men and women alike. I think some of the girls are about to faint, visibly leaning into their friends and husbands for support when I flash them my smile.

It's boring. The only woman I want to see losing her mind is already next to me, ready to go over the edge as soon as I twist the dial higher.

And I do.

"Silas – oh!" I read her lips again. She's leaning back in her seat now, her hips squirming like mad.

Can't resist putting my hand on her thigh and squeezing it hard. I stare her down in between smiling at the crowd, throttling the controls back. Just enough to leave her on the precipice.

"You don't come until I say you do," I growl, leaning over to whisper in her ear.

She looks at me like she wants to sink a knife in my throat. Smiling, I suppress a laugh, wondering what the media jackasses are capturing right now through their lenses. The video online later ought to be *very* interesting.

We turn the corner, circling the next street, rolling down another double row of people screaming at us like we're rock stars about to bang out their favorite tune.

Everyone except one asshole, anyway.

A big, surly bastard in a trench coat rushes my car, hate twisted on his face. Secret service acts fast. I see them throw the fucker down on the pavement, a boot pressed firmly in his back. His sign slips out of his hands and hits the curb, right-side up.

NO MORE GREED.

NO MORE LIES.

NO MORE KING.

I don't even bat an eye at the ridiculous slogans written there in thick black ink. I turn to Erin, wondering if he scared her, but she's in another world. She's balls deep in pleasure, lost there so deeply she's forgotten what pain and fear mean.

She's simply gorgeous. I pause, taking a good, long look, before I decide how I'm going to bring her off for good. Squirming, bucking her hips shallowly in her seat, desperately trying to milk the last burst of pleasure in the toy that sends her over the edge.

"What did I tell you, Princess? Can you hear me?" I say softly, placing my hand over hers.

"You're killing me. Please, Silas. *Please.*"

"Please what?" I smile, wondering how filthy and crazy she can get when she really wants it.

"I'm not going to…I can't fucking say it. God, you're a bastard!"

Guilty as charged. My thumb slides across the little wheel in my pocket, but only for a split second, teasing with such sharp vibrations I'm sure she can feel it in her clit.

My dick leaks more pre-come in my pants. I hope like hell there isn't an improved press conference after this. The entire kingdom is going to see my hard-on if I don't get a chance to fuck her first.

"Sire, Mister Nelson from the Daily Eagle is just ahead," Vic cuts in. "We'll do our very best to let him get too close, but you know how aggressive he can be."

Yeah, I do. The motherfucker ambushed me last year in my own nightclub, dancing with no less than Serena when I was drunk off my ass. The rumors that hit the press the next day didn't help me, or my secretary's ridiculous crush.

"Let him come up," I tell my chief.

"Your Highness?" He looks behind him in the seat, both his eyebrows raised.

"You heard me. We have nothing to hide."

Slowly, he turns back around, and whispers something into the radio to security. Perfect timing. I see Nelson's giddy, goateed face staring from the curb. The idiot steps out onto the asphalt with two assistants, all their cameras flashing.

That's when I throw my arm around Erin, pull her close, and smash my lips down on hers.

Sometimes, the only way to tame a tiger is to give the damned thing its red meat. I'm giving him exactly what he wants – the photo of a lifetime. Serving up huge, juicy steaks with this kiss, so hot and sudden I think we're going to set our custom made Rolls-Royce convertible on fire.

Her sweet, dark eyes are narrow. Lids half shut. Begging.

Not yet, beautiful, I tell her with my kiss. *You don't get it unless I see how bad you want it.*

Show me.

Her desperation tastes incredible. When I try to break the kiss so I can smile to my subjects some more, she doesn't let me. Erin throws her little hands around my neck, digs her nails into my skin, and bites my lower lip.

Fuck, doesn't she know I'm going to bite back harder? We're practically stripping off our clothes and fucking in the seat before it's over. I wonder if I can shut down the bullet shoved inside her, make her come with just my kiss.

It's goddamned tempting, if only it wouldn't ruin all the fun.

I have to break the kiss. *Have to,* before I roll around, push between her legs, and take her in broad daylight in front of several million people.

I've always had a bit of an exhibitionist streak, certainly, but even I'm not that big a freak.

I'm winded when I break away, settling reluctantly back into my seat.

My tension has nothing on hers, though. Erin has her eyes pinched shut, gently bobbing her hips, after the leverage she needs for sweet release.

My heart starts pounding. The car rolls on, reminding me I'm the sole heir to an entire kingdom someday. Lesser men would swell up and prance like peacocks at the prospect.

Not me. With Erin on the brink of coming next to me, it's nothing.

I'm not after power over anyone except her, and her next O. My fingertip burns against the remote, stuffed into my pocket, while I look back across the crowd and wave with my very best.

A few more Republic First disruptors go down when they come for the motorcade, tackled by my boys. A couple thousand more people get my smile, my wink, my grey gloved hand waving their way with grace and reassurance.

I don't have the soft, motherly air Her Majesty brings. But I can tell the people I won't let them down. They're safe, happy, and prosperous with me, whatever the media jackals and the protesters say.

"Sire, the King Winston bridge is coming up next. Several ministers there from the EU, China, and India are waiting. They're scheduled to meet you after the parade, as planned, and we've given them one of the best spots in the city to observe your arrival."

"Of course. Wonderful work, Victor." I see him glowing in the rear view mirror.

That pride's starting to rub off on me, but not because I

give a damn about the old, robotic diplomats waiting to shake my royal hand. Slowly, I turn to Erin, a smile creeping across my lips when I see the sweat building on her brow.

She's dying to come. Lucky her, I'm finally going to make it happen, just as soon as the dignitaries are in sight.

I slide across the seat, coiling one hand around her shoulder. "I'm going to kiss you, love, and you're going to give it up. *All* of it."

"Silas, God yes…please."

Please. Fuck, now she's showing me.

Holy shit. Her big brown eyes are huge, pleading, completely mine. She's still begging, and I'm worried I'm going to lose it in my trousers when I bring her off like I promised it.

Fuck it. My free hand slips into my pocket while the other tightens on her shoulder, squeezing her so hard it should hurt ever-so-slightly. I clench my jaw, rolling my thumb against the wheel, just as I see the tall, shadowy figures of men and women in fine suits standing on the huge stone bridge.

"You can't look at me like that, Princess," I whisper, hearing a moan slip out her mouth. "You keep that up, you're going to make me fall in love. Don't, for both our sakes. I don't know how to deal in hearts – only in the best fucking sex you'll ever have in your life."

I'm sweating like mad, saying shit I know I shouldn't. Don't know whether it's my slip up or my finger gliding across the wheel that sends her into heaven. The wheel cranks as far as it can, making me think I can hear the little toy vibrating inside her when we pass through a quiet break in the crowd.

"Oh. My. God…Fuck!" Those are the only four words I can make out when I feel her start shaking.

She clenches my suit, hangs on for dear life. She comes, harder than I've ever seen her explode. My head leans on hers, pushing her mouth to my wrist. I let her bite it so she won't scream while the tsunami I've unleashed in her body sweeps her into another world.

"You're bad for me, Princess," I tell her, hoping my dick won't rip through my trousers just watching this. "Look at you. Coming for me, coming like mad, soaking the fucking seat in front of all these ministers and ambassadors. I ought to pull you down on my throne, and spank your hot little ass until you scream."

She squeals against my skin. Rocking in her seat, gushing underneath that dress, coming until she can't even breathe.

It's too much – for everyone. My dick barely holds onto the fire raging in my balls.

Vic clears his throat in the front seat, and the idea of being discovered back here throws cold water on my desire for a split second.

My eyes shift off the beautiful woman twitching next to me. He's talking into his radio, not looking back at us in the mirror, thank fuck.

I don't start turning down the intensity until she whimpers. Then my lips smash down on hers, sucking whatever pleasure I can from her mouth, awed by the burn of her teeth marks on my wrist.

What the hell is happening? Playing pretend isn't supposed to be this wild.

It's a fake engagement to a fake wife, and the f-word is sounding extra hollow the more it's said.

Fake, fake, fake. Fuck.

Fake isn't supposed to bring my cock to the brink. Fake damned sure isn't supposed to make me admire every inch of her when she's buried in her orgasm. Fake definitely isn't kissable when she comes down from it, looks up at me, and sucks my eyes into hers with a single blink.

I'm starting to freak out, but I don't show it. I just kiss her harder, until she stops moving, and I make sure the remote is turned to off.

"Time to stop playing slut and do Princess again," I say, taking her hand as I sit back in my seat.

"Really? You haven't realized how talented I am yet?" Erin sticks her tongue out for a split second. "I was born to multi-task."

"Careful, babe. The cameras are watching every second."

Absurd advice, after I just gave her one of the best orgasms in her life on film, and we both know it. She looks at me, smiling, shaking her beautiful head.

"You're so ridiculous. Did you mean what you said about love?" Her tone turns more serious. "When we were in the heat of the moment, I mean…"

I don't know. I'm about to wiggle my way into some wishy-washy, half-assed escape when royal duty sweeps in to save me.

Our car stops. Erin's passenger door pops open, and I see her valet standing there, holding the door. "They're waiting next to the conference center, at your convenience, Your Highness."

She flashes me another quizzical look just before we slide out. I've bought myself some time, but she isn't going to let this go.

I never should've ran my mouth. Hell, I should've kept the strange thoughts and feelings from invading me, speaking their evil out loud.

Meeting these ministers and smiling pretty for the cameras might be the easiest thing I do all day. Who knew making this woman come her brains out in the riskiest, hottest way ever would have such a steep price?

Her touch doesn't betray anything when I take her arm. About a dozen dignitaries stand at attention, waiting for us at the end of the bridge, next to the conference venue.

Most of them bow when we approach. The others shake hands. One big Russian diplomat I've met before lets his gaze linger on my wrist too long.

"I trust you're in…good health, Your Highness?"

I smile, slipping my hand into my pocket, hiding the reddish impressions Erin's little teeth have left in my skin. "Never better, Sergei. Too much rock climbing last week in the highlands."

He nods enthusiastically. "Da, da. They used to bring us to the Urals for training in the army. Amazing how the mountains look so beautiful, but cut so deep, no?"

"Yeah."

Yeah. He doesn't have a fucking clue.

* * * *

Several hours of trade talks and a dinner fit for a Roman emperor later, we're back at the palace. I've passed the dignitaries off to the kingdom's trade minsters to iron out the fine print on several new agreements.

Technically, it isn't royalty's role to get involved in politics, or make any real decisions like this for the nation. In practice, we've been charming the best and brightest from all over the world to see things our way for at least a hundred years.

Erin hasn't said much since dinner. I saw her drinking lots of water, barely touching the champagne, which tells me the gift I gave her in the car practically sucked her soul out. Or at least half the water molecules in her sweet skin.

Best of all, I'm not done yet. Far from it.

Next time, we'll come together, and I'll banish this painful swelling between my legs that's been taunting me all evening.

"So, we're staying here tonight? Not going back to the castle?"

I shake my head. "Not while I'm in charge. You slept like a baby in the chamber last night anyway, love."

She doesn't deny it. I can say the same thing, really, which is weird.

I haven't felt so at home in the palace since my parents were still around. Before I was old enough to realize the picture perfect days they gave me as a boy were lies. Before those days became hellish nights where they fought late into the darkness, storming off to separate rooms when they were finally exhausted…

My old place at the castle has lost its charm, and it's not just because I'm effectively head of state with grandmom in the hospital.

I think about my old club downstairs, the parties I hosted in the huge lounge, endlessly stocked with fine scotch and even finer women.

It doesn't do shit for me. Something's changed big time, because nothing does it anymore.

Nothing except getting Erin Warwick naked, sweaty, and moaning even touches my crank.

She pulls ahead of me, holding my hand, making her way to the big staircase that will take us up to our room. I stop her right there.

"Hold up. I have a detour in mind," I say softly, taking her in the opposite direction.

My dick jerks. I'm crazy for doing this, but when will I get another chance?

I can't ignore the fantasy I had in the car while I teased her pussy raw. Fucking her in the throne room, the holiest, most taboo place possible, where there's always bound to be somebody around.

Except for tonight because I have an idea.

We walk quickly, and I guide her through the ancient passages, careful to avoid the places where I think the guards are likely to be on night patrol. Erin's eyes go wide when we're stopped, standing in front of the huge handcrafted door. Two honor guards come to attention and salute.

"At ease. I'd like to show my lady the throne room while there's some peace and quiet. We won't be long."

"Aye aye, Your Highness."

My greedy grip tightens on her hand. She knows what's coming – both of us, naked and grunting like animals while we fuck on gold and gemstones. Completely surrounded in the luxurious rapture that can't be duplicated anywhere else.

I won't get another chance like this for years, maybe decades. Her Majesty will be home soon. If the day comes when I'm King, there will always be someone posted inside, waiting for my royal ass to get parked in the seat and take care of business.

It's the first time I've been inside it by myself since I was a kid. I look around, letting out the slightest whistle when the huge doors behind us slam shut.

The fire isn't even lit. I have to walk over to the fireplace myself and start the gas.

There's no Patricia, no Victor, no foreign emissary in shock and awe from standing in front of the richest royal family in the world.

There's nobody. Just the ghosts of everybody who ever wore this crown, probably staring in horror at what I'm about to do. Maybe a few of my ancestors from the middle ages are cheering me on – the old Kings were notorious bastards, scoundrels who'd fuck the finest woman in every village in between their dirty orgies.

"So, why are we here?" She says nervously. Like she doesn't already know.

I turn, taking her into my arms, pressing my lips to hers

for a good, long minute. "We're here tonight because of what I said in the car."

Staring, she cocks her head. It's adorable, and it really fucking shouldn't be.

I let out a long sigh. "Look, love, I've never been great with with words. Actions mean more. If a man can't show you what he means, what good is he?"

I take her hand, lead her over to the huge golden chair in the center. My butt hasn't touched the ridiculously comfy burgundy cushion since I was twelve years old, but now it does.

I sink down, feeling lightning roll up my back, pulling Erin onto my lap. My hands roam her curves, doing circles on her thighs, resisting the urge to rip right through that dress she has on.

"You can't be serious!" she whispers sharply. "Silas, of all the things you've done, *this* is too much. We can't get caught – I can't. You're not telling me anything. Why are we here?"

"Like you don't already know, love. I haven't been in this room informally for years," I say, quickening my circles on her legs. Her thighs shift open, and my cock pulses again. "I was a little shit in my early teens."

"You? Never." She rolls her eyes, pushing playfully against my chest.

I catch her wrists with my free hands. Pulling her closer, we kiss before I continue my story. I'm not sure where the hell it's going, considering the blood rushing to my temples, making me hear the heartbeat that's pounding in my balls.

It's hard to think about anything except how bad I want my cock in my Princess.

"I snuck down here with a smoke bomb when I was a kid. Thought I'd throw it in the fireplace and let the white smoke roll out the palace chimney, get it thick over the city, in mom's memory. It was about a year after she died. Got the idea from watching the Pope being elected, watching the white smoke roll out the Vatican. That fucking counselor they hired, I wouldn't tell him anything. Words wouldn't help me then, and neither would any shrink. Thought I could remind myself and remind the country she isn't really gone, as long as we remember."

She blinks raw emotion. "That's a little more touching than I expected. So, what happened?"

"It was the wrong kind of smoke bomb. The damned thing detonated in the fireplace and blew the glass doors to hell. Guards rushed in, thinking it was a terrorist. I never heard the end of it from dad, my nanny, and the prick who kept hounding me to talk through my feelings."

"That prick might've been right," she says, moving a finger up my chest. "You can drop the asshole act sometimes, Your Highness. I know there's more to you now than what they show in the tabloids."

"Yeah, you'd better, after we've been more than skin deep." My hands go straight to her ass underneath that dress, squeezing.

Christ, she looks like an angel. She's soft, smiling, and teasing me the way my cock loves.

"With some things, words aren't enough. What good does

it do to tell you I'm deadly, crazy serious about all that crap I said in the car? That it wasn't just my dick doing the talking?"

Her eyes are huge now. I hug her tighter, dragging her fully into me on the throne, until our foreheads are as close as our lips.

"It's getting real between us, Erin. So goddamned real it's the only thing I taste, think, and feel when I'm able to. Or, hell, maybe when I'm supposed to be paying attention to everything else that comes with being heir to this throne."

"Silas…"

My name comes out in such a low whisper, I wonder if she knows what the hell to say. I don't give us a chance to find out. I reach up, press my finger snug over her lips, and keep on speaking.

"I know what you are. You're a walking, talking, cock-teasing risk, Princess. The biggest one I've ever wanted in my life. I could waste the next few hours telling you all about my feelings. Or, we can do it my way, and I can show you just how far I'm willing to go. Don't know yet if your pussy's magic, or what, but I know I can't let it go. I won't. Not for fucking anything."

Show me. Her eyes are screaming for it, begging with the same intensity they did in the car when I teased her to the edge of her O.

I'm going to push her right off that cliff a few more times tonight.

My finger drops away and my hand goes behind her head. We kiss in sweet, sexy silence, filling the void with passion.

A woman shouldn't taste this good. I can't get that honey richness out of my mouth when my lips own hers again and again.

My other hand paws at her breasts, angrily tugging on the fabric, rolling her nipple through the layers. She leans back while I hold her. Moaning, struggling for breath, already grinding her hips on mine.

My dick's been denied all day, and he won't take a second more of this. Gently lifting her off my lap, I lower her onto her knees. She goes down like a good girl, reaching for my cock the instant I start working the zipper.

"Suck." It's one word, beautiful as it is filthy. "Suck me so dry I can't even see straight, Princess."

Cool air surrounds my free cock for about two seconds before it's bathed in her silky, intoxicating warmth. Scotch on an empty stomach wouldn't hit my brain half as hard as this.

I'm grunting, clenching the arms of the throne, while my swollen head disappears behind her lips. She's been paying attention during the last few times I've let her do it.

Her tongue teases me before moving in for the kill. Erin pulls me in, moaning on my length, bobbing her head up and down, until my balls are about to pop.

Faster. Hotter. More tongue swirls around my massive cock, focused on that sweet spot underneath my tip.

I can't help myself. My hips start moving ragged in her face, fucking her mouth as hard and deep as I can without hurting her.

She loves it. I can see her nipples through the dress, hard

and pleading, aching for my mouth as much as my cock begs for hers.

"Jesus. Erin, baby, you're going to make me –"

I never get it out. She starts pumping my thick base with one hand, reaching up with the other to pull on my tie. It's so fucking hot and possessive I lose it on the spot, especially when she slams her face down on my dick, pulling me in halfway, teasing me with that glorious tongue.

Fuck!

Her pressure doubles when I start groaning. I'm leaning back in my family's throne, grinding my teeth like sandpaper. I'm coming.

Fire spits out my balls and my whole damned spine goes electric.

This was my idea, yeah, but I can't believe it's actually happening. I'm coming so hard I see stars for at least the next minute, watching my seed spill out her mouth. Her little hand catches the excess before it spills on her top, giving us away once we step outside.

It's so intense, so good. I jerk her up as soon as the wild spasms in my dick soften.

I'm not done yet. I have to fuck her again, right fucking now, or else I'm going to do something worse.

What's worse? Something outrageous, like saying the dreaded L-word.

Yeah, Prince Silas Bearington III is losing his mind, but he hasn't gone so batshit insane he's letting himself say *I love you* to a Princess who was just pretend a few weeks ago.

My hands tear at her furiously, helping her out of that

dress. She's never looked more beautiful than she does now, naked before me, bathed in the golden glow reflecting on the amber walls.

"Tell me you're on something so we can fuck like we should."

"Yes. IUD. I've had it the whole time," she whispers.

Everything I need to hear. It's an invitation to her bare pussy. It's all I can tolerate as I jerk her up, tearing down my pants, bringing her on my cock.

My hard-on never fades. It needs more, it needs her, right fucking now, or else I'm going to start climbing the walls and swinging from the two hundred year old crystal chandelier above us.

She grabs the high seat of the throne behind me for leverage when I start pumping in and out. It's hell stopping ourselves from the moaning, the groaning, the screaming. The door looks like it's as thick as a vault, supposedly soundproof for royal happenings in here, but even I'm not crazy enough to test it, bellowing as loud as I can.

I grab her hair, wrap it around my hands, and pull those chestnut locks tight. I swallow every little noise leaving her mouth.

A dozen strokes in, she's coming. She's so hot, so responsive to every thrust inside her, it's like she was made for me.

A thought so ludicrous it turns me into a fucking maniac. Maybe a maniac fucking.

I don't know who I am or what I'm doing, buried in her to the hilt, moving her hips up and down my cock with a speed that defies gravity. Her gorgeous tits are flopping from my chest to my face each time she moves. My palm slaps her ass several times, forcing her on faster.

Faster, goddammit! I won't stop until we've blown out every circuit in our bodies. Not before we're drunk and stupid and so sated on pleasure I'll have to request help just to carry us out.

I'm surprised I last as long as I do. All the stamina I've built up over the years is about half what it should be when I'm fucking this woman.

She's in the middle of her second climax, clutching my shoulders, tearing her lips off mine and arching her back, when magma churns in my balls. I can't stop it. Don't even fucking try.

"Keep coming, love. Keep coming on this dick that owns you, the one you've been waiting for your whole life. Come the fuck with me!"

Erin cries out, losing control, and so do I. I don't think about the noise or the guards or anything else.

I'm too busy shooting every damned drop up her bare, clenching pussy this time, pouring my royal seed in her womb.

I can't worry about anything outside us, except how fucking *right* this feels. I'm coming inside her, coming in my Princess, coming so rough I can't roar loudly enough to drown out the thunder roaring through my body.

Even when it's over, with my come pouring out of her, I don't pull out. My cock stays hard while the rest of me is spent. My arms hold her against my chest, one hand rifling through her hair. I need to touch it, smell it, bury my nose in it to bring myself back to earth.

"Silas...do you think they heard us?" She gestures to the door behind her, wiggling her ass, tempting me all over again.

"If they did, it was worth it. I don't give a damn if we end up on social media tomorrow with our bare asses hanging out in this room. That kind of sex is worth it. You're worth it, love."

Smiling, she looks at me with those irresistible brown eyes, and kisses me again. "I thought you were insane before."

"You don't anymore? Guess we're making serious progress."

"No," she says, her cheeks flushing red. "I'm starting to understand. And I think...maybe...this could become more than pretend."

So do I. I've confessed too much today to say it.

But she knows exactly what I mean when our lips connect for the thousand time, salty and sweet as ever. We fuck two more times before we finally clean ourselves up as best we can and step out.

I nod to the guards. They return my salute, staring ahead like statues, just as they've been trained.

We're taking the stairs slowly, one by one, up to our room. The men back there don't show any signs they've noticed anything. I hope they've heard us the entire time, as twisted as it is.

Sex like ours, in that room, is once in a lifetime. Fuck secrets.

What we have is so exquisite, it deserves witnesses.

XIII: Royal Interruption (Erin)

I wonder if I died in that ridiculous royal parade, coming so hard I passed out and never woke up in the fancy car.

The last two weeks have been heaven. Fancy dinners, tours around the capital fit for a Queen, perfecting my royal smile in front of the tireless paparazzi cameras.

Then there's the sex.

Toe curling, gasping, sheet soaking bliss. Every day. Every night. Every time we're alone, or sometimes just barely.

Sex that shakes the bed, the shower, the stone bridge in the royal gardens. Anywhere and everywhere Silas decides to lay me down, taking down my panties with his teeth, claiming what's his.

It doesn't matter whether it's hours, or just a few minutes. I can't tell anymore who's more addicted to who, and I don't care.

Yesterday, on our way home from a royal military memorial, nobody knew I had the gold clamps on underneath my dress. Silas looked extra dashing with his formal uniform on, the purple rose and diamond crosses he'd earned in the war shining brilliantly.

The warrior Prince barely waited until we were in the nearest alley to conquer me. He held my hands by the wrists, hiked up my dress, and fucked me as hard as he could, those tiny golden teeth digging into my breasts with every thrust.

It took the edge off the somber ceremony that came before. I notice he's drinking less, barely touching more than an evening scotch, or maybe a few glasses of wine with dinner.

I wasn't sure before, but now? It couldn't be more clear.

I'm his new addiction.

His escape.

His Princess – with more benefits by the day.

Today, he's away, visiting Her Majesty. I haven't seen Queen Marina since she returned to the palace, except for a brief glimpse when everyone lined up to see her. She's slower, a little more shaky than before, still on bed rest half her days.

But she's doing better again, and things are starting to feel as normal as a life of royalty, wealth, and power can be.

Her Majesty isn't the only one. My last few calls with dad were just like old times. He tells me he's in remission, so swiftly and suddenly he probably won't have to go under the knife again.

It's nothing short of a miracle.

I even talk to my mom, so busy with work she's been completely out of the loop about my impending marriage to a billionaire Prince. It's clear she doesn't care about my life either, muttering half-thought complaints about her latest cases and business deals while she types on her keyboard.

So, I don't bother to fill her in.

Let her find out when the wedding invitations hit the mail. Just a matter of weeks now.

"Madame, Miss Hastings will see you, at your convenience." Dean calls lightly through my door, gentle as ever.

"Thanks! I'm almost ready."

Ugh. Will I ever be? I don't really want to sit down alone with Serena, the bitch, and deal with her nasty attitude again.

Too bad she's still the sitting press secretary. I'd better get used to it, too, because this Princess thing means a woman needs a high tolerance for assholes.

We're going to have breakfast with the Queen next week, a halfway public affair that will have more cameras than usual covering it due to her health.

I can't screw this up. Meaning, I have to put my own feelings aside, and work with Silas' old crush to make sure I don't curtsy to Her Majesty at the wrong time, or accidentally walk in front of someone who should go through the next door ahead of me according to royal tradition.

There are a thousand and one mistakes waiting to be made in this position. However 'normal' this life feels, I'm very new to being a Princess. I won't even pretend I've figured it out yet.

As soon as I'm done, dressed in a nice business dress and a blouse, Dean takes me downstairs. My guards stop outside the same small press room Silas and I used before for our prep work to face the cameras.

Was it really only half a season ago? It's all come together so fast, and changed me in more ways than I can count.

The door shuts behind me. Serena sits at her desk with coffee, a tablet and a stack of papers on the small desk next to the ancient stained glass window. Brilliant reds, oranges, and yellows dance across her skin, making her look more evil than she already does.

"Oh, there you are," she says, flipping her hair back. Something about that not-quite-English accent sounds extra haughty coming from her.

She steps out behind my desk, gesturing to a chair, towering over me on her tall black heels. New heels. Like something she's bought just to rub her limited power in my face.

I sit down and muster up my best look that says *don't. I'm not taking this crap again.*

"Just tell me what I need to do so I don't screw this up," I say, a small prayer that maybe we can get this over with quickly.

Serena sits on the edge of her desk and narrows her eyes. "Protocol, protocol, protocol. I'd say you should've been doing that from the very beginning, but I certainly can't control what Silas lets his women get away with."

"Don't you mean His Highness?"

She purses her lips. "Sure. Anyhow, the Queen's tea

service is always a very sensitive and traditional event. This one, more than ever, knowing what we do about her health. You, madame, are expected to be at the Prince's side the entire time. Smile and wave to the cameras. Don't, under any circumstances, talk to reporters. You know how nosy they can be, I'm sure, since that's the direction you were heading before you found your Prince."

"I still am," I say. My fists tighten on my lap when I see her give me a surprised look. "I'm going to be writing a book sometime after the wedding. All about my experiences, the beauty and kindness in this kingdom, falling in love with Silas."

"Don't *you* mean His Highness?"

I blink at her angrily, wondering what the hell she means. As his fiancee, I'm not required to use the royal title. I'm sure of it. I looked it up weeks ago.

Serena tips her head back and laughs, tapping her heels like the evil witch she is. "That was a joke, dear. Lighten up. God, even in the backrooms, they say you come off so tense, so cold. The press wants another Lady Bearington to adore like Silas' poor mom. So far, you're coming dangerously close to falling flat."

Falling flat? I'll show her *falling*, preferably by shoving the bitch off that desk if she doesn't shut her mouth...

"Oh, and you're going to have to send your manuscript to me, as soon as you have it ready. I'll go over it with Perkins, the palace's lawyer, strictly to ensure you haven't said anything that would cast the crown or the kingdom in a bad light."

"You're kidding, right? You make it sound like this isn't a free country. I think I'm entitled to write whatever I want, so long as it isn't libel. There's no reason for me to insult anybody, much less my own husband and his family."

"Nonsense. You're entitled, dear, to writing anything you damned well please. What you're not entitled to is publication, if the palace deems it's going to be a problem. Still thinking like an American, I see. If you want to be a Princess, you'd better start acting like it, and thinking like one as well. That means leaving the free speech on demand crap on the side."

I've had it. I stand up, look her in the eye, and let it roll.

"Why are you constantly so fucking insulting? What did I do to deserve this?"

She gives me a blank look. "We both know why, dear. You're abandoning your dreams to take over mine. Marrying Prince Playboy, heir to the throne, in a country you know next to nothing about."

"That isn't true! I'm reading every damned day, when I'm not busy traveling, or talking to all the great people he introduces me to. I –"

"It isn't my place to judge, or to alter anyone's decisions. I'm here to whip you into shape so you don't embarrass Her Majesty and cost this family its throne. Look, I'm being as open and honest with you as I can. There's no sense in hiding it. I'm *trying* to get over him. Someday, I know I will, and then it'll be all business."

"Like it should be now? I should tell Silas myself."

"Go ahead. He still reports to the Queen, as long as she's

258

breathing. He won't get rid of me." She smiles sweetly, a shark-like grin that makes me want to punch her stupid face. "The great thing about being in this position means I'm privy to all kinds of dirt. Silas won't take the risk. Not when he's tying the knot, thinking about hanging up the partying, and becoming King in the next few years. Or is he? Maybe that's the latest load he's decided to feed you. He'll say anything and everything to charm you into having his way. Trust me, I know from experience…"

I don't say anything. I'm blindsided, wondering if I should interpret this as a threat. She isn't that crazy…is she?

"Oh, I'm terribly sorry. I meant *His Highness*. Is that better, my Lady?" Sarcasm drips off every word like poison.

"I need to go," I say, knowing it's true. I need to get the hell out of here before I do something I really regret, like risk a drag out fight.

It would be worth it just to put this asshole in her place, too. If only it weren't for the scratches and bruises I wouldn't be able to hide before the Queen's tea in a couple days.

"We aren't finished," Serena snaps, trying to lock me down with her pale blue eyes. "If you'll sit, my Lady, we can go over exactly what you should expect. I'll even do it without being a bitch. I am a professional, after all."

It takes every fiber of patience in my body to park myself back on that seat and stare at her. For the next half hour, she becomes another person.

She talks about the history, the pushy journalists to watch for, and the demeanor each person should have when they're enjoying this high royal honor. I actually listen, biting my tongue the entire time. It's easier because she lives up to her word.

She muzzles her inner bitch, and I gag mine. I wonder why she can't be like this all the time.

"Are we finished?" I say, when she stops talking and grabs the French press next to her, pouring more coffee into her china cup.

"For now. See, my Lady, that wasn't so bad, was it?"

"No. We might be able to make this work if you could hold that attitude a little more often."

She kills my hopes with a single smile. "What would be the fun in that? I'll tell you what I can do, though."

We lock eyes. If I could choose any superpower that moment, it'd be the ability to shoot daggers out my pupils.

"I'll go along with this," she says quietly. "Just do my fucking job without letting my feelings get in the way. Because I'm damned good at it. It's most certainly *not* my place to screw up things between you and Silas, or prevent this ridiculous wedding from happening. I'll let you find out for yourself what it's like to be used and cast aside like rubbish. He always does it to his girls, sooner or later. You've just gotten a little further than most for reasons I'll never understand."

I don't jump her, or slap her, or tackle her on the floor and start ripping out her hair. Every evil little fantasy burning in my brain gets doused just long enough so I can stand up, turn around, and walk out the door without seeing her venomous smile one more time.

"Everything all right, my Lady?"

"I want to see the Prince," I tell Dean, letting him wonder about the pain that's curdling my face. "Take me to him."

The guard frowns. "Mister Chambers told me His Highness won't be available until after four. He's at the Air Force base, awarding several men today. I can take you there if you're willing to wait until the ceremony's finished."

"Sure, sure. Whatever. I'll wait however long Victor says."

"I'll fetch a car and a security detail this instant, madame." He's already got his phone out before I walk past him.

I need to talk to Silas. I have to get him to discipline Serena, or fire her, or just let me spit in the bitch's face.

It isn't just personal, although it's definitely that. She's so busy talking about protocol and making sure traditions happen like they should.

I'm not going to take this when I'm officially wearing Silas' ring. If I let her walk all over me when I'm officially Princess, or God forbid, Queen, I'll never live it down. I *have* to put this bitter woman in her place, and demand some respect when she insults my soon-to-be-husband, too.

By the time the pitch black SUV circles up with Dean and several others inside, I'm seething. I don't say a word as I climb into the back, tearing a bottle of water from the ice.

I have to cool myself down before I talk to him. I swear.

If I don't, something absolutely crazy is going to happen.

* * * *

I sit in a back row, insisting on a subtle space cleared by the guards so I don't bother the families. Watching Silas up there with the Royal Air Force pilots helps stifle the anger. It's so somber, just like the other times I've seen him wearing his uniform, around other military men.

He takes this soldier stuff *very* seriously. It's beautiful, really, showing a side he wants to pretend isn't there.

This is my man with his shields down. The man I want to marry behind the magnificent tattooed body and the king-sized cock. The hero, the veteran, the worldly gentleman with the filthiest mouth I've ever imagined.

This is Prince Charming, the war hero, incarnate.

I wait patiently, until he's finally done. A few of the families below us whisper about me and my entourage. I try to shrink down, not wanting to take the moment away from them.

When the ceremony is finished, and the captain is leading his men off the runway with their wives and kids, Silas sees me.

Surprise. He doubles his speed, walking through the small gate held open by the guards.

I climb halfway down the metal seats to meet him. He grabs me, holds me in those tender, powerful arms, and banishes my woes in a single kiss.

If only they'd stay gone.

"What're you doing here, love? I would've been home in another hour or two."

"Serena."

One single word, and his face tightens knowingly. "What did the bitch do now?"

"She insulted me, insulted you, and I'm not going to take it anymore. I'm afraid she's never going to let it go. Whatever she thinks the two of you had. She won't stop being a bitch to me, every time I'm supposed to meet her for those briefings."

"She won't be easy to replace, Erin." He frowns, thinking it all over. "I'll probably have to get grandmom's approval, simply because she's been a favorite for several years. Shame, really. Old Henry, her predecessor, never would've treated you like trash. I *knew* I made a mistake with her. Whatever, I'll do what it takes to sort this out."

"That's all I'm asking," I tell him, squeezing both his hands. "I don't need her fired if you think there's some way to make her shut up and show some respect. This isn't an ego clash. I just can't wait and wonder if she'll ever stop questioning us with every other sentence that comes out of her mouth. It's not her place, and it's rude as hell."

"Forget it," he growls, sliding one hand down to the small of my back, pushing me against his chest. "She's gone. I'll get Her Majesty on board, one way or another. I've got to be careful not to stress her too much, seeing how she's in recovery. Still, I'll find a way."

"Oh." I look down, suddenly embarrassed. I hadn't thought of that. "Well, if you think you can do something."

"Babe, don't even ask again. I'll put the bitch in the

dungeon and give her a talking to myself, if that's what it takes to shut her yap."

I'm laughing. "You're joking, right? You don't really have a...dungeon?"

He smiles. Yes, that familiar, slightly wicked, damnably handsome curl of the lips.

"Hasn't been used since the eighteenth century, love. I think it's time we made an exception."

"Don't!" I slap playfully against his chest. "Seriously. She's a bitch, but she isn't a criminal."

"She's a demon in my book," Silas growls. "*Nobody* fucks with my princess."

He brings his face closer, gently grabs my face, and tips my lips to his. I can feel his breath on my skin, and I'm already getting wet.

"Don't worry, I won't torture her. I won't even scare her unless she really lays it on thick. I'm not letting this go until the palace has a new press secretary. Anyone who insults my wife, my Princess, isn't fit to clean the fucking stables."

"Wait, stables? You have horses?"

He laughs. A deep, baritone, belly busting sound that's like music to my ears.

"What's a Prince without his white horse? After the wedding's over, I'll take you on a trip to Saxon castle in the south. You can meet Eddy, the stud I used to ride when I was a boy. Only animal on this island who's more hung than me."

He's insane. I'm slapping his chest again and trying to wiggle away, laughing, but nothing could ever escape these arms. Silas' lips take mine, harder than before.

It's a kiss that tells me I'm going to be reminded just how big the favorite part of his anatomy is tonight. Maybe reminded at least five times.

God, yes.

* * * *

He talks to Serena, but he doesn't tell me what he's said. It's morning, several days later, less than an hour before we're due to arrive for tea with Her Majesty.

"You've got nothing to worry about anymore, love. She's been taken care of. Gently, I assure you."

"So, she's not in irons over in Grace tower?" I nod my head out the window toward the high spire across town, supposedly attached to Silas' castle by a secret passage.

"I wish." He shakes his head. "I do have principles, whether you want to believe it or not. There's only one woman I want to see writhing in restraints, and she sure as hell isn't Serena."

He steps up, cups my chin, and silences my next round of sass in a powerful kiss. "Mmm. Now, you're making me wonder who."

"Bullshit." His hand glides down my back, lifts off, and smacks my ass. "You know."

I do. I'm reminded every single day how much he wants me.

We're about to kiss again when Silas' phone goes off. "Yeah?"

I watch his face go dark and tense. He swears under his

breath, turns around, and whispers a few more words into the phone. I don't move until he ends the call and stuffs the leather and gold clad unit back in his pocket.

"What's wrong?" I ask, hoping it isn't the Queen's health.

"Fucking protesters. Again." He paces around me angrily, moving to the window, staring out across the city.

I join him. The streets are teeming with little crowds, tourists and pedestrians, mostly people milling around the palace so they can catch the royals setting off for tea. It's been all over the morning news, Her Majesty's first public event since coming home to the palace.

"I don't understand. What is it they want, Silas?" My hand squeezes his shoulder, trying to be reassuring.

He's bristling with so much rage he won't relax. "They'd hack off our heads if they could. Fucking maniacs, all of them. I'm sure half the bastards are hoping they cause grandmom to have another stroke so the crown falls to me, and they can have their damned referendum."

He isn't just speaking anymore. He's growling, each word more angry than the last, sending chills up my spine.

"I'm sure it'll be all right. It seems like there's nothing but sympathy for the royal family. If they do anything crazy, the public will turn on them."

I'm trying to talk with confidence. But truth be told, I know very little about the emotions wrapped up in the political situation here.

That has to change, and soon. Everything's becoming less theoretical by the day with our wedding approaching.

Silas looks at me, his eyes full of flickering blue fire. "I'll tell you something, love. These shit-stirrers are lucky we're not the monsters they claim. If we had the rights and powers we enjoyed five hundred years ago, they'd be rotting away with rats and moldy bread crusts by now."

Silas' phone chirps again before I can respond. "Shit, time to get downstairs. They want us to leave early, considering the situation. The biggest idiots have been cleared away from the palace grounds, at least."

I nod, grateful for the small progress. When he takes my hand to lead me out, his grip is tight, almost as intense as the day our first press conference turned into disaster.

"Sire!" A soldier in camo fatigues salutes the Prince when we're outside, heading for our big white limo. We have a military escort, more than just the usual security services, as I can see from the Humvees with heavy guns mounted to the sides.

Silas nods, helps me into the car, looking around him the entire time. My instinct makes me want to run my eyes over the people gathered just outside the gate as well, in case I see any impending violence.

I'm stopped in my tracks, though, because suddenly I'm face-to-face with Queen Marina.

"How are you, dear?" she asks, sitting across from me with Patricia and several bodyguards I don't recognize.

"Perfectly well, Your Majesty!"

Yeah, if perfectly well means stressed as hell.

"You look much better. I'm pleased to hear you're on the mend," I say, while Silas climbs in next to me.

Is there anything worse than trying to make small talk with a Queen?

"I still have a few good days in me to serve this kingdom," she says, twirling the platinum and gold tipped cane in her hand. "Silas, what's eating you, boy?"

"The protests," he growls, as if it isn't obvious. "Can't stay off our damned backs for a single minute."

I lay my hand on his. Patricia gives us both a sour look. Next to me on the other side, Victor clears his throat uncomfortably.

"They're entitled to their opinions. They certainly won't be allowed to stomp their feet or smash up my property. However, what kind of kingdom do you think we'd have if we didn't allow a place where people are free to express the unthinkable?"

"Yeah, maybe you're right," he says, clenching my hand tighter. It doesn't sound like he's being honest. "I've been worried about you lately, Your Majesty. That's all."

"Take your minds off me today, please." She pauses, looking around at each of us. "That goes for everyone in this car. Today, we have a chance to show our people that we're peaceful and united. I trust no one here wants to screw that up, and too much thought my way isn't helping the situation."

It's hard not to laugh. I wonder if she knows she's riding on a powder keg.

Peaceful? United? It won't take much to blow it all sky high.

"We'll be at Milton's in five minutes, Your Majesty,"

Patricia says. She snidely one-ups Victor, who'd been pulling out his phone to check the time.

"Wonderful. Miss Warwick, you'll be pleased to taste the finest tea in Europe at our traditional spot today," Her Majesty says.

"Oh, yes!" I clap my hands together, praying it won't ignite the tension in the air. The grin on my face feels crazy. "I love, love, *love* a good cup of tea."

I'm trying harder than I ever had in my life to diffuse the invisible rage.

For a minute, nobody says anything. Then Silas relaxes his grip on my hand and starts to laugh, shaking his head.

"Yeah, tea. I'm going to tell them to make mine so damned strong I go blind."

* * * *

I think things are going...well.

Unbelievably well, perhaps. We've just sat down at a private table reserved for the Queen. The media bombards us with camera flashes of our first orders before they're shuffled out the door, leaving us alone.

They won't see us again until we head back to our car, all smiles, Silas gently helping his grandmother down the steps. It's going to be a picture perfect end to a picture perfect photo op with so little drama people will fall asleep when it rolls across their newsfeed.

That's what I'm hoping for, anyway.

Our tea shows up in no time while the royals talk about Silas' dealings with diplomats in Her Majesty's absence.

Mine is black, velvety, sweet and citrusy. It's heaven in a cup, a million times more soothing than the shot of something stronger I'm sure Silas is craving.

"Erin helped with the trade ministers from the EU," he says, eyeballing me while he sips from his cup. "They were very impressed with her candor and beauty when we rolled in to meet them at the foot of the bridge."

Oh, God. He's referring back to the day I came in front of half the capital, clenching his hand, squirming in my seat.

I smile delicately at Queen Marina, trying to pretend nothing unusual happened. I can't believe he's teasing me like this. If he's hoping I won't go anywhere near his dick tonight, he's doing a great job.

"Yes, I believe the media is taking a slow, but steady liking to our new lady," she says, looking at me. "Of course, she won't be fully in their eye until the wedding and the ceremony where she's crowned. We're moving to the right place for this kingdom and our family. It just takes time."

I watch her too perfect false teeth take a huge bite from a flaky croissant. My stomach growls, and I'm mustering up the courage to eat in front of the Queen when the door behind us flies open.

My appetite goes completely cold when I turn around and see who's there. Silas bolts from his chair, whipping around so hard it tips over, hitting the floor.

"What the hell are you doing here, Serena?" he growls.

My heart skips several beats. I don't know if the rage boiling in his eyes is more directed at her, or the guard who let her nose her way in.

So much for picture perfect. The bitch smiles, staring at me, slowly coming closer.

"It's really a shame I have to do this. You were all doing so well on your way in. Heeding my advice about tea today, no doubt."

"I'm not asking again," Silas rumbles, his eyes shifting nervously to his grandmother.

I'm quietly praying he won't go nuclear. Jesus, he can't.

Queen Marina doesn't need this stress right now, especially with more bodyguards rushing in, surrounding Serena before she can totally reach out table.

"You thought you could get rid of me. You did what you had to because the American girl decided she didn't like my attitude. I get that, Silas. This isn't about us anymore. I'm here today to protect the kingdom and Her Majesty's honor. Just another patriotic, helpful subject, hoping for the best."

"Your Majesty?" Patricia looks angrily across the room, gesturing to the guards, making them form a wall between the intruder and the rest of us.

"Let her come forward. Pat her down first. I want to know the meaning of this."

Silas does a slow, maddening pivot. His face says it all. *You can't be fucking serious.*

I have to stop the mushroom cloud that's about to turn this room to ashes. I bolt up, wrap my arms around him, and hold him tight. I can feel his huge muscles bulging, trembling ever-so-slightly, his caveman instinct to kill and protect on overdrive.

No, I mouth to him, as soon as his eyes swing to me. *You can't.*

I'm worried he's going to fling me aside and go for Serena's throat. The guards have finished their pat down, and she's walking past, straight through us, taking a seat at the fucking table like she's part of our group.

"Your Majesty, I hope you'll forgive me. You know I've served you to the best of my abilities for years. That's the only thing I want to do here today, one last time, before I'm on my way out and –"

"Enough. Why are you here?" Queen Marina's royal blue eyes are blazing now. I think she's a second or two away from having the guards haul the bitch out after all.

I hope. Just like I hope it happens before her health takes a hit.

"I've been doing some research before Silas came to me last night and told me I'd never serve the royal family in any capacity again. Lots of research, before he called me a cunt to my face, and swore he'd have me locked up if I dared defy his royal orders."

My jaw clenches until it feels like my teeth are about to pop. If she's looking for sympathy, it isn't going to work, no matter what Silas did or didn't say.

It's a miracle he's staying quiet. He feels like granite in my arms, a statue ready to come to life and throw Serena out the nearest window if she makes one more wrong move.

"Now, you've all seen the op eds in the papers. The ones that wonder if this wedding is illegal or not, according to the kingdom's laws and traditions. I've talked to several lawyers, and I'm certain it is, but I won't bother going into that because there's still a shred of doubt." She pauses, reaches for my glass, and takes a long, agonizing pull.

Yeah, the bitch is drinking my tea like a hummingbird. I'm about to ask Silas to restrain me for my own good.

"We have our own lawyers, the very best in the nation. Whoever you've spoken to, they can't possibly be better," the Queen snaps. "If you have nothing more important than this nonsense, I'll ask you to find your way out, this instant."

"Oh, Your Majesty, I wouldn't be here if that were the case." She sets the teacup down loudly. "I've been talking to some doctors in Mexico about Miss Warwick's father."

My face goes dark. I'm afraid to check my own pulse and discover proof my blood just froze.

"As we know, he's very been very sick, but he's on the mend. What's very interesting is the funding." She turns away from the Queen, staring up at us, tucking her blonde hair back in that almost flirty and completely antagonizing way. "You see, Silas, I know you didn't pull the money out of that little trust stipend you like to use on liquor, parties, and gifts for you women."

"I don't have a fucking clue what you're talking about, woman, but you're going to be sued for every word you say. I'm keeping track, starting now."

"Sued? Ha!" Her shitty grin only gets bigger. "The only one who's going to be suing anybody will be Suzie Q. Public. Probably led by the Republic Firsters. For all their flaws, they've got some powerful legal contacts. Seriously,

Your Highness, what were you thinking? Using a public account on this medical bribe for your whore of a wife?"

She shakes her head slowly, mockingly sad. I want to slap her stupid face until it's spinning like a merry-go-round.

"Did you really think you could just snap your fingers and Victor could pull money from wherever, without getting caught? In this case, the royal wildlife fund, which receives several million a year from public tax dollars for wilderness and recreation? It almost worked, I suppose. You probably wouldn't have gotten caught if I hadn't been motivated to follow every single transactions. Thing is, my Prince, I did. And the scandal will *kill* Her Majesty when I feed it to the press."

Silas spins around, turning me with him. He's eyeballing Victor now.

"Your Highness...I...there wasn't enough in your private account at the time to cover a private, unscheduled trip to Mexico and the extensive treatment Mister Warwick received. Your trust fund wouldn't have disbursed additional money quickly enough when time was of the essence to save his life. For the record, the nature fund in question only receives partial public reimbursement each year. Most of its money comes from admission fees to the parks, and I was certain it wouldn't be a problem. This is, of course, entirely my fault, and I'm deeply sorry."

Silas isn't listening anymore. Serena stands up, drifts past us again, looking over her shoulder as she heads for the guards.

I can't bear to look at the Queen. She's probably as speechless as I am. I'm fucking devastated, hurt and confused, hanging onto him like a helpless monkey.

"This all could've gone down so differently, once. I really did love working for the palace, just like I used to love you, my Prince. Who knows where life will lead us once you're a pretender to a throne that doesn't exist anymore, but it's a shame we'll never cross paths again. We could've been something beautiful."

"Don't let this fucking bitch leave," Silas growls to the guards.

I hear several other chairs scrape across the floor. The Queen, Patricia, and Victor are all talking at once. Serena starts screaming the second one of the men in the suits grabs her arm.

The whole world spins, catapulting my field of vision around and around until I'm going to be sick.

I can't do this. I have to get out of here. I need to move my feet out the door beyond all the commotion, before I pass out.

It's a miracle. I do better than just power walk because something makes me *run,* without tripping on my heels or my skirt.

Silas yells after me once. But the guards are too busy with the anarchy all around them to think about catching me, and he never gives the order to chase me down.

I burst through the doors and run across the hallway. The teahouse is attached to an old hotel, where I crash down on the seats in front of a TV, burying my face to hide my tears.

Serena has the perfect bait to destroy everything that matters to him.

And it's all my fault.

For the first time in weeks, I want to be home. Back in North America, wherever dad is, consoling myself on being a good daughter because I don't know if I can be a good wife.

I can't be a good Princess.

God. There's something on TV. I see it through my blurry eyes, a scary scene outside the palace. It's the protests. They're still happening, live.

Two men tangled together in a crowd, fighting. One wears a black shirt with a big, red X through a gold crown held by the double-headed eagle.

Another man has a purple lapel pin for the Queen, but it's hard to make out. His shirt looks bloody – probably from the broken nose the protester gives him before the police throw him to the ground, jabbing a taser into his side.

This kingdom is a mess. And it's only going to get *worse* when Serena drops the bomb, assuming she makes it out of here without being able to sue royal security for assault.

Everything suddenly feels radioactive. It's killing me, shattering my heart in a way I've never known.

I don't want to leave him. Really, I fucking don't, more than I've ever wanted to avoid a thing in my entire life.

Doesn't matter. I can't ignore the sick truth gnawing at me deep in my soul.

This kingdom, this family, is going to tear itself apart if I stay a day longer. I won't watch that happen, even if it causes my heart to shrivel up and die.

I can't be his Princess – with benefits, or without. I can't be anywhere on this island anymore.

XIV: Melting Point (Silas)

She's gone, gone, gone like a fucking ghost, and it's all my fault.

Nobody knows where she rushed off to. I couldn't go after her when that bitch, Serena, was still standing there throwing barbs, threatening to ignite a new stroke in grandmom's poor brain with every evil word.

Her Majesty let her say her piece – her load of total bullshit. Then security escorted her out.

All while I stood there like a chump. Frozen.

Paralyzed like I haven't been since facing the damned war, except even mortar blasts never turned me to stone.

I'm back at the palace in my private office, staring at the bottle of scotch laid out on my desk, next to the crystal glass. My fingers shake so much each time I take a good, long look, imagining how good it'll feel to have the familiar heat in my guts. I grab myself by the wrist, clenching my teeth, snarling like a wild beast.

"No. No, goddamn it. You're going to find her, and you're not falling back on bad habits. She can't be gone."

But she is.

It doesn't matter if security tells me exactly where she's gone over the next few hours. I can feel it in the pit of my stomach, my woman pushed over the edge by forces she can't control. Leaving me here to my tower, just like some dark Prince in a fucking fairy tale.

Those stories have happy endings, at least. Once she's outside the island's airspace, my power is limited. I'll never be able to bring her home without causing an international incident. I can't anyway, after Serena turned our whole royal world upside down.

Drinking won't fix this.

Hell, not even grabbing that traitorous bitch by the throat and squeezing the life out of her will solve anything at this point.

Nothing besides feeling Erin's perfect, pink lips under mine is going to make it all right again.

The drug I need isn't here on this desk, taunting me in the face because it used to solve my problems, and doesn't do shit anymore.

Growling, my arm swings through the air, pushing the scotch and glass onto the floor, along with an antique clock and several paper weights.

My raging heart won't stop pounding. I have to make sure I'm not hallucinating when I hear the faint rap at the door.

"It's open," I say, sitting back in my seat, adjusting my tie.

Vic slinks in like a scorned cat, pausing when he sees the mess. "Your Highness – is everything all right?"

"You know the answer," I growl. "Send in whoever to clean this up when you're finished. I'm done having my temper tantrum, I'm sure."

I motion to the seat across from me. Victor takes it, stepping carefully over the shattered glass.

My arms press against the desk, and I stare at him, the words I want to say burning my tongue. "You know where she is, don't you? Tell me."

"She took off in a private jet this evening, sire. Chartered, rather than royal. The plane was heading for Mexico, I'm told, surely so she can join her father at his treatment center. No one thought to freeze her access to the accounts, seeing as we were otherwise preoccupied…"

"Yeah, with making sure Her Majesty didn't die on the fucking spot after everything that bitch said."

"Indeed." Vic nods, eerily calm, and pulls an envelope from his pocket.

My eyes shift down, watching as he slides it over to me. My fists and jaw clench simultaneously before I pick it up, rip it open, and pull out the lengthy typed letter. It only takes me thirty seconds to scan it before I've got the gist – and I don't like it.

"You're not quitting on me," I tell him, slamming it back down on the ivory surface.

"Your Highness, we both know that's the most reasonable course of action. Perhaps my departure will make things easier for the crown, legally speaking, in the matter Miss Hastings plans to bring forward. My mistake provided her with ample fire to burn the palace to the ground. I can't live with that. I've failed you, my Prince, and I fear I'll never recover from these grotesque missteps."

I almost snort. The only thing that looks grotesque right now is how pale and dead his face is. It takes balls to hand in your notice at a job that's your whole reason for living.

"Sire, if you'll permit, I'll do my very best to find someone worthy of this position so this never, ever happens —"

"Enough." Pulling the paper off the desk, I tear it neatly in half, crumple both halves, and throw them in the basket at my feet. "You're not going anywhere, Vic. It was an honest mistake. One I forced on you by setting up this arranged marriage. When I told you to help her old man, it wasn't real between us. Not at first. Believe me, man, it's worth more than my own damned crown now."

He looks at me and nods, a faint smile lining his lips. "As you wish, Your Highness. I'll serve you faithfully."

"Yeah? Then start by finding Serena and bringing her ass back here for a talk."

My valet blinks, surprised, shaking his head.

"You heard me. I want to set this crap right once and for all. Nothing illegal – we've already done plenty of that." My fists clench, wishing I hadn't passed on the scotch. "I need to talk to her. Alone. I'm going to find out how much it costs to make a deal with the devil."

After a moment, Victor nods. "I'll keep it as quiet as I can, sire. A security detail will be going out shortly to find Miss Hastings and bring her here."

"Good. I'll meet you both downstairs. Tell me as soon as she's arrived," I say, watching as he stands up to leave.

"And Victor…I want you to speak more freely now, man to man, instead of reminding me I'm your master all the time. We've known each other too many years, worked under the same roof. It's high time you started calling me Silas."

"Of course, if that's your wish…Silas."

I wait until the door closes before I smile. He could barely choke out my name.

Some things in this world just aren't going to change.

Doesn't matter. I won't let Erin go without bringing the greatest fight of my life.

I didn't give up booze and pussy to quit my whole reason for getting off them, and starting to live for the first time in my life. I *need* my woman, my love, my princess. God willing, I'm bringing her home, whatever it takes.

* * * *

Several hours later, I'm pacing slowly on the patio overlooking the royal gardens, one more place where this unlikely poached my heart like a lion ripping into an antelope.

I don't look behind me until I hear the door open. Then I whip around and see Vic with several guards, standing in front of the bitch herself.

"Give us some privacy, boys," I say, motioning Vic to the corner, to stay outside. "Serena, take a seat."

She looks at me haughtily, colder than the icy late summer night. I don't see that man-eating smile on her face until she sits down, relishing in the power she thinks she's got.

"Well, I didn't think my message had actually sunk in. Have you finally come to your senses, Silas – or will we be seeing each other in front of a royal judge next time?"

"You've schemed this entire thing, and it's all bullshit," I say, glaring. "I'm not here to play games. I want your terms, short and sweet, so I can forget about this and work on bringing my girl home."

Her face sours. Unmistakable jealousy.

Christ.

She *still* wants me at some level. My guts twist in disgust.

Sure, I've woken up with that *what the hell were you thinking?* feeling more mornings than I care to count. When I remember fucking the woman sitting across from me with her evil grin and pointy witch heels, it's visceral.

"You're going after her? After she's ruined you, and the drama she's brought threatens a fifteen hundred year old dynasty?"

"Yeah. Already told you, Serena, I'm bringing her home. That's what you don't get. She's *mine.* All your threats, your nastiness, every damned legal decree on the planet – none of it's going to stop me from going after her. They're nothing in the face of love."

"Love?" She whips her head around and spits it out like a curse. "*You?* Prince Playboy in love? You've lost your mind, Silas. I'm not stupid. I can't believe this, and I don't have to trust a word of it. You're not playing me a second time. Look, I *know* you took this girl on improve your image after what the Queen suggested. We talked about it together. We put the same idea in your head. If only I'd known it would've taken on this absurd life of its own!"

"Nobody's getting played tonight except me because I'm offering you a deal," I say, stepping toward her. "Sometimes, you get blindsided when you least expect it. I brought Erin in for reputation management, business, it's true...and that all ended awhile ago. We found love. What we've got, after spending so much time together, it's real."

Real. The demon in front of me pinches her eyes shut like I've just driven a dagger in her chest.

"Do you really want to know what I want, Silas? Or did you just bring me here for torture?"

"Told you, I want a deal. Whatever the fuck it takes to make you drop this lawsuit and never hear from you again. Name a price," I growl, hoping like hell she finally will.

"Forget that stupid American bitch! How about that? You obviously don't care who you get to play Princess. Do it with me, instead. Make me your bride. I'll play along with anything you want – the drinking, the parties, the women – anything and everything. Just as long as you take me and forget all about her!"

Fuck. I'm taken aback. The crazy in this woman's eyes shines brighter than the moon.

"I can't believe this." I shake my head. It was a big fucking mistake bringing her here, thinking I could reason with her.

"No!" Serena comes closer. "It's not too late, Silas. You can get yourself out of this, do something for both of us. You can –"

"I'm not marrying you, bitch. Unless you want to name

a price in dollars, Euros, or fucking rubles, the deal's off. We're through tonight, and forever."

Her face goes bright red. It looks like there's shame heating her blood, but I don't think this woman is self-aware enough to feel embarrassment.

"You're making a *huge* mistake, Prince. I won't let you live this down. You want to marry her? Fine! You can do it with *nothing* left to your name except millions in debt, and your crown in the gutter. That's where you really belong." Raw anger hisses out her lips. "I truly thought you were better than this. Silas, you're a stupid man. A monster."

"And you're a fucking lunatic, Serena. I've got everything on the line, and I'm going to fight. You want to talk stupid? That's trying to blackmail a Bearington by thinking I'd ever let you get anywhere near the throne."

I barely hear her scream before she rushes me. Then there's a whirlwind of little fists beating against my chest. Her heels kick me in the shins while I try to grab her.

She's hitting me with her purse, reaching into it. She's so skinny and quick it's hard to get a hold. I don't want to hurt her, much as my baser instincts would like to.

I grab her, fold one arm around the stomach when she's turned away from me, just as she screams, reaching into her purse.

Something sharp scrapes my arm when she flails again. I don't have to time to see what, because Victor is on us, ahead of several guards.

"Miss Hastings! Let go! For God's sake, you can't assault the Crown Prince of Saint Moore! You must –"

He makes a sad, strained sound. I've finally got a lock on the bitch, knocking that little metal thing in her hands to the ground. It's hard to see in the darkness, but it looks like a brass keychain made to wrap around the knuckles for self-defense.

I notice the red spot spreading in Victor's abdomen about a second before he tumbles to the ground.

"Shit, Vic!" The guards catch up to us then, thank fuck. "Get this bitch out of here!"

She's still snarling like a wild animal, throwing every obscenity in the book at me, while they drag her out. I hit the ground, pressing my hand over the valet's wound.

Damn it, there's blood.

A lot of blood. I'm roaring like a lion for a doctor, vowing the bitch is going to pay big for what she's done.

"Your Highness...Silas...don't let me fail you again. I can't —"

"You haven't failed me in anything, friend. You just took a psycho's blade that was meant for me. That's doing more for me than any of these slow goddamned guards."

He isn't speaking anymore. Blood keeps leaking all over my hands, and suddenly I'm back in Afghanistan, covering my Lieutenant's gash from a mortar round.

Everything goes numb in my head, like I'm detached, watching somebody else. There's nothing except my hands trying to stop precious life from leaking out of his veins, shaking him every few seconds, trying to keep this man awake and alive.

Medics show, seemingly out of nowhere. I step aside, my

hands covered in gore. I won't go back into the palace until they've got him out, on his way to an ambulance.

If Vic dies, I swear to holy hell I'm going to tear that cunt's head off myself.

They're hoisting him up on a stretcher, rolling him back through the greenhouse, when I see someone who should *not* be here.

No, *two* very out of place someones. Serena stands there in plastic handcuffs, held by two guards, glaring hatefully at me. Like I didn't just stop her from tearing my servant's throat out.

The other person is Her Majesty. Grandmom looks like she's just woken up, standing in a regal white flowing gown, without a single piece of jewelry on her royal skin.

"What's the meaning of this, Silas?"

My fucking heart sinks. This night couldn't get any worse. Oh, except for having to admit that I'd tried to strike a deal with Serena Hastings behind her back.

"I tried to talk to Serena," I tell her, not knowing where the hell I should begin. "Things went bloody crazy. She attacked me, and stabbed Victor."

"You're telling her I struck first, you bastard, after everything you said?!" Serena screams against the wall, beyond deranged. "It was self-defense! I'd do it all over again! I swear, I'll –"

"Get her the fuck out here!" I roar to the guards, wishing it were just as easy to dismiss this whole evil situation.

"Belay that order," Her Majesty snaps. "She isn't going anywhere until you tell me exactly what's going on in my palace, Silas."

I'm screwed. If I hide the truth, it's only going to piss her off more, and that might tip her health into the red zone.

The truth, that's all I have, the only thing that hasn't been shot to shit by the last twenty-four hours.

Okay.

"We know what happened at tea, grandmom. Erin's gone. Dealing with this bitch ripped her heart out, sent her running to Mexico, to be with her father. Can't blame her, honestly. I pushed this on her. In the beginning, this whole wedding was going to be a fraud." I pause, watching as my grandmother's matching blue eyes go huge. "It isn't that way anymore, Your Majesty. I swear on every single thing I've got. We were just playing pretend, Erin and me, a selfish plan I hatched to save my image. I took your advice, and I wanted to take the pressure off you so the kingdom would think I'd be fit for the crown someday."

I take another breath. Every drop of blood running through my veins feels like it's on fire. I wonder if anyone's ever spontaneously self-combusted from a confession before.

"Go on." That's all she says, tapping her exuberant cane against the stone floor.

Fuck, why isn't she saying anything? I clear my throat and do as she asks.

"I know it was wrong. Just like the way I tried to bring Serena here. I tried to negotiate some way to pay her off tonight so she'd leave us all alone." I close the distance between grandmom and me, never breaking eye contact.

"They say love causes people to act like idiots. I didn't understand that until just recently. After our pretend engagement became real, little by little. I'm going after her, Your Majesty. Nothing means more to me now."

Boom. Right between the eyes. I'm amazed my grandmother remains silent.

"Do whatever you need to. No hard feelings. I'll resign my crown, my title, give up every damned Euro and dollar in my accounts. You can make my cousin in Sealesland heir to the throne, and I'll never step foot on this island again. I'm sorry as hell to leave Serena and her crap on your plate, grandmom, but I'm not sure what she can do after cutting into Vic like that. I'm sorry, but I can't wait any longer. I have to go soon."

"Silas...shut up." She blinks, letting out a sigh that sounds like she's been holding it in for a fifty years. "There's an awful lot I'll never understand about you. If the last twenty-five years have taught me anything, it's that. But I do understand a man and woman in love, as well as an intruder in the way. There's nothing more to explain, son. You're free."

Her old, bony hand lands gently on my shoulder. *Free?*

"Find her. Bring her back. She'll make a beautiful Princess for this kingdom, and you're going to make a better King than I'd believed, one day." Her head turns, focusing her gaze on Serena, up against the wall. "I'll deal with this despicable traitor myself. You, boy, follow your heart."

I'm smiling. Leave it to the royal wannabe bitch in the corner to kill the mood.

"That's it? Are you fucking kidding me? You're mad! All of you! The Republic First idiots are right. This crown deserves to fall, for the good of the country. I'm going to do everything I can to make sure that happens – just watch!"

Nobody moves except grandmom. I watch her, heading for Serena and the guards at a slow hobble. I barely hear what she whispers to Dean and the other boys until I step up.

"Turn her around, please," Her Majesty says.

Serena won't stop seething. She's disrespecting everything she ever swore to serve. Fucking hypocrite.

I'm standing by, hoping grandmom knows what she's doing, dangerously close to this psychopath. Serena opens her mouth to bitch again, but nothing ever comes out.

Her Majesty's soft, wrinkled hand slaps our ex-press secretary across the face. It echoes through the greenhouse like a gunshot.

Everybody stops, stares in shock. I hope those guards remembered to keep their grip on the asshole.

"I've had enough of your mouth!" Grandmom says, turning to Dean. "Take her to the auxiliary holding area. We'll deal with the police report there. I'm going to come clean to the ministers about everything that's happened here tonight, but I'd like to make certain Miss Hastings doesn't set one foot onto the streets until she has a qualified doctor and a parole officer assigned."

"Auxiliary holding area?" Dean looks at the other guard, smiling. "Right away, Your Majesty!"

That's the formal name for the five hundred year old dungeon underneath the palace. An off-the-books prison that isn't supposed to be used except for overflow in times of war or national crisis.

Serena doesn't even spill any more venom as they're hauling her out. I think we're all too stunned to do anything. Grandmom slowly turns to me, leaning on her cane, like slapping Serena has sapped her energy.

"Why are you still standing there, Silas? Don't you know where your lady has gone?"

"I have a good idea," I say, walking up to her while Patricia comes out the door and grabs my grandmom by the arm, helping steady her.

"Take the first royal jet you see to Mexico, then. I'll handle the rest of this nasty, nasty business."

I nod, more than ready to head for the airport. But I stop first, and throw my arms around the old woman.

We've always been distant. That's the way it is between a royal living legend, and a man who hasn't been fit to fill her throne until just recently.

But tonight, we're family. One and the same.

We're Bearingtons. Always just, savage when we need to be, and determined as the mythic eagle stamped on my chest until the day I die.

* * * *

One Week Later

It's a resort. I'm on the highest level, overlooking the cancer treatment center, an unassuming facility at the edge of this luxury circus.

It's taken me several days since landing to find out where she is. Special intelligence had to track her down at my request because she'd chosen a small hostel outside the resort zone.

Smart, if she wants to disappear completely. It costs me and my men some effort.

I could've confronted her at the hospital, sure, but the visiting hours are always irregular. And the last first impression I want to make on her old man is seeing me begging her to come back.

That's right. Prince Silas Bearington III, ex-soldier, badass, biggest swinging dick in Europe, is ready to do whatever it takes to tear my heart out and hand it to the woman I love. Even if it means crawling to her on my hands and knees.

I can't lose this girl. I can't fuck this up.

I *can't* go home without her.

I won't walk away, even if I have to spend years in the Americas convincing her we're meant to be together.

My small, but devoted security detail would never let me slip into city without them. But I do it anyway, taking a taxi. I keep my t-shirt and my shades pulled tight, praying nobody will recognize a billionaire Prince among them.

Thankfully, there's not as much celeb gossip here as the States.

The taxi driver stops in front of a dirty, ancient looking building. He mutters a few words in Spanish, telling me the price and wishing me well.

I pop the door, stuffing the biggest tip he's ever gotten

into his hand on the way out. He calls after me, wondering if it's a mistake or I'm positively *loco*. I don't bother stopping.

It's early morning, just after five o'clock. Nothing's stopping me.

The place isn't as dirty inside, but it's not exactly up to Western standards either. Instead of rooms, people are gathered in huge wards by gender, with privacy curtains to pull shut at night.

The woman at the desk can't give me a precise spot where I'll find Erin. She turns her nose up, though, muttering about that wounded American girl, the one who's kept several other girls up at night with her crying.

I've come to the right place. I creep into the women's section, careful to only take the quickest peek behind the curtains. Stealth combat training comes in handy here. I'm still expecting one of them to see me for a second too long, and wake up the whole room screaming.

I see her as soon as I peel back the last little curtain in the corner. I'd know that body I've had wrapped around me anywhere.

Fuck, she's beautiful. She's sleeping, the faintest morning light seeping through the curtain, falling across her dark hair. I push past it and wait there until she stirs.

At first, she doesn't see me. When I move my hand up to rub my face, she jumps, jerking up flat against the headboard.

"Silas? You can't be here!"

"Believe it, Princess. I've come for what's mine." I step

up to the bed, pulling her into my arms.

She's too stunned to fight for the first few seconds. Then she starts twisting like mad, wriggling away, throwing me off.

"What the hell's wrong with you, love? Sorry about the surprise. Didn't have much choice."

Her tits look like ripe fruits swinging in that gown. My dick swells for the first time in what feels like forever, begging for the pussy it's craving something fierce.

"No. You're *not* supposed to be here. You can't be. I'm going home to LA with dad in just a few days. He's about to be discharged."

Folding my arms, I smile through the dim light. "He's cured? Great. I knew the magnificent bastards here would come through for him. Guess I'll be booking a flight to LA next, too."

Those lips I want to ravish all day drop. Her sweet head shakes, amusement and sadness written all over face in one warring symphony.

"No. No, Silas. This is crazy. I left Saint Moore behind, and I left you, too." She looks up, tears wavering in her big brown eyes. "I can't be responsible for tearing that place apart. It isn't my country. Whatever else we had, I corrupted you. I set you up for doing dumb things that let Serena weasel her way into threats. No more."

"You're wrong, love. Serena's been dealt with. The crazy bitch tried to stab me, missed, and hit Victor instead. She's done." While she's staring me all shocked, I throw my arm around her tighter, pulling her into my embrace. "He's okay. Recovering at the royal hospital. Lost a lot of blood."

"Jesus."

"Yeah. Grandmom's going to come clean about the money that was moved around. I'd bet everything that nobody in the parliament has the balls to say boo about it. Anybody running for election has done a hundred times worse, and the Queen's popularity has never been higher."

"What about yours? Does the kingdom know anything?"

I pause. "They know you haven't been seen for a few days. They know the former press secretary stormed out of tea with us. The tabloids are starting to bark, saying our wedding's off, that the whole thing was a fickle fucking sham from the start. Look at me, Erin."

I tilt her face up. She's crying now, biting her lip, shaking her head weakly. She's telling me *no, no, no*, fighting her basest instincts.

Ask me if I care. I'm going to remind her what we have, take her home with me, and show her why she's never running away again.

"I don't care how rough it gets. I'd dump my crown for you, love, without hesitation. What started on a lie, it's too damned real to give up. We both know it."

She's too hurt. Too conflicted. She still won't look at me.

I push my fingers gently into her jaw line, tip her face up, until she finally opens those beautiful eyes. Mine lock on like hawks, holding her gaze, showing her the want.

I'm not afraid to open up anymore. I'm showing her

what no woman's ever seen, the gnawing want for her, blazing down to my very soul.

"Erin…"

"Silas…I can't. It's wrong. We're not right for each other…I realize that now. We're too different. It's never going to change, not in a hundred million years. We don't belong together. I know it, and I think you do, too."

"Enough. You're wrong, love, and I'm going to prove it. Kiss me, then tell me what you just said isn't bullshit."

I don't give her time to turn away. My lips crush down on hers, hungrier than they've ever been, relishing the sugary sweetness of her lips like it's the last time.

Because if I can't convince her, it might be.

I might be going back to Saint Moore empty-fucking-handed.

No. No! I won't let that happen, no matter how much heaven and hell I have to pay.

Our tongues touch. I take hers, twine it around mine, feeling the same electric heat we had the very first time. We're reliving every kiss in this one.

Every fight. Every tease. Every night we ever fucked, plus the very moment when fucking blurred into making love.

I used to hate that phrase, 'making love.' It sounds like some stupid flowery shit prudes use to convince themselves they aren't after just as much nasty, glorious pleasure as the rest of us.

But with her, the woman I have on my lips, I felt it a few times. I want – no, need – to feel it again. Have it over and over and over for the rest of my life.

It hurts like hell to pull my lips away, but I have to. Need to hear her answer. She's lost in my eyes again, too screwed up to speak.

"One word, babe. That's all you've got to tell me right now. Say you're coming home. Say we still have a wedding to go to. You want to be mine, I can see it shining clear as day in your eyes. Erin, love, it doesn't have to be complicated. Just tell me we can get past this, all the evil, stupid things that happened. We can be husband and wife. Prince and Princess. Real, not fake, so fucking real it seems like everything else in this world's a hollowed out ghost. You're feeling it, love, yeah? Tell me you are."

It takes her a few seconds. Several terrible, heart wrenching seconds that almost turn my heart into a black mass of dripping tar.

Then she says it. "Yes! Okay, maybe we can make this work, you bastard. It hurts too much to lie. I love you."

"Prince Bastard has a damned good ring to it, love, as long as that's what you're calling me in bed."

"Better than Prince Hung," she whispers.

The next time we kiss, I feel her smiling underneath my lips. This love tastes better than ever before.

* * * *

A couple days later, we're planning to embark, returning to the kingdom, hand in hand. She's happy to be in my room and out of that cramped hostel. There's just one last unfinished item on the agenda waiting for us at the treatment center.

"Here we are again, Tom. You're holding all the cards for this interview, though, trust me," I say, sitting next to my princess, holding her hand.

"Yeah, and they're all Jokers. Wilds. I still can't believe my daughter is about to marry a Prince. Right out of a fairy tale."

Erin's father looks good for just surviving hell. He's lost some weight, looks like he could use some red meat to put color in his skin, but otherwise, he's doing better.

"Oh, daddy. It's surprisingly normal," she says, squeezing my hand. "No glass slippers or evil witches here."

I'm sure her dear old dad's read plenty in the tabloids and trash blogs. But he doesn't have a clue what we went through to get here, approaching our happily ever after, if only we can get his blessing.

"Your Highness, marriage aside, I owe you my life," Tom says, nodding respectfully. "If it hadn't been for you, for this place, I doubt I'd be fit to see my daughter again. Much less walk her down the aisle. They do that in Saint Moore, don't they?"

I smile, straightening up in my chair. "We have our own traditions, yes, but there's plenty of room to make accommodations for the bride's family."

"So, you're in, daddy?" she whispers excitedly, bouncing her knees a couple times.

We've spent the last two days fucking our brains out, catching up on what we've been missing. Damn if every gesture she makes, every movement rippling her curves, doesn't make my dick throb for more.

"LA can wait." Tom stands up, without so much as a

tremor, walking over to embrace her. "I'd be a fool if I weren't there to see you off. Also, to remind His Highness that he's going to have hell to pay if he ever hurts you, disappoints you, or screws you over. I don't care if I wind up in a dungeon for spilling blue blood."

He gives me a sharp look. One I respect. I nod, pulling Erin's hand fully into my lap, protective as ever.

"It's just Silas now, Tom. No more of that Highness crap. Save your threats for somebody who needs them," I say, bringing my woman's hand to my mouth. "I know my reputation. I've played around and shamed myself more times than anybody will ever know. All that's behind me now. The only woman I'll ever need is right here next to me. I'll make her happy if it kills me."

My lips brush the back of her hand. They're both smiling, staring at me, making the whole room light up with more than just the hot, airy Mexican sun seeping through the windows.

"I know you will, son. I've done my share of interviews before the Big C laid me low, and there's a good chance I'll do some more. I know what a changed man looks like. I'm staring at one now."

It's ridiculous, but Tom's words mean more than they should. He's right.

I've changed, and it's all for her. The old Prince Silas with his gold booze and endless pussy is never coming back. May he Rest In Peace.

The new Silas, the man I've become...well, his story's just getting started.

It's going to be fucking incredible.

XV: Royally Ever After (Erin)

Several Weeks Later

"You're beautiful, baby. I'll make sure you don't trip in that thing," dad says, holding my arm, waiting for the massive cathedral doors to open.

"You'd better! There are probably like a hundred million people watching. I don't want to give them something to laugh about my first official day as Princess."

"Forget it. We'll be fine."

My nerves make me wonder. He tightens his grip on my arm, making me smile. He's really regained his strength, plus several pounds this past month, returning to the vibrant man he used to be.

Everything else? Jesus, it's happening.

I'm really here. Standing at the door to a thousand year old cathedral with my literal Prince waiting at the altar. Wearing this long, flowing, angel white gown with twenty-four karat gold trim all over it.

Then there's the diamond tiara I'll get after my ring. The heavy, jewel studded thing that tells me there's no turning back the instant it goes on my head.

"Ten seconds, my Lady." Dean stands at the side, one hand near the piece attached to his ear.

Two burly guards on both sides of the doors finally make eye contact. They start to pull the massive doors open with a squeak that would make an ancient tomb jealous.

I've got this, I tell myself, remembering rehearsal. *Just listen for the cues.*

The first one, there's no missing. A dozen coronets blow the world apart, piercing the sky, proclaiming our love to the universe.

Dad starts moving before I do. I follow carefully, one foot in front of the other, down that long, rolling burgundy carpet that seems like it stretches a mile. There are too many people on both sides of the aisle to look at any of them too long.

Dukes, duchesses, priests, diplomats, and heroes. Famous celebrities, billionaires, scientists, politicians. All wearing suits and formal dresses that could easily give mine a run for the money.

The full orchestra fires up. Medieval stone walls and stained glass shake softly, sending the heavenly, unbelievable notes up to the domed ceiling and back down again. It's an echo unlike anything I've ever heard.

I'd stop and admire the breathtaking beauty. If only I weren't the star of the show, I could stop and enjoy it longer.

"Keep going, darling. We're almost there," dad whispers when we've closed half the distance.

I won't let my eyes fix on him until they're good and ready.

There he is, as if from a dream. Silas.

More dashing than ever, dressed in his royal finest, a navy blue dress uniform with a red sash and medals criss-crossing it like stars. He's waiting for me with a smug, smackable smile on his face.

His tongue comes out, almost imperceptibly, rolling across this lips for a fraction of a second. Yesterday, he teased me about tying me down and eating my pussy all night for our honeymoon. If he's doing it again, however silently, I *swear* I'm going to flip.

Dad's hand lets go a few seconds later. I have to walk the last few steps alone, up the tiny stairs, holding my breath as I take the steps.

Silas reaches out, grabs me, and pulls me up. "Christ, you're gorgeous. Almost too hot to take to bed, love. Almost."

Yeah fucking right, the wink he flashes says.

I won't even smile at his crap today, however much I want to. Cameras watch every move we make, perched from every corner. He's already violated several rules the new press secretary drilled into our heads during practice.

Keep it formal. Respectful. Subdued.

The last one, subdued, never made sense to me, anyway. There's nothing remotely subdued about this hundred million dollar display of royal luxury.

Queen Marina sits behind us on a temporary throne, ready to do her part. Silas takes my hand in his, and we turn to face the priest, just as the final choral voices behind the music die down.

"When two hearts become one, bound in royal blood, a kingdom rejoices," the priest begins. "A people lives by its sovereigns, and dies by their absence. Today, we are gathered here with full confidence that we will live. His Highness, in all his love and wisdom, restores his line and our nation by binding his heart to hers. Will you both hold your right hands and swear before God, before the Queen, before your very lives?"

We both lift our right hands. A choral note swells high. It's so drawn out my arm starts to hurt by the end, but I keep it up, my heart banging in my ears. I'll do anything for this handsome man next to me.

"Your oath is your word, true and immortal as steel and diamond. Your Highness, do you have the ring?"

"I do." He reaches next to him, swiping it from the lavish pillow Victor holds out. Silas' valet looks so much better than he did just weeks ago, when he had to use a cane while the stitches in his side healed.

"Will you claim this woman, today and forever, for your crown, your country, and your future children?"

"I will, and I do."

His words echo proudly through this insanely huge place. Then he's shoving the ring on my finger, instantly adding weight to my hand with its gold and oversized diamonds. Breaking tradition, he brings my hand to his lips, closing his eyes.

He kisses it while the priest frowns, trying to pretend

this isn't happening. I can't help it, I let myself smile now.

What would this wedding be if there weren't a few things uniquely Silas mixed in? It's ours, after all, not just the country's.

"Erin Warwick, will you wear this ring into the next life, for your Prince, your nation, and all the children that will come from this day?"

Silas squeezes my hand and flashes me an excited look. *Great,* like he really needs to think about baby making even more.

"I will, and I do," I say solemnly, trying hard to keep this as formal as they'd like.

"Then you're now man and wife, and Her Majesty will finish the rest."

Two aides have to help her up. Queen Marina crosses to the altar, and we bow. I mean *completely,* down on our knees, so low I can't even see when she grabs the diamond tiara off its resting place.

"By my title, my will, and my wisdom, I crown thee Princess Erin June Bearington," she says, bringing it down on my head, her old hands shaking very slightly. "And speaking informally, as one woman to another, you're as perfect for this country as you are for its future King."

Everything stops. Silas and I both look at each other, doing a double take, before we stare at the Queen.

She's just gone off script, wearing the most mischievous smirk I've ever seen on her royal lips.

"People of Saint Moore, this day is all about Silas and Erin joining in marriage, and I won't steal their light. I've chosen to do something that will make everyone remember and cherish their love forever."

About a thousand gasps and hushed, excited murmurs rumble through the crowd. Silas reaches for my hand, gripping it, pulling me up as he stands.

"Grandmom?" he says softly. No one has a clue what's happening.

Queen Marina leans into the mic, lifting both hands above her head to the crown. "I've served you all faithfully with my very best for sixty three years. Regrettably, my health is failing, loyal subjects. I won't give you anything less than my finest. My ministers will be briefed, and the paperwork has already been drawn up by the palace. By midnight tonight, I will formally abdicate the throne. It's only fair that my grandson should stand next to his beautiful bride, wearing the highest crown, a new royal couple for our kingdom in an evolving age."

The choir starts to sing over the murmur in the crowd. They've probably decided it's the ceremony's end, like it's supposed to be. Truthfully, nobody really knows what to do after the shock and awe Her Majesty just dropped. Her ex-Majesty?

I'm clenching Silas' hand while Queen Marina lifts the heavy crown from her head, shifting it toward Silas, who bows his head low.

It's on his head. King, in all but name only.

I'm going to have a heart attack. I don't know what to say, so I just stand there, while Silas shares one more look with his smiling grandmother.

Then he turns to me, his eyes narrowed, that huge golden crown sitting just slightly crooked on his head. "Love, let's not forget the most important part."

I don't remember what he means until he jerks me into his embrace. Fortunately, my lips do it for me.

We kiss, with more fiery passion than there's been at this altar in hundreds of years.

He kisses me long, hard, and hot. He kisses me while the crowd goes insane and cameras tip over in the commotion, with guards rushing around, settling down the madness breaking out all around us.

The orchestra and choir both keep going because they don't know what to do. It's a beautiful, chaotic confusion that's strangely fitting.

For us, it's easy.

We're finally official, and Silas isn't going to take his lips away until heaven itself knows it.

* * * *

Several Hours Later

The official crowning ceremony can wait, or so we've been told. Silas insisted on it with the royal cabinet, and they gave him their blessing.

He's chosen a secluded spot for our honeymoon, thank God, a different corner of the northern shore, next to the most amazing mountains I've ever seen and an extinct volcano. The royal helicopter has nobody in it except us, and our pilot, who's going to drop us at the cottage and go.

We'll be left alone to the wilderness and our own hearts for the next two weeks. Plenty of time for the media to remember how to breathe. More than enough for Queen Marina to tie up loose ends, and close out everything before Silas has the reigns.

The scandal with Serena never even got off the ground. The Republic Firsters are probably seething because nobody cared when they jumped on it, stealing the headlines for roughly two seconds, before wedding madness swept everything else like a tidal wave.

There's certainly something crazy sweeping through me right now, every time his thick, strong hand brushes my wrist.

He's going to kill me with desire before we land. Silas and I share looks that say a thousand words, numbing any need to shout at each other over the helicopter's blades.

I'm going to fuck your brains out, his eyes say.

Not if I melt yours first. That's what mine say right back, while I'm biting my lip, grateful that I'm down to just one layer of casual white royal fabric.

It's so intense I can barely stop to appreciate the gorgeous scenery, swelling up all around us.

"Three minutes, sire! I'll take us down," the pilot says over the radio.

A lot can happen in three minutes. Like smoke rising between my legs, the fire only he can see, tempting him to go as deep as he needs to put it out the minute we're by ourselves.

You're a knockout, he mouths. *Beautiful as sin.*

I'm a Princess now. Isn't looking pretty part of the job?

He grins. Devouring my sarcasm in that cocky, sexy, possessive smile.

He's going to eat me alive tonight. I'm going to adore every single second.

Silas reaches over, grabbing my hand as the chopper bounces to a stop. The pilot switches off the blades. We're unloaded in no time.

It's awesomely silent out here. There's a glacial lake at the foot of the mountains. Nothing but a few distant bird calls to remind us we're on planet Earth.

Turning around, I see him helping the pilot. He looks so ordinary, lugging our stuff in, everything the royal service hasn't prepared for us several days before. Silas jokes with the pilot like they're old friends.

Smiling, I know I didn't marry him because he's a Prince. I hitched my life to the man behind the title, gold, and diamonds, the one who's struggled to get a grasp on his kingdom simply because of who he is.

Yes, he's had his demons. I've watched him slay them, one by one, until he can see me with those clear blue eyes I love. Every glance, I'm swept away.

Silas waves to the pilot, and guides me to the cottage's porch. We both watch as the helicopter lifts off, disappearing into the sky, leaving us to ourselves.

He embraces me from behind, pressing his hard-on into my ass. "Finally. Love, you don't even know how hard it's been keeping it in my pants after seeing how you looked at me at the altar…"

"Yeah?" I twist in his arms, turning around, rolling my hands up his shoulders. "I think I might have some idea. There's something sexy about a man in uniform, and yours was the best I've ever seen."

"Too bad I didn't pack it," he says with a smirk. "Only brought a few changes of clothes. We're not going to need them with all the time we'll be spending naked."

"Aw, really? I thought we were just here for the scenery," I tease.

Growling, Silas runs his hands down my back. He stops at my ass, clasps my cheeks, and squeezes them hard.

"Fuck the gorgeous views, Princess. There's nobody around here for a few hundred kilometers. We can scale the volcano wearing nothing, if you'd like, as soon as I'm done fucking you raw."

Yes. Please. My eyes say it all.

He grabs my wrist and leads me inside, kicking the door shut behind us. Inside, it's rustic, cozy as a lodge, just I imagine. We wind our way through the old rooms to the master suite overlooking the lake. It's on the second floor, really just a giant loft with a bed, a few cabinets, a hot tub, and a lovely looking bathroom attached.

I stop when I see the bed. It's even bigger than the ones in the palace, with tall black pillars reaching up to the ceiling, lion heads carved in every post.

"Hmm. I see we'll have an audience," I say, sticking my tongue out.

"I wasn't joking about the restraints, beautiful. You're going to need them to hold your legs open after you've come on my tongue ten times."

"Silas...don't tease." I can't tell when he's joking.

He sounds so deadly, excited, and serious. I'm going to find out *how* serious when he grabs me, pushes me onto the bed, and starts tearing away what's left of my wedding dress.

Our lips collide the whole time. I can't keep my mouth off his. I'm moaning, panting, begging for his touch.

He's swallowing everything I give him. All my breath, my love, my fire, pressing the massive erection in his trousers against my bare pussy. The teasing doesn't end when he pushes me to the center of the bed, dips over the bed, and reaches into one of the heavy oak drawers under it.

"Legs out. Before that pussy soaks the sheets straight through." I surrender.

He takes my feet, one ankle at a time, and puts them in the leather loops. Each one goes to a pillar, stretching me wide open for his hands, his mouth, whatever he desires.

I'm losing it when he looks at me again. Silas presses his hand firmly against my pussy, but he doesn't slide his fingers in. He just teases my clit in slow, evil strokes while his lips press mine.

"Please – please!" I'm in heat, pleading, by the time he starts his trek down my body.

My back arches each time his mouth pulls at my nipples. He sucks them rough, plumping my breasts, grinding his thumb a little harder against my clit.

"No, Princess. Not yet. Got to make me believe you need it," he growls, kissing down my belly, then across my right thigh. "Make me believe you *need* this mouth. Then I'll make you squirt so hard you're seeing stars."

Oh, hell. Doesn't he know he's close to doing that without even putting his mouth between my legs?

I'm twitching. Moaning. Shifting my hips side to side, aching for his touch, just a few lashes of his tongue to give me sweet release.

His licks and kisses wrap around my thigh, circling ever closer.

Closer, closer. God, please, closer!

Every muscle I have quakes as he slowly, tauntingly moves to my wet center, replacing his hand across my mound with hot, feral breath.

"Did you think this Princess thing was easy?" he whispers, mischief whirling in his eyes. "Bet you didn't know it means giving this sweet cunt up to me anytime I want it, Erin. Any place. Any fucking way. You're about to forget that 'no sex' rule ever existed."

Forget the rule? I barely remember my own name.

I'm about to explode. He pushes his face in just then, opening me with his tongue. Licking wild, sucking furious, taking my clit like he owns it, because he does.

Pleasure's coming, stealing me away.

Going. Going.

Gone.

My body tenses up and my legs shudder. The straps holding them open do their job, their tension adding an extra thrill to the orgasmic wave ripping through me.

My spine turns to flame. My hips pump, riding his face,

over and over and over. I can't press the back of my head into the mattress anymore.

There's nowhere to run. Nowhere to hide. Nothing to do except scream, and let it wash over me.

This is a tongue fuck truly fit for a royal. Sheer, mind bending ecstasy in full control for the next five minutes.

His hands and mouth won't stop. Just when I'm coming down, they stoke my flames again, pushing me back to the edge.

He's licking me even faster this time. Even harder. My clit disappears into his mouth, throbbing against his tongue, and crackles like lightning again.

I'm coming so hard my vision goes red, then white. I see dark, fiery spaces in between.

Stars. Just like he promised.

Is nothing impossible for this man? The answer's probably *no,* because about ten seconds later, I feel a dam break somewhere mid-orgasm.

I'm coming again.

Coming!

Except, this time, there's a distinct heat. A wetness that soaks my entire pussy and leaks out of me onto the sheets, his face, everywhere I can feel it through the numbing ecstasy that's ignited my blood.

The bastard has me gushing. Another promise fulfilled, one that says my body will do anything for this man on command.

I don't realize I'm clutching the sheets, nearly ripping roles through them, until he moves away from my quivering legs.

Silas comes up wiping his face, his smile more sexy than ever. Of course, that also means more arrogant.

"Hope you liked your first wedding present, love," he says, slowly taking down the restraints. "We'll get back to these later. But I want your legs wrapped all the way around me when we fuck. I want you to pull my dick so deep I don't see a drop of come slipping out when it's over."

There's that heat again. Impossible, as it is incredible.

"You're the King," I tell him.

"Not officially," he says, slowly undoing his belt. "That won't happen until we're home, and I'm formally crowned. You'd better believe it doesn't matter in this bed. I'm fucking like a god, love. Like I own every single inch of you because we both know I do."

I'm about to mouth off, try to deny it, when he drops his pants. That huge, magnificent cock coming into view always silences me.

It's a thing of awe. And it's about to be mine, as soon as it's inside me, pumping its way to a few more earthshaking climaxes.

He's completely naked, on top of me, dragging my legs up over his shoulders. Our eyes lock fierce while my chest rises and falls.

I want him more right now than any woman should. I want my Playboy Prince, my bastard, my husband.

I want to fuck him today, and then every day for the rest of my life.

"Oh, God," I moan, just as he starts rubbing his swollen cock against my pussy. "Go, Silas. Please. Fuck me."

"What's that, love? Didn't hear the magic word."

He's going to make me say it. I try to hold out as long as I can, stroke by stroke. But when he starts to dip the very tip of his cock into me, pulling away before I get his fullness, I'm helpless.

I surrender, and then some.

"Please." My eyes pinch shut as he gives me another inch. "Yes, fuck, *please!*"

My legs shake harder on his shoulders. He grabs them, holds them still, and gives me another feral look.

"I'm in a giving mood today. Must be that hot, tight married pussy wrapped around my cock."

He thrusts deeper. Sweet heaven.

At least, Silas fucks me. It's a slow building storm, strengthening one stroke at a time, lifting me a little higher each time he pushes into me. His hips crash into mine each time he pulls back and glides forward.

"Harder," I grunt, teasing him.

"Harder?" He pauses, grabs my nipples, and pinches them tight. "Like this?"

He almost pulls all the way out. Then he slams himself into me so hard my breasts shake in his hands. I'm moaning again, enraptured.

His wife.

His Princess.

His whore.

He's taken what I said like a challenge, and I'm in trouble now. The most decadent, tantalizing kind of trouble a woman can get herself into.

His cock slams into me so fast and hard I can feel his balls slapping my ass. Silas' hold on my legs tightens, and he's growling, fucking me over the edge.

"That's right, love. You'd better come for me again. I'm not giving it up until you're begging me to stop."

Oh, shit. Hell!

I'm screaming. Clawing at his chest. My pussy pinches his cock so hard the stars return, beautiful as they are scary. Coming shouldn't feel this good.

My heart shouldn't throb this intensely for any man. But it does, and it will forever with my Prince.

Our fucking becomes hotter, so swift and fiery, it's blinding. I'm deep in my zone, locked when he reaches between my legs, thumbs my clit, and lets his hand go berserk while he power fucks me into the next century.

Coming! Yes, it's insane, but it's happening again.

Somehow, I hear him growling his words in between his thrusts, savage and forceful. He's whispering in my ear, driving deeper with every word, beating his balls against my ass.

"Knew I'd make you mine the second we made that deal, Princess. Fucking knew it. Good thing you love it."

I do. And he isn't done.

His hips piston faster. I've barely recovered from the last orgasm before he starts on a new one, jackhammering his cock into me. It's bigger, hotter, and faster than ever before. My pussy tingles for his come, totally engulfed in flames, praying for the only thing that can put them out.

"Silas!"

He grabs my chin and pushes his lips on mine, holding my face. Crazy doesn't even describe what I'm feeling anymore.

"You think it's hot now? Just wait, love. I'll be making you sing when we're so old and gray they're printing us on the kingdom's money. I'm going to keep fucking you. Going to keep owning every beautiful piece of who you are. Going to put a baby in your belly soon, Erin. Then another, and another, and another…"

Oh…fuck! I grab him so hard I probably scratch his shoulders.

Neither of us care. Thinking about him planting his seed deep drives me over the edge.

My hips go wild, joining his in the frenzy, bucking back at his length as hard as I'm grunting. His cock drives deep, just to the edge of my womb, and swells.

Coming! Coming! This time together, fused together, twitching as one.

"Fuck!" Silas cries out, losing himself in me.

His cock heaves everything from his balls deep inside me, flooding me with his heat, his essence. My eyes roll back in my head. It's so intense I can't even breathe, let alone scream.

Time flies like mad. Soon, I'll be off the birth control, letting him own me in the most primal way a man can for real.

For now, this is great practice.

"Christ, I needed that. Every second of you, love," he whispers, drowning me in tender kisses.

I'm still coming down from my climax. Very slowly, he softens, and then pulls out.

Laying on his chest, he holds me in his huge, tattooed arms. We're spent, at least for a few minutes, and it's marvelous.

"Did you really mean what you said about how you knew the first time?" I ask, letting my eyes feast on his perfect body. Every contour, every muscle, is smooth and strong as steel, like God himself reached down with a chisel and sculpted him for me.

"Don't think I'm allowed to wear the royal crest on my skin if I didn't believe in destiny." He smiles, resting his forehead on mine. "Fate. There's something to it, after all."

His smile is contagious. We kiss again, only breaking away when his hand gently cups my cheek.

"You're meant to be my Princess forever, babe. Mine, with more benefits than I dared imagine. Love you, Erin. Love you like nothing else in the world, like nothing any money or power will ever buy. Love you so fucking hard and real it's never changing. Never fading. Never going anywhere. Not in this lifetime, or the next."

"Silas…I love you, too." My heart flutters.

He's right about the benefits – more than he knows.

It's amazing where life takes a woman. I never thought I'd wind up married to a Prince, shaking off the best sex of my life, surrounded by a gorgeous kingdom I've just started to explore and understand.

Incredible as it is, it's nothing compared to how his words have changed, down to their very roots.

'Princess with benefits' used to make me want to slap the smugness off his face.

Now? It's the magic phrase that sends my lips to his like magnets.

We kiss. Long and sweet. Tender as our love itself.

This stopped being pretend a long time ago. It's real, and I'm proud to belong to my Prince with benefits forever..

Thanks!

Want more Nicole Snow? Sign up for my newsletter to hear about new releases, subscriber only goodies, and other fun stuff!

JOIN THE NICOLE SNOW NEWSLETTER! - http://eepurl.com/HwFW1

Thank you so much for buying this book. I hope my romances will brighten your mornings and darken your evenings with total pleasure. Sensuality makes everything more vivid, doesn't it?

If you liked this book, please consider leaving a review and checking out my other erotic romance tales.

Got a comment on my work? Email me at nicolesnowerotica@gmail.com. I love hearing from my fans!

Kisses,
Nicole Snow

More Intense Romance
by Nicole Snow

FIGHT FOR HER HEART

BIG BAD DARE: TATTOOS AND SUBMISSION

MERCILESS LOVE: A DARK ROMANCE

LOVE SCARS: BAD BOY'S BRIDE

RECKLESSLY HIS: A BAD BOY MAFIA ROMANCE

STEPBROTHER CHARMING: A BILLIONAIRE BAD
BOY ROMANCE

STEPBROTHER UNSEALED: A BAD BOY
MILITARY ROMANCE

Outlaw Love/Prairie Devils MC Books

OUTLAW KIND OF LOVE

NOMAD KIND OF LOVE

SAVAGE KIND OF LOVE

WICKED KIND OF LOVE

BITTER KIND OF LOVE

Grizzlies MC Books

OUTLAW'S KISS

OUTLAW'S OBSESSION

OUTLAW'S BRIDE

OUTLAW'S VOW

Deadly Pistols MC Books

NEVER LOVE AN OUTLAW

NEVER KISS AN OUTLAW

NEVER HAVE AN OUTLAW'S BABY

SEXY SAMPLES:
STEPBROTHER CHARMING

I: Hit the Floor (Claire)

Visiting Club Zing is supposed to be my last hurrah, a post-college escape before the long summer falls across Seattle, and ushers me into grown up land. It's supposed to be my last girl's night out before distance makes things a whole lot harder.

So, why the hell can't I keep my eyes off *him?*

"What's up, Claire? You're nursing that thing like you're about to go away to Saudi Arabia for a year!" My best friend Dana points to my Long Island iced tea and lifts her own. "Come on! Put it down and keep up with me, girl. This is *our* night!"

Sighing, I raise my glass and clink it against hers. "Cheers," we both echo.

Somehow, I'm not feeling it. I've never liked goodbyes. And I *really* don't like this other bastard stealing away the attention my bestie deserves, even if he's moving around the club like he owns the place, sculpted to leave more than a few pairs of panties scorched.

Who am I kidding? Is this seriously how it ends?

By now, I'd normally be holding back the tears and hugging Dana's shoulders while she takes her stompy boots out to the dance floor. I don't understand how she wears those things so gracefully – they look like something German soldiers used to march in – but they always make her the center of attention when she busts her moves.

I'm going to miss her stupid purple hair and how she can't let go of the goth look, even though she's pushing twenty-two, just like me. Hell, I'm going to miss this place. Mostly, I'm going to regret wasting this precious time with my eyes glued to the devil by the bar, the giant towering above everybody else.

It's so obvious I can't hide it anymore. Dana grins at me after a long, dizzying sip on her drink. She spins around and follows my eyes.

"Jesusss, Claire! Don't tell me you've never seen the owner before? Haven't you seen him?"

"Nope, never." I shake my head. "That's the boss man? He's so young…"

My friend waves a hand, flashing the bright purple nails that match her hair dye. "Pssh. You'd own this place if your daddy was a billionaire too. That's Tyler Sterner. Playboy for life and easy on the eyes when he's actually here doing his job."

My brow furrows. Seriously? This guy barely looks older than we are. It's even more amazing I haven't seen him around campus or here on our earlier outings. He's got the kinda body any woman with a beating heart would notice *anywhere*.

He's at the end of the bar, slapping some older, balding man on the back and laughing. Two plastic looking girls are at his side in short skirts, their ruby red lips and pearly white teeth grinning at him like statues.

Massive is a gross understatement. He puts everybody else in his shadow, even the other well-built guys next to him.

He looks like something from another age in the neat suit jacket wrapped around his broad shoulders. An aristocrat, maybe, remembering all the paintings I studied for my art history minor.

Except country gentlemen didn't get this built in the old days taking strolls through the hills and chasing after foxes. No way. Mister – what's his face? – Sterner looks like he's been pumping serious iron and eating big to get big in all the right ways.

The harpies next to him step aside for drinks, and I get a view of his tight packed torso. He's a Greek god from head to toe, a six foot something goliath with a beast of a jaw and blue eyes that look like they're there to put out the fires he's bound to spark in every girl who looks at him. The quirk in his lips and the messy wave in the dark hair on his head matches the self-assured way he's leaning back against the stool.

Something tells me looks are deceptive, as they usually are. This Tyler might look like Prince Charming, but I have a crazy feeling he's more like the ultimate rogue with the way these chicks are eyeing him.

"Hey!" Dana reaches up and snaps her fingers in my face. "Seattle to Claire Frost – come in!"

It's nothing new, she's done it a million times before when I space out. I always push her hand away and get annoyed. Tonight, I just smile, knowing how much I'm going to miss her crap.

"There are plenty more hotties here who'd actually give us the time of day, if that's how you want to roll this evening," she says with a grin. "Check out that one!"

I follow her finger to the dance floor. There's an edgy looking boy with a few too many piercings and a swirl of thick ink around his eye that makes him look like an Amazon warrior.

Ugh. Just her type – not mine.

I'm all for edge and ink, but I like to be able to feel a man's bare skin too beneath his decorations. I nod, take a long swig of my tea, feeling the delicious vodka and rum bathe my belly in fire.

"You go on. Looks like he's eager for a dance," I say, flipping my wavy hair back.

"Oh, no, you don't!" Dana wags a finger. "Come on! Shake your pretty ass. It'll be fun now that you've got the good stuff in your system!"

"Dana, Dana, Dana!" I keep calling her name as she jerks me out of my seat and pulls me toward the dance floor, but nothing's going to stop her tonight.

It's our last good night at our favorite club. I'm heading north tomorrow to take a few weeks off at my mom's house before the big internship begins. I landed a paid gig with Cascades Now!, an environmental lobby with an amazing reputation for landing awesome consulting work. It's half of the equation I need to jumpstart my career – the other fifty-percent is coming from my mom, former three-term

Congresswoman, Amanda Frost.

As for Dana, she's off to Portland for her MBA. Really, I think she just wants to embrace the city's weirdness. There's no doubt whatsoever she'll fit in great with Portland's eccentric scene and endless supply of food trucks.

I'm trying not to think about the future. It's uncertain and exciting and so damned unnerving sometimes I feel my stomach churn. Thankfully, the alcohol hits right as we step onto the floor, numbing everything in its sweet fire. Everything is a glorious distraction up there, and it's easy to see why my friend is a dance-o-holic.

"Go, go go! Shake it like you're going blind!" she chirps.

I laugh, wondering how many drinks Dana had before I showed up. We're definitely going to need a taxi home after tonight.

I move my hips, mimicking her movements. The dress I've picked out is too tight to dance comfortably – or maybe I've just let all the senior year stress add a few too many inches to my butt. Regardless, I hit it hard, and the liquor in my system helps me feel like I'm not making a complete jackass of myself.

It feels good to move – especially when dancing helps me lose track of Prince Not-So-Charming. I don't even see his freakishly perfect jawline hovering over anyone now.

And I'm not the only one who's lost track. Nobody's paying attention to me, as usual. Several eyes are on Dana, though, including the grown up emo kid who's been circling us on the floor like a shark, his silhouette whirling through the throbbing bass and neon lights.

"Hey, little mama, you got a name to go with those moves?" He finally sneaks past me, and he's hitting on her so obviously I start to laugh.

"I'm nobody's mama!" Dana pushes playfully against his chest, and then he grabs her with a grin, pulling her into his arms. "If you want to dance with a grown woman, then step the fuck up. Don't give me that crap. Show me you've got some skills yourself!"

I watch them whirl and twitch in each other's arms. Dana flashes me a drunken wink while I try to cut in with the small talk. That's the cue we've worked out for each other to make ourselves scarce, but it's always been Dana who makes off pretty. Or should I say makes out? Fucks and moves on?

Nobody ever dances with me for more than a minute before I freeze up or shrug the idiot off as a complete asshole.

I've never been into easy, forgettable dick like my best friend. Ugh, and she's already grinding up against him. For a second, bright red jealously burns in my veins. I wonder how it comes so naturally to her – she's had a gift for free, uncomplicated lovin' ever since our freshman year in the dorms.

Whatever. I hope to God my grown up desire to play the dating field seriously before I jump into bed with some bastard will pay adult dividends. They've got to, right? I need to believe all this waiting around for the perfect man isn't for nothing...

I'm spinning, listening to people blabber drunkenly and

laugh. The hard rock switches over to some techno stuff, and the lights go insane, doubling their speed. I'm not even wearing heels and I stumble, nearly losing my damned grip on the floor.

Plowing into the huge shadow in front of me feels like slamming into a brick wall. He reacts quickly.

His arms are around me in an instant. My cheeks burn first, and I've got about three seconds to figure out how I'm going to apologize for smacking into him before I look up. When I finally do, my heart stops.

It should've been predictable as hell, yeah, but when it happens, it doesn't soften the blow one bit.

I'm staring into Tyler Sterner's glacier blue eyes.

He looks at me for what feels like a whole minute as I start to stammer and tumble back. His lips – those evil, kissable, suckable lips! – pull up like horns, exposing some adorable dimples on his cheeks. Who knew Prince Charming had the devil's smile?

"Shit, babe, you look like you've never been out on the club floor before. You had one too many, or what?" He steps close to me again, throws his hands around my waist, and jerks me close like we've already been intimate. "What's the matter? Don't tell me I'm right. Can't believe an ass like yours doesn't have a few good moves."

My mouth drops. I try to speak, but the words won't come. Flushed, stunned, infuriated doesn't begin to describe the shock turning my blood to ice.

I can't believe these are his first words to me – his *only* words – if I have anything to say about it.

"Come the fuck on," he growls, starting to grind and sway with the music. "Move with me, baby. I wanna see *everything* shake through that thing you've got on. I like to see what I'll be bouncing later when I'm balls deep inside you."

Jesus, and here I thought Dana's new buddy was way too forward. My brain can't process what's happening, and my confusion rolls out in a laugh.

I start laughing and try to double over, but he's holding me too tight. I hate admitting the asshole's hands feel good on me, but I guess that's part of the charm. If you can call it that – my Prince is about as charismatic as a swamp toad.

Does he seriously think he's too good to skip cheesy pickup lines? Does he always just jump right into how he's going to fuck a girl?

"What's so goddamned funny?" He says, that stupid sexy smile on his face finally pointing down. "Don't tell me you've been hitting E or some crap. We don't allow that shit here. Listen, I'll toss your ass out and find whoever the fuck sold it to you if that's why you're laughing your damned ass –"

I slap his chest. "I'm laughing at *you,* idiot. And I've had exactly one Long Island iced tea this evening. Not exactly an illegal substance, last time I checked."

"Whatever. You here to laugh your pretty head off or dance? I'll even forgive the idiot remark if you shake it like I think you can. You've got the right stuff, babe." He stares me up and down like I'm a piece of meat, making zero effort to stop his eyes from lingering on my cleavage.

He bends me around in his arms, making me do a turn so he can get a perfect view of my ass. I've never felt completely *undressed* by a man until now.

The smart thing to do is target his face with my next slap. But his hands zip down my back and cup my ass, giving it a sharp squeeze, perfectly timed to the way the music starts to throb again.

Asshole! I shoot him a furious look, but it's really directed inward. I can't believe my body purrs happily with the raw, caveman way he's grabbing my goods. I don't understand what the hell he's doing to me.

I jerk backward, breaking his grip. Tyler laughs, marches forward, and grabs me by the wrist as I'm trying to get away. "Okay, okay. We'll take it slower, beautiful. Give me another try. I'll keep my hands off anything hanging like ripe fruit while we're on the floor. Promise. That shit can wait 'til later when I've got you all alone."

My hand twitches in his, hungry to deliver the slap that'll get me the hell out of this place. Of course, I don't do it. His smile draws me in, and I catch Dana out of the corner of my eye, pressed up against the emo boy with her lips on his.

Sigh. I slip back into his kinder, gentler grip and start to sway my hips, about the most conservative tempo anybody can keep to match the song. I try to keep my breasts and hips well away from direct contact with his washboard body.

"I'm Ty," he says after a minute. "This place belongs to the family, in case you didn't know why everybody's making room for us."

I blink and look around while he folds his arms around me. Crap, I hadn't even noticed. It's true. Half the people are gawking right at us, like we're skating on ice. Half the guys look fearful, or else so jealous they're about to hit the ground and worship us.

I shrug, trying to hide the heavy weight on my shoulders. "Well, I guess a nice, private dance won't hurt."

He laughs. It's rich baritone and it resonates deep in my ears, turning my blood to lava. "Babe, this isn't exactly what I'd call private or dancing. Now, we can do the horizontal dance in my personal suite later if you want. You don't know it, but I've had my fucking eyeballs glued to you all night, and they're gonna melt right outta their sockets if I don't see you naked. I'll bet you turn into a fucking whore when those panties come off…"

His voice drifts into a growl. God damn. How does he do it? I thought my anthropology class taught me Neanderthals were extinct. Except, now there's one with his arms around me, talking dirty in my ear, keeping his hands low enough to be polite – but still so fucking close to my ass.

Too close. And having them one inch away from crude and uncivilized makes me think savage thoughts to match.

What will I do if he puts his hands there again? How will I react if he goes further, pulls me into him, grinds his undoubtedly huge cock shamelessly between my legs? Who the *hell* am I becoming in this man's filthy grip?

I jump. The music stops. He swoops in like he's aiming for a kiss, and I fight like hell to break his grasp. I need to get him off me before I lose my mind.

This is officially too much.

It's just as well too. Out of nowhere, two plastic looking bimbos come trotting up and grab his shoulders. There's one on each side massaging him with their long, bright nails.

The redhead on his left leans over, and I let out a little gasp as she touches the tip of her tongue to his earlobe. "You said you'd be off the dance floor by now, babyyy," she whines. "Is this girl joining in or no?"

"Hold up. I need another minute." He jerks out of their grip and steps up to me.

I don't know how the hell I manage to keep my palms folded down instead of hitting him, but I do. He's shown his true colors several times over tonight. But it's not hard to see it's who he is – a rich jackass who's made Club Zing his personal kingdom – just like Dana told me.

I feel like a fucking idiot for dancing with him. Jesus, I *let* him put his hands where nobody else's have ever gone before, even when I'd started to get hot and heavy with a few college guys.

"Babe, come on…"

No. I run the instant I hear his voice. I hop off the dance floor and push through tight crowds on my way to the table. Halfway there, I look over my shoulder and do a double take. The psycho bastard is actually *chasing* me.

I can't believe he won't take the hint. Or maybe he doesn't want to. Maybe he can't believe someone is actually saying no, showing him what a disgusting pig he really is.

Reaching for my glass in the unlikely event I need a weapon, I spin around and face him, just as he reaches my table. "Look, Ty, I don't give a crap if you run this place. Stop following me. I'm *not* interested in you."

I almost choke when I say the last part. My brain agrees, but my body twists, calls me out as a liar.

"Hold up. I'm sorry we went too fast. I didn't mean to make you scared. I just figured you were used to the business that goes down here between a man and a woman on a good night like this." He runs a hand through his dark hair. "There's something I gotta ask you…"

For some reason, the gesture softens my heart a little. He looks genuinely hurt. I shouldn't be hearing another thing he has to say, but I sigh and lean in, letting him bring his lips close to my ear.

"There's room for one more in my private suite, babe. You wanna be part of my first foursome?" He reaches around and cups my ass. "I wanna make these other sluts jealous when they see what we do. I'll fuck you 'til you scream and break their fucking eardrums."

That's when I lose it. My hand flies up and lands on his powerful jaw. I slap him as hard as I fucking can. Giving in to the urge feels incredible.

I can hear the crack over all the club noises. His lips twitch and he steps backward, drawing one hand to the hot red welt blossoming on his cheek. It's like time locks up.

For a second, we stare at each other. I swallow, knowing I'm in deep shit. But I wouldn't take it back for anything. *Nobody* treats me like this – especially not this pompous, strange prick who's obviously used to getting his way too much for his own good.

Ty tips his head back and starts to laugh. I think I let a growl slip past my lips, wondering if he's some kinda sociopath. Nothing seems to get to him. Absolutely fucking nothing.

"Asshole!" It tears out of my throat. Too bad it doesn't stop him.

He's still going, chuckling dark and deep like I just leaned in and whispered the world's dirtiest joke.

When he finally recovers, wiping his eyes, he reaches into his pocket and slams something down on the table. "Thanks for the laugh. You enjoy your evening, baby. Door's open upstairs anytime if you change your mind about that foursome."

He turns smartly and disappears back into the crowd. It's good he moves fast. I swear, one more second and I would've whipped the glass right at his stupid smug face. My heart's racing like mad, probably faster than it has since I gave up tennis my sophomore year.

I need to sit. Sliding back into the seat, I set down my glass and reach for whatever he's left behind. I don't know why I bother.

It's an envelope. When I crack it open, I gasp. Inside, there's at least three crisp one hundreds and a bunch of smaller bills. I consider stuffing it into my purse and taking off, leaving Dana a text to explain my disappearance whenever she's done with lover boy. But I promised we'd go home together, and I really don't want Ty the Jackass to ruin my last night clubbing with my best friend.

I hold up a hand, waving a server over. Ten minutes later, I've got two fresh Long Island teas in front of me and a couple shots of high end vodka.

"Fuck you, Mister-Asshole-Sterner," I whisper, lifting the first crisp shot to my lips.

I don't stop until the entire club is spinning.

* * * *

"Claire, holy shit!" Dana hisses. "You look like *hell*, girl."

I crack my eyes open and feel a cool compress sliding over my forehead. The first thing I smell is Dana's perfume, now mingled with the thorny scent of the emo kid. I look up and see her hair. It's all messed up.

In my dumb state, there's a pang of jealousy. Why can't I walk out of a place like this just once with Dana's sex hair? Then I remember the only asshole who wanted to fuck me tonight, plus two other girls simultaneously.

My head jerks. Dana leans down, wiping my brow like a concerned sister. I suppose she is.

"Jesus! Take it easy." She frowns. "Don't tell me you've been sitting here alone all night drinking?"

"What time is it?" I groan.

"Quarter to two. The bar's about to close. Hang on, I'm going to see if I can still get you some water!"

I yell out to her, but she's moving too fast. Jesus, my head keeps pounding. I know I've been out at least an hour. Fastest, swiftest hangover in the world – just my luck, right?

My stomach lurches as I stand up. I try to make it to the

bathroom before she gets back, but it feels like my knees are jelly.

I manage to make it just in time. The bathroom is halfway down a long hall with a big fancy burgundy door at the very end – probably leading to the kitchen or some VIP lounge. I wash my hands and stumble out, but not before I crash into the second asshole of the night.

I look up. They say karma's a bitch, but I think it's deja vu.

Ty's huge chest stops me like concrete, except this time it's almost bare. He's got a robe halfway open and draped around his shoulders. I catch a glimpse of some wild geometric designs going around his neck, above what looks like a tiger or panther in full roar on his breast.

"Fucking shit. Didn't think I'd run into you again tonight, babe."

I barely stop myself from sticking my tongue out. "I didn't think so either – and I'm really sorry that I did."

Predictably, the bastard laughs. God damn it. The laugh I loved at first now just sounds like nails on chalkboard. Well, if scraping an old blackboard could be deep, sexy, resonating –

Stop. I can't let myself think another positive thing about this royal dick.

"Christ. I can smell the booze rolling off you, babe. You need a ride home or something?"

I shake my head furiously. Big mistake. It only makes the pounding in my head worse. While I'm frozen, he reaches up and tucks a few stray hairs back against my ears.

I'm drunk and hungover, but I'm not dead. My hand shoots up, pinches his forearm, and I rake my nails down him. Just like a feral cat.

"Fucking hell!" Ty growls, steps back, and hits the wall. "Don't be a bitch. I was just trying to make sure you're –"

"What? Okay? Yeah, I was, until you decided to get in my face tonight. You fucked up my last night in this city with my best friend!"

He tries reaching for my shoulder, but I dodge him. Looks like I'm not the only one drunk tonight. Except there's the unmistakable smell of women all over him. Sickly sweet sex and perfume. He must've fucked them for hours.

My stupid brain wants to think about it too, but I won't let it. I try to get away as fast as my feet will carry me.

Then my heel catches on an unwieldy step going up the short staircase and I tumble.

I brace myself for a lot more pain when I hit the floor – except it never comes.

I fall right into his huge arms like a damned fairy tale. Okay, now I'm *really* pissed.

Ty flattens me against the wall as I fling my elbows against his hard abs, screaming my frustration. It doesn't faze him.

"Shhh. Quiet, babe. Just relax." His voice rolls low, soothing, dangerously close to my ear. "Let me walk you out for a taxi. Just need to get a shirt on. I never got your name."

"No!" Hellfire flows through my elbows again, and I

stab him in the guts, as hard as I can.

I can't even hope to hurt him. I don't care if he's trying to help. I don't trust this jackass, and I need to get away before he drives me insane. I shove my elbows into his rock hard abs two more times, squirming like a madwoman.

He's just stunned enough to let me go, and I practically crawl up the stairs. For some dumb reason, I stop and look back, using the banister to get back on my feet.

There's a wicked sneer twisting his lips. He looks at me like something he's just stepped in, shakes his head, and shrugs. "Fine, babe, do it your way. Go the fuck home. Get some sleep."

My stomach heaves. I'm terrified I'm about to lose the liquor left in my belly all over the place. I fight back the urge to vomit and watch him stomping back to his room.

I feel like total shit. I've made an ass of myself way too many times tonight, even if it was partially this dickhead's fault. I call out to him and stumble forward, back down the stairs, before I know what I'm doing.

"Wait!" My voice echoes down the long corridor.

He stops when he's almost to the burgundy door and turns, waiting for me. "Is there any way I can hit you back for the money? I spent it, and I shouldn't have."

Brutal guilt. Shame. Typical for a Frost girl, especially one who grew up seeing her mom slandered every two years for re-election. But I don't want to owe this fucker a dime, even if we're talking about my own internal good karma counter instead of money.

"You don't owe me shit," he growls. "I paid you for the

laugh, just like I said. No different than any other entertainment tonight. You wanna give me something? Go home and rest like I told you. You're not Club Zing material."

"You're not my boss." I try not to shake my head, though it's impossible when this ham-fisted apology is the dumbest idea in the world. "I just want you to know I'm not a bitch. I'm not a bad person."

He looks me up and down. Slowly. His eyes zero in on my cleavage, and I flush.

"Does that mean you changed your mind about the foursome?" He steps close, and next thing I know, I'm back against the wall. Fighting but not really fighting as he moves in for a kiss. "Shit, I'd settle for one on one at this point. Drunk and pissed, you're still fucking hot."

Hot. Nobody's ever called me that before. It's the only explanation for why I let his vile lips connect with mine.

This isn't a kiss. This is a fucking explosion on my lips. My entire body tenses up, muscles clench, everything below the waist writhes like I'm made of snakes. I moan just as he presses his tongue in my mouth.

Of course, I've read about sexual tension in books and seen it on the big screen. I just didn't think it really happened, not like this animal spark igniting between us.

His tongue twines with mine and his lips move rougher, faster. My palms are on his back and my fingers go jagged, tearing at the skin underneath his thin robe. I can't decide if I want to hurt him or make him fuck me.

The unbelievable hard-on I feel grinding on my thigh

definitely says he's willing.

I'm about to come completely undone when my legs kick hard. I knock my knees on his and shove my hands to the wall, twisting and flattening myself, crazy to get away before I do something I'll *really* regret. The other shit that's happened tonight is an afternoon sprinkle compared to this hurricane staring me down.

"Don't!" I yell, pushing against him when he comes close. "Really. I mean it. This was all a mistake...I need to go."

"That's not what your body says, babe. I know a girl who wants to fuck when I see one. Hell, I can *taste* how bad you want it."

I run. This time, I don't stop. I'm like a hummingbird darting up the stairs and through the bar, grabbing Dana by the wrist.

"Hey! I've been wondering where the hell you went. I've got your water if you want to down it before they –"

"We need to go. Right now, Dana. *Now, now, now,*" I whisper, urgent as all hell. "Let's find a cab."

The rest of the night happens in a blur. Dana makes me crash at her apartment, and she doesn't let me sleep until I take a multivitamin and swallow three huge glasses of water.

I keep telling her I'm okay. I whisper something about a guy being too aggressive, too close to me when I'm drunk off my ass.

I don't dare tell her it's Ty, or that I practically invited the last collision with the sex-crazed jackass.

I'm already stuck in enough crap. I can't imagine telling

her how good his lips tasted on mine.

At some point, she stops interrogating me and throws a blanket over me as I'm lying on her couch. I pass out and sleep like the dead until my phone screams me awake in late morning.

* * * *

"Claire, it's Mom. Just making sure we're still on for lunch?"

Of course we are. The universe has decided to make me pay for last night.

I inwardly groan, wishing I could pass out for a few more hours. I'm alone in Dana's place. My friend went out shopping and left me an extra key to lock up if I decide to leave, as the note on the counter says.

"Yes, mom. I'll be there."

"Oh, good!" her high, almost sing-song voice makes my ears ring. "Don't be late. I've got some *huge* news to tell you."

Huge? As if *big* isn't enough? I hope to God she isn't going to say she's launching her Senate run early. I can't deal with the stress of that, especially the media storm it'll bring, when my first summer as a real adult has barely started.

"Honey, what's wrong?" Mom pauses, oh-so-concerned. I'm surprised she can't smell the vodka through the phone.

"Late night with Dana. Nothing to worry about. I'm just shaking off all the fun."

"*Claaaire.*" She clucks her tongue in that haughty,

disapproving way she's always done. "You need to start taking better care of yourself. You're out of college now. When I was your age, I was struggling just to keep my head above water. I didn't have time for all night drunken –"

Blah, blah. Fuck you. And blah.

Shaking my head, I slam my phone at the edge of the sink and wash up, listening to her lecture me about all the thrills and dangers of being a young woman. I want to cut the speaker phone, or else drown the fucking thing in the sink.

"Mom, I know. I hear you. Let's not talk about this, okay? I really want to have lunch and figure out the ride back to Tacoma. I haven't seen you for a while, and I actually want to. I just don't want you treating me like a total idiot."

"Yes, Tacoma…" She trails off oddly, and I don't really understand why.

Maybe admitting she actually counts freezes her cold in her tracks. Mom and I haven't really been close since I was a teenager. Her last couple terms in Congress were a blur. There wasn't much hanging out with her staying in DC half the year while I was stuck here for school.

Then when she left the US House and came home, she was always busy with something, and I can't say the desire to reconnect has been crazy pressing until now.

"All right. You know I'm only hard on you because I love you."

"I know. So, Carbonari's at one?"

"No, no. I thought we'd try something new. There's this

great new wine bar a little north of the city."

She gives me the name and I almost fall over. It's a budget buster for me, and way beyond anything my frugal-minded mom normally indulges too.

Damn, now I really know she's contemplating that early Senate campaign. She's going to bribe me to soften the blow.

"Okay, I'll be there. Uh, you're paying, right?"

I exhale relief when she says yes, because I'd be going home hungry if she wasn't. It's a miracle I'm not ass deep in loans like my friends, but hitting the classes hard hasn't left me much time to work, and my bank account looks really pale.

Slipping out of Dana's apartment, I lock up and slide the key back underneath the door. Then I'm in my car, struggling for oversized shades to blot out the blinding sun.

My eyes don't want to let go of what happened last night. They're throbbing like mad, making me re-live all the stupid memories at Club Zing. My mind won't get off him the whole way to the wine bar.

I can't believe I kissed a total asshole. And I *definitely* can't believe I let him put his hands all over me, however brief. Jesus, what would've happened if I'd been so fucking drunk I said *yes* to Ty's gross advances?

Shaking my head makes my eyes feel better, so I'm practically swaying to the music buzzing out my radio the whole trip. Last night needs to be my last big drinking binge ever. A tall order, I know, because right now a glass or two of wine sounds awfully good, if only to take the edge off.

The place is even fancier than I thought. If it's not the Senate campaign, I wonder if she hit big in Vegas. Mom was gone there for a whole month up until my graduation. She's a gambler by nature, which I guess is what makes politics so appealing.

I can't say I'm immune to the same adrenaline rush — and certainly not to finer things. When I walk into the place, it's heavenly. The light potpourri of high-end wines blends with well-cooked steaks and starters. My stomach growls something fierce, reminding me I haven't eaten since a quick dinner last night, before meeting up with Dana.

"Honey! There you are!"

I turn toward Mom's voice and see her sitting in a stylish tall booth. And — what the hell? — she's not alone.

I can't get a good look at the guy next to her until I slide into the free seat. When I do, he looks vaguely familiar, but my brain can't place him. He's about her age, broad shouldered and generally well built with just a hint of a gut. His face is nice, except he's rocking some thick ass glasses that make him look like my Chem 101 professor.

"Claire, this is —"

"Gary Sterner." He smiles, jabs his hand toward me. I take it, and he gives me a powerful shake. "I sincerely hope this isn't too rattling for you. Your mother assured me this would be the best way to make an introduction, so…here I am!"

I can tell by the way he's talking that this guy is a blend of distinguished rich guy and slightly awkward nerd. My stomach starts to tighten up when I think about why the hell's he's here at all.

"Don't tell me…this is your new campaign manager?" I blurt it out and guzzle water. Jesus, my throat's so dry from last night.

I just want to get this disaster over with, and find out how royally fucked our family's going to be for the next year.

Mom laughs, loud and a little childish. She gives my question a big fat no by wrapping her arms tight around the rich geek's neck – way closer than anything that would be professional or platonic.

I frown. Mom hasn't dated in ages. Hell, being a strong single woman who survived after being left by the anonymous deadbeat who made me was always a big part of her election narrative.

"No, honey. Gary's much more special than that." She pauses and looks at him. Talk about puppy love. "I…I don't know how else to say this…"

Holy shit. I'm sitting up so straight my spine hurts. Mom's never at a loss for words.

"Claire, your mother's a married woman now," Gary finishes for her. "I know it's sudden –"

"So sudden!" Mom squeals, squeezing his arm with her hands. "We didn't want to make a big spectacle. Gary's got way more cameras to worry about than I do. Claire, I cut my trip to Vegas short for this. As soon as he proposed, we headed up to Alaska on his jet. Had ourselves a small, private ceremony in Denali Park. It wasn't even a ceremony, really – just us and a priest, maybe a few grizzlies roaming around behind us. It was beautiful."

346

No joke, I can feel my heartbeat in my eyeballs. It's like they're about to explode. I grab my water and swallow the whole thing, tipping the glass up high so it blocks my view of them.

"Claire, honey? Are you okay?"

I don't answer until my cup empties. The glass bangs the table hard when I set it down. I shake my head for like the hundredth time today.

"I'm...Jesus Christ, Mom! Married? I didn't even know you were seeing anyone!"

She frowns. It pains my heart to see the big smile melting like that.

Fuck. I don't like it, but I can't bring myself to totally ruin this special moment. I reach past Gary's hairy arm and pinch Mom's.

"It's okay. I'll get over it. It's just going to take some getting used to, that's all." I try to be reassuring.

Gary clears his throat. "Yes, well, I apologize again for dropping this on you without any formal notice. It was a whirlwind, Claire. One thing I'm never going to be sorry for is putting a ring on this little lady's finger. I hope you understand – we're really in love. I'm going to take the very best care of your mother."

They lean in and kiss. There's that stupid head shake again. My prim, upbeat, and always guarded mother is acting like a goddamned teenager. It's seriously freaking me out.

I lift my hand and summon the waiter over for more water while the two love birds are at it. Mom doesn't even look up while I order a glass of good Malbec and another pitcher. Like, an entire pitcher of water, just for me.

"I don't get it," I say, stopping until they're both looking at me again. "Gary, you mentioned something about media? Jesus, I thought this whole thing was about my mom's Senate campaign."

Mom smiles and pushes a finger to her lips. "That's our little secret, baby. And it's one I'm not ready for quite yet myself."

Gary looks at her and winks. "Come on, Mandy. I think I know all about your ambitions, and I'm right behind you all the way. You're going to make us all proud."

Mandy – fucking Mandy? Is he serious? Nobody's called my mom anything besides Amanda or Miss Frost or Representative for as long as I can remember!

"Gary!" Mom clucks her tongue.

"Just teasing, dear, I'm sure that decision's a few years off. Your mother was talking about my own little paparazzi issues, Claire," Gary says as I start massaging my temples. "Since 1997, I've been the founder and CEO of –"

"Spree," I cut in. "Fucking Spree. Of course."

Mom gives me a stern look at my language. Whatever. It's just as well because my wine shows up along with two other glasses they must've ordered before I arrived. Perfect distraction.

"We've been using your site since I was a kid," I continue. "God. Your company's a household name. That must mean you're loaded, right?"

Mom's mouth drops open. Gary laughs and clinks his

glass gently against hers, giving the sparkly champagne inside it a swirl. "It's okay, Mandy. The girl deserves some slack. It's not every day your mother marries a billionaire online mogul without warning."

Christ. He can say that again. I have to stop and drink half my Malbec before I'm able to speak again.

"So, how long have you guys been dating?"

"It's been – what? – seven or eight months?" Mom looks at Gary and smiles. "We actually met at the big industry dinner in DC about a year ago. Gary came to me personally for some help moving things forward in Washington. I was on my way out and happy to take some risk with his drive to grow Spree because it meant more jobs and more revenue. One thing led to another and…well, here we are today."

Yeah, here we are. Just where the hell is *here?*

I can't place myself in this reality anymore after they both set off this bombshell in my face. What's really insane is how sure and lovey-dovey they seem. At first, I thought it might be a marriage of convenience, something old people with years in business and government do. America doesn't have blue bloods, but it definitely has aristocrats.

And yet, the man sitting across from me with his brilliant features and graying hair is a *much* different kind of royalty than anything we've ever been. A Congresswoman's salary doesn't mean insta-millionaire, especially when she's not taking kickbacks. Mom stayed fairly clean for a politician.

Her new hubby, on the other hand, is a billionaire.

Billion with a capital B. I can't fathom it, but I'm going to have to try.

This is the new normal, isn't it?

"Claire, are you sure you're okay?" Gary's tone is almost fatherly.

Holy shit. Fatherly. That's right – he's officially my new step-*father*, something that didn't hit me in the face until now. Staring at the huge diamonds on Mom's finger helps drive it home too when she turns her hand and they catch the light.

"I'm fine. I'll be okay, I mean. It's just a lot to take in after a long night out."

"Of course it is, honey. Don't worry. We'll all mull this over at a big family dinner soon enough. I just wanted to give you a chance to find out in a nice, relaxed atmosphere."

Ha ha, Mom's so funny today. The way my heart's beating, I'm not sure I'll ever be able to relax again. I look at Gary, narrowing my eyes.

"So, what's your story? I hope Mom isn't like your fourth wife? Have you been married before, Gary?"

Another scolding look from Mom. I feel kinda bad, but there's no fucking way I can be polite. Not when my whole world keeps crashing to smithereens. My brain racing a trillion miles an hour strips away the mind-to-mouth filter. Naturally, that makes me think of the asshole and his smothering kiss last night.

Gary laughs, patting my mom's hand. "It's okay, Mandy. Really. I like curiosity. Claire, you'll be pleased to know your mother's only the second woman I've ever called my wife. And I intend to make sure she's the last."

I raise an eyebrow, breathing an inward sigh of relief as more water shows up. I pour it and start sucking it down. My body needs it, plus it might just keep the nuclear reactions inside me from going off.

"What happened to number one?" I ask in between sips.

"Skiing accident. It was terrible. I still think about those times – where does it all go?" Gary shakes his head. Finally, someone else's turn to do it. "I was a young man with a startup and a five year old son in those days. There wasn't time to mourn. The only saving grace is I wasn't such a popular guy then – the media left my family alone. I wasn't on their radar yet. It was up to me to raise my son alone while I built my company. I'm pleased to say it all worked out. Mostly, anyway."

I nod. Okay, maybe Gary's not such a weirdo with a silver spoon hanging out of his mouth after all. I gnaw on some bread while they make goo-goo eyes at each other again.

Shit. I hope the spark wears off at some point like all relationships. It's going to be a *long* fucking summer if I have to see this all the time.

Munching isn't helping my stomach much. I have to really focus on drinking my water and trying to remember what Dana taught me about meditation from her yoga classes to keep from spitting wine up all over the table.

"Honey, you're *sure* you're okay?" Mom gives me the look of death, demanding I tell her the truth.

"I think I need to rest. Let my brain recuperate after it's

been blown right out my ears. I hope you don't mind if I cut this a little short. I just want to go home."

Gary laughs and looks at me. "You're perfectly welcome to join us at our new home, Claire."

New home? Oh, shit. I hadn't even considered that, but it does make a scary kinda sense.

Mom nods. "It's way better than our old condo. I think you'll like the house – Gary had his maid set up a room for you, Claire. You'll find everything you need there, and if anything's missing, just shout. I'll be putting the old place in Tacoma on the market soon too – it's peak buying season, after all."

I throw down my napkin and stand up. I really want to whip it right at them and scream until every wine glass in this fucking restaurant breaks.

It's one thing to have my whole world turned upside down, but now they're telling me the only thing I can really count on – *home* – is somewhere else?

"Don't worry about driving. We'll take care of your car," Gary says. "I already told my driver to wait for you out front. I figured you'd need a little time to be alone and get settled in. You'll find my place in Bellingham very comfortable, Claire. My chauffeur will have you home and be back here to pick us up in no time."

Jesus. Bellingham's like an hour north on a good day. They must be planning to sit here for a good long while and drink, maybe make out or something nasty I definitely don't want to see

I do the only thing I can in this situation. I plaster on

my biggest, fakest grin and shake Gary's hand.

"That actually sounds good right now. Are you sure you'll be okay getting my stuff home? Everything I brought off campus is in the trunk."

Mom beams – probably relieved I'm making a graceful exit instead of an explosive one. "Of course! We'll take care of everything, baby. Gary's a good man. When he proposed, I told him you're my number one. Our marriage doesn't change that."

"And I told her I want the whole enchilada," Gary says, reaching for my hand. "Mandy's family is mine now, Claire. I know it's going to take some time, but give me a few months, and you'll see I'm right. I always am."

I give him one more weak smile and get the hell away before I'm drowned in their affection or the billionaire's arrogance. True to his word, there's a sleek black sedan waiting out front with a neat looking driver, who gets out and opens the door for me as soon as he sees me coming.

My only regret as I slip into the car is that I didn't have more water, and more wine.

* * * *

One thing's for sure – Mom and new Step-dad aren't bullshitting about the size of the house. When the car rolls through a gate that's like twice as tall as I am, I know I'm in trouble.

There's a guard shack. An honest-to-God security checkpoint just for billionaire Gary, and I guess that includes Mom and me too.

The man in the guard shack smiles and waves us through, just as friendly and perfectly behaved as the driver. The place looks like a modern castle sitting on the coast. Powerful waves churn just over the hills, and I see one of the cleanest Washington beaches ever below.

On the other side, it's flanked by the most blinding, beautiful green the Pacific Northwest has to offer. The incredible foliage hanging around the house reminds me all our rain has its advantages.

"Miss Frost," the driver says, almost like he's about to salute me when we pull up. I step out through the door he's holding, gawking at the monstrous palace for a good thirty seconds.

Then my stomach twists again, and I'm forced to move, if only to get inside and use the bathroom.

The key Gary gave me works. It's a card, just like at a hotel, and apparently there's an app to let your phone unlock the door too. I wouldn't expect anything less from a tech mogul.

Luckily, there's a bathroom nearby. It has about all the fine finishes I expect. I do my business, wash up, and run cold water over my face. What little I've seen of the house so far makes me feel like I need to purify myself just to be here.

When I step out in the hall, the first thing I hear are footsteps. Thinking I'm alone, I jump. But that's stupid, I tell myself. I already know Gary has a housekeeper and who the hell knows what else — and I'd better get used to it awfully fast since this is my new home now.

He also mentioned a son…and didn't really say much else about him. Is he living here too?

I head down a long hall with these awesome murals, hoping it brings me to the kitchen. It does. The massive refrigerator has a whole shelf filled with drinks – mineral water, fancy juices, kombucha, and some other tasty looking imports I've never seen before. It all looks good, but I know I need more water.

Always more. My stomach won't forgive me until I've replenished everything the last two days have drained from my system.

I head through the other opening in the kitchen, ready to explore at least this little part of the mansion. There's a dining room, and then a hallway leading to what looks like an awesome living room. There's leather furniture, the biggest glass windows with a perfect view of the ocean, and –

Oh, hell. There's a young man standing right in the middle of the room, dripping wet from a workout, shirtless. He's ripped and tattooed as all hell. It looks like he's just come in from a run, or maybe using the gym – wherever that is.

I set my drink down on the nearby counter nervously and hold my hand up to wave. If he's Gary's son, I never thought I'd be meeting him like this. I hope it's not too awkward.

Only one way to find out.

"Hi, there. I'm Claire."

The boy turns around. His piercing blue eyes dart right

through me like a bullet to the head.

"Fucking shit," Ty says, breaking into a princely smile.

Fucking shit is right. I barely have time to reach out and catch myself next to my drink before I go crashing to the floor.

Look for *Stepbrother Charming* at your favorite retailer!

CPSIA information can be obtained
at www.ICGtesting.com
Printed in the USA
BVHW040235071021
618404BV00022B/430